A BETTER TOMORROW FOR THE EAST END LIBRARY GIRLS

PATRICIA MCBRIDE

Boldwood

First published in Great Britain in 2024 by Boldwood Books Ltd.

Copyright © Patricia McBride, 2024

Cover Design by Colin Thomas

Cover Images: Colin Thomas

A CIP catalogue record for this book is available from the British Library.

Paperback ISBN 978-1-83518-031-0

Large Print ISBN 978-1-83518-030-3

Hardback ISBN 978-1-83518-029-7

Ebook ISBN 978-1-83518-032-7

Kindle ISBN 978-1-83518-033-4

Audio CD ISBN 978-1-83518-024-2

MP3 CD ISBN 978-1-83518-025-9

Digital audio download ISBN 978-1-83518-027-3

This book is printed on certified sustainable paper. Boldwood Books is dedicated to putting sustainability at the heart of our business. For more information please visit https://www.boldwoodbooks.com/about-us/sustainability/

Boldwood Books Ltd, 23 Bowerdean Street, London, SW6 3TN

www.boldwoodbooks.com

In memory of my lovely mother Joyce Johnson who was a true cockney

1

The library doorway darkened as a tall, muscular figure hesitated on the threshold. Backlit by the sun, his silhouette dominated the entrance, broad shoulders seemingly spanning the frame. Stepping forward, the man looked around uncertainly, keen brown eyes darting from the circulation desk to the readers sitting amidst the stacks. Despite his commanding presence, he lingered hesitantly, appearing almost nervous to enter the library. It wasn't his rich brown skin that made him stand apart. Generations of immigrants meant that Silvertown was an area filled with a variety of people from across the globe. What was striking was his height and obvious strength. In war-torn, threadbare Silvertown, his crisp white shirt and neatly pressed trousers looked almost ostentatious. He cut an imposing figure, yet his shifting gaze held more apprehension than menace. With a wary glance outside, the stranger steeled himself and stepped towards the desk.

'Can I help you, sir?' Cordelia, the head librarian, asked.

'I sure hope so, ma'am. My name is Eugene Miller. Do you let folks like me join your library?'

Cordelia immediately knew he was referring to his skin colour. The Yanks, as they were called, had recently arrived in Britain to join the war effort. Already, there were stories of fights between black and white American soldiers. Some of them came from areas where colour segregation was still normal and expected. Newspapers reported that some white Americans got upset that black Americans were not segregated in the United Kingdom. Rumour had it they were especially infuriated if white women went out with black soldiers.

'We have no segregation here,' Cordelia said and pushed a form towards him. 'If you'd like to fill in this form, we can set you up with a library card straight away.'

'Thank you, ma'am,' he said and headed to the nearest table.

One of her assistants, Mavis, walked towards her. She'd just finished restocking returned books on the stacks. 'He's a good-looking fella,' she whispered. 'Gotta be a Yank. Wonder what 'e's doing around 'ere.'

Jane, the other assistant, was busy getting ready for the children's reading session, setting up tiny chairs they'd rescued from bombed schools, and finding books to appeal to all ages. When she was ready she joined the other two. 'We need to think about how to keep the children occupied during the school holidays. They start in two weeks.'

Just then, Mr Miller returned with his form. 'I hope I've done it right, ma'am,' he said, handing it to Cordelia.

She glanced at it and nodded. 'So you've got accommodation near here, I see,' she said, trying not to sound too surprised.

He nodded. 'We're not going into action just yet and we're allowed to find our own accommodation until we do. My folks came from round here way back. I'm hoping to find out more about them. So I'm just staying here for a while while I do some research, then I'll move nearer my base.' He paused and rubbed his chin. 'Do you have any books on the history of the area I can borrow?'

Cordelia should by rights have asked one of the other two to show him where the books were. She had a pile of paperwork waiting to be tackled on her desk. Not least was how to make the budget balance. But something about the man made her want to spend more time with him.

'Follow me and I'll show you the right section.' As they walked to the relevant section she was aware of a tingle in her body she hadn't felt since her boyfriend Robert left for duty in North Africa. 'You can borrow two books for up to two weeks. Bring them to the desk when you're ready and we'll stamp them.'

'Thank you, ma'am,' he said with a sweet smile, and turned to look at the books. Feeling something she couldn't identify, Cordelia went back to the desk. 'I'll leave him in your hands, Mavis. Now, about the summer activities for children. Do you have any ideas, Jane?'

Jane flicked through a book that had been returned, checking for marks. The variety of writing and drawings borrowers did in the books was sometimes amusing but often infuriating because they took ages to remove. 'Well, we can carry on with storytelling and arts and crafts, but I had another idea. How about a reading competition?'

Mavis looked at her in amazement. ''Ow would that work then? They're all different ages and you can bet your bottom dollar some of the little blighters would cheat!'

Rubbing out some doodles done in pencil on the side of a few pages of the book she was holding, she sighed. 'I expect you're right, Mavis, but we'll be the most popular people in Silvertown if we keep them out of their mothers' hair.'

'May I join your conversation, ladies?' The newcomer had moved near them without them noticing.

Cordelia, who still hadn't gone back to her office, asked, 'Do you need any help finding books, Mr Miller?'

He smiled at her and she experienced that tingle again, one she quickly suppressed despite noticing his cologne, woody and fresh, which reminded her of walks in the woods.

'Please, feel free to call me Eugene. Before the war, I used to be a teacher for kids in primary school. I have some experience with keeping young minds engaged. Perhaps I could offer some suggestions? I can't offer to teach them though. I'll get court-martialled if I'm not on duty when I should be.'

Mavis and Jane hadn't noticed the newcomer and exchanged glances, intrigued by his offer. Cordelia nodded, curiosity piqued. 'We'd love to hear your ideas, Mr Miller.'

Eugene leaned against the desk, his presence commanding yet approachable. 'I found that a scavenger hunt was always popular with my students. You ladies are familiar with the contents of the library. You could create a list of items or facts for them to discover within the library's books. I always found the sense of competition got them even more active than asking them to work alone. If you can manage a prize or two, they'll be really engaged.' He paused for a few seconds. 'I've been here long enough to know about your rationing. At the base we have cookies and candy you may not get. I'd be happy to donate some for prizes.'

Jane's eyes lit up. 'What a brilliant idea! We could have a different theme each week – history, nature or whatever. They'd love it.'

Mavis folded her arms in front of her chest. 'But when would we find the time to do something like that?'

The man glanced at Cordelia, and again she felt that flutter of excitement. 'I am free at weekends, so I could help next Saturday. You're open until lunchtime, aren't you?' Even though Mavis and Jane had been speaking to him, his reply was directed to Cordelia. Mavis and Jane looked at each other and Mavis raised a knowing eyebrow.

Just then, the library door creaked open and a group of children burst in, their laughter filling the room. Jane quickly gathered them around the small chairs in the children's area, herding them like a professional shepherd.

Eugene watched with a smile. 'You have a lively bunch there and some of them look as poor as the kids I used to teach.'

Cordelia nodded in agreement. 'This part of London is very poor as you'll have worked out. We do our best to help.'

Mavis had been listening to the conversation but glanced at the clock. 'Well, I'd better get on with restocking more books. I must walk miles every day.'

As she walked away, Eugene turned back to Cordelia. 'Thank you for making me feel welcome. It's not always easy being... different.'

Cordelia met his gaze, her heart aching with empathy. 'Here at the library, we believe everyone deserves to feel welcome. Times are hard enough.' The sound of children giggling got their attention. 'Jane is brilliant with the little ones,' Cordelia said, trying to ignore the pull of Eugene's deep brown eyes.

When she began working in the library, Jane had been timid, rarely speaking her mind. She had been the opposite of Mavis, who was outspoken and bold, taking no nonsense from anyone. That meant Jane was often in her shadow. Cordelia soon noticed what was happening and set about giving Jane tasks to build her confidence. She'd never be as blunt as Mavis, but Cordelia sometimes thought one Mavis was enough anyway.

'We look forward to seeing you again soon, Mr Miller,' Cordelia said with a smile.

'Please, call me Eugene,' he repeated, and looked around

again. 'How about I come next Saturday and help with the scavenger hunt unless your very capable colleagues have got it all sorted out.'

'We'd love that,' Cordelia said, and watched him with a feeling of unfamiliar loss as he walked out of the door carrying two books.

While they'd been talking, several library users had been following the conversation with interest. And Cordelia watched them as best she could while distracted by this attractive man.

When he'd left, Mrs Grey marched up to the desk, eyes blazing. She was a regular library user and a member of the library sewing circle where she frequently put people's backs up.

'I'm telling you now,' she said, her eyes narrowed and chin jutting out. 'You give me any books that... that... creature has handled, and I'll throw them back at you!'

Her friend, Mrs Giovanni, a plump Italian woman whose hair was tied up in a bun on top of her head, nodded and muttered, 'You tell 'em, Nellie!'

The three librarians looked at Mrs Grey in amazement. Memories of the Cable Street Battle were still fresh in Silvertown minds. Local people had stopped the fascists, led by Sir Oswald Mosley, from marching through the area. That battle had been about the fascists' hatred of Jews.

Cordelia stepped forward and looked Mrs Grey in the eye. 'This is a library for anyone who signs in and wants to use it. We do not discriminate on the colour of skin, the country people come from, or their religion.'

Mrs Grey blustered, her breathing fast. 'That lot, they're dirty, everyone says so. Bringing all sorts of diseases over here...'

Mavis and Jane stepped forward, one either side of Cordelia. Cordelia indicated for them to let her deal with the comment.

Mavis would probably have thrown the woman out on to the street by the scruff of her neck.

'Mrs Grey,' Cordelia said, struggling to keep her voice level and calm. 'That is simply not true. You should be ashamed saying such things. I have had to ask you to keep your opinions to yourself in this building before now.'

Mrs Grey sneered, her top lip distorted. 'Oh yeah, and what if I don't?'

'Then I shall have to ask you to find an alternative library. Perhaps you'll be happier elsewhere.'

Mavis had been struggling to keep her mouth shut, something she never found easy. Finally she could hold back no longer, her tone unyielding. 'And you, Mrs Giovanni, your skin isn't lily white, is it? 'Ow would you feel if people treated you like your friend 'ere is treating that man?'

Mrs Giovanni's defiant stance evaporated like dew on a summer's day. Her cheeks went red and she fiddled with the handle of her bag, taking care not to look at anyone.

Mrs Grey glared at the three librarians. 'I've never been so insulted in all my born days.' She looked at her friend. 'Come on, Maria, we're not welcome here. We'll find a library that has a better class of people.'

When she'd gone Mavis turned to Cordelia with a wicked glint in her eyes. 'Better class of people? She obviously doesn't know your father is a lord!'

2

———

'You're late this morning. Is everything okay?' Cordelia asked, concern in her eyes. Mavis's punctuality was legendary.

Mavis grunted as she took off her coat and hung it up. 'Only a leak in the damn roof again,' she said, frustration in her voice. 'It may be summer coming up but it still rains. I 'ad to get old Jonny from the next street to bring 'is rickety ladder round to fix the roof. The people upstairs weren't a bit 'appy with water dripping on their bed; they asked me to get it fixed. They knew I'd find someone to do it. It needed doing before my place got wet too.' She ran her fingers through her damp hair, the cool droplets falling on her shoulders. 'Slipped tiles again, 'e said. They need fixing on properly, that's the trouble.'

Mavis's problem was a familiar one and Cordelia was only half listening, worrying about all the work she still had to get through. 'Shouldn't the landlord see to that?' Her voice was still tinged with concern about the amount of paperwork to be done and the grim state of the budget.

'Huh! You think we ever see the landlord? That'd take a miracle and we're short of them in the East End. 'Ardly know who the so-and-so is. But one thing I know for sure, 'e'll be somewhere warm and dry.'

Unnoticed, Miss Unwin, a regular library user, had come to the desk, her worn-out shoes hardly making a sound on the wooden floorboards. As usual she wore a brown felt hat and brown coat with brass buttons. 'Yes, you're right, Mrs Kent. He'll be taking our money and doing nothing for it. I have exactly the same problem. My plumbing doesn't work half the time and no matter how often I complain, nothing happens.' She paused and got out her hankie. 'It's embarrassing to have to go next door to use their toilet. But the rent still goes up. Me and me neighbours all have problems that never get fixed. The council should do something about it.'

Signing a form, Cordelia absent-mindedly looked up again. 'Does anyone ever complain to the council? Presumably they could get the landlords to do something. Don't they have to approve them or anything?'

'I've written to them twice,' Miss Unwin said, her voice tinged with disappointment. 'They've never replied though.'

A cough behind them made them all jump and turn round. The regular library user they informally called The Professor stood there, looking unsure if he should speak. His gentle countenance and ready, shy smile immediately put the women at ease. He wore a pair of wire-rimmed glasses held together with tape on one arm, and his eyes sparkled with curiosity and intelligence. Wisps of grey hair peeked out from under his well-worn tweed cap and his chest-length beard was salt-and-peppered. He wore his usual tweed jacket, past its best, but which still gave him the air of being a scholar of some sort. And as sometimes happened, he wore a bow tie, this one forest green with white spots.

'I think I may have something to offer your conversation, if I may intrude, ladies,' he said, looking at each of them in turn. 'I'm something of a scholar, an amateur one these days, but I like to keep up to date with what's happening.'

Miss Unwin touched his arm lightly, her eyes filled with gratitude. 'We'd be very grateful for anything you could tell us, sir.' She hesitated. 'I'm afraid I don't know your name although I've often seen you in here.'

The Professor nodded his head. 'My name is Berger, but to be honest I'm often referred to as The Prof and I'm very happy with that.'

'So how can you help?' Cordelia asked, surprised to find he liked being called the name they had secretly used between themselves.

He took his hankie out of his pocket and, removing his glasses, took his time cleaning them before putting them back on. 'If you decide to do anything about your unfair rents you need to know a bit about the law. In nineteen thirty-nine, the government brought in the Rent and Mortgage Interest Restriction Act.' He paused, his gaze fixed on all three of them. 'It means that no excessive rent increases are allowed without good reason. If your landlords are not doing repairs, then there is no good reason to raise your rents.'

Mavis scoffed. 'Ratbags, the lot of 'em!' she said. 'What can we do about it, Prof? Will the council 'elp?'

The corners of The Professor's mouth turned down. 'That's an excellent question, Mrs Kent. In theory the council oversee this issue and deal with problems but with the war on, many councils are dealing with more pressing issues and it often gets overlooked.'

'That's what I said,' Miss Unwin replied. 'They ignored my letters. Not a dicky bird out of them.'

The Professor straightened his bow tie. 'Let me know, ladies, if I can be of any further assistance. I'm here most weekdays.'

He was about to go back to his seat but Cordelia spoke before he took a step. 'Professor, I hope you won't think me rude asking, but I sometimes wonder what you're studying. Is it something you used to teach?'

His eyes lit up with memories of standing in front of mostly eager students. 'I used to teach law. You may have guessed that. But these days I like to spread my learning further. I find it helps to keep my mind active. At the moment I'm engrossed in the subject of psychology. It's utterly fascinating learning how the mind works. But I won't detain you any longer. I expect you have plenty to think about.'

When he returned to his seat the three women looked at each other, at a loss. 'I have no idea what we could do,' Miss Unwin said sadly. 'There's got to be something.'

For a minute or two they stood deep in thought.

'Hang on,' Mavis said. 'The dockers 'ere go on strike some-times over their pay and working conditions. Perhaps we could go on strike. Not pay our rent. The buggers would soon take notice then.'

Cordelia frowned. 'But how would that work? If you refuse to pay rent, surely your landlords would evict you.'

All three were silenced by her comment. Their plight seemed hopeless. Then Miss Unwin spoke up. 'That's a good idea, Mrs Kent, but it would need to be a lot of us not paying at the same time or it won't have enough impact.'

The other two women looked at each other. 'It'd take a lot of work to get enough people involved,' Cordelia said, shuffling her papers. 'Something to think about. I'm sorry but I'll have to leave you to it. I've got things that must be done before the end of the day.'

'Would you be willing to talk about it some more with me, Miss Unwin?' Mavis asked. 'It's not the sort of thing you usually do.'

Miss Unwin smiled widely. 'I may be an old surplus woman now, but I used to get into all sorts when I was younger. I'd love to get involved and I think it's time we were on first-name terms. My name is Emma, and I know you are Mavis.' She did up the buttons on her coat. 'Shall we meet over lunchtime tomorrow to think some more about it?'

That evening Mavis walked to collect Joyce, the six-year-old she had recently adopted. The sun glowed softly through a thin veil of clouds as she stepped out into the bustling high street, clutching her worn handbag. The usual Silvertown smells hit her – wafts from the Thames and the factories that lined it, everything from the Tate & Lyle sugar refinery to a glassworks that fabricated glass for military purposes. She skirted around a large crater in the road, a stark reminder of the German bombs that had fallen a week earlier. Instinctively she looked up, relieved to see only silver barrage balloons drifting this way and that, and no dreaded Nazi planes.

The bombings were less frequent but the memory of over two hundred and fifty non-stop days of death and destruction were still fresh in the minds of the tough East Enders.

Planning what she and Joyce would do that evening, she turned a corner and almost walked in front of a lorry heading to one of the factories. She coughed when it belched out a sooty cloud of exhaust fumes as it passed. The experience made her remember the home Joyce had lived in. Set in a small Essex town, there was plenty of countryside and no unhealthy smells like they lived with every day in Silvertown. Had she done the right thing bringing her here, Mavis wondered regularly. Here,

Joyce had love and affection. She wasn't simply one child amongst many.

As always happened, she looked forward to being with her daughter again. She'd been worried that the adoption board might not think she was a suitable person to adopt her. Mavis wasn't well off and rented only half of the run-down house she lived in. But Cordelia had helped her identify what she had to offer and given her tips on how to complete the many forms demanded. She would always be grateful to her boss for that.

The government provided plenty of nursery places since the war started, including places after school. But like all the other children, Joyce was usually tired and not at her best at the end of a long day. It was many years since Mavis's son, Ken, had been a boy. She still remembered some of the techniques for keeping a fractious, tired child calm though.

He was far from a child now, instead a soldier stationed in Scotland. She thought of him every day, hoping he was safe and happy. He'd been a cheerful lad until he got in with the wrong crowd. She was absolutely determined not to let that happen to her new daughter.

Putting aside thoughts of him she hurried towards the nursery, glad she had queued for food for their tea in her midday break. Keeping a tired child happy in a long queue was something she tried to avoid at all costs.

As Mavis turned the corner to the nursery, the sound of children at play drifted from the playground. She smiled, always loving those merry sounds. But as she got closer, a teacher met her at the door looking worried.

'I'm afraid Joyce had a fall during playtime at school,' she said. 'It's just a bump on her head but she was upset for a while. The teacher put a cold flannel on it and cleaned it up. I just thought you'd want to know.'

Children fell over all the time in their hurry to get from place to place so Mavis wasn't worried when she saw the small wound, even though Joyce was making the most of it. Their relationship was still fairly new and Mavis had to resist the temptation to give her treats because of the injury. She forced herself to ignore that urge. That way you would teach a child to always play on any little cough or cold, never mind a bump on her head. She knew plenty of adults who did that.

As they walked hand in hand towards the gate she overheard two other mums discussing the increases in rents. She hadn't realised the rises had been so widespread. Did one man own all the houses, she wondered, or had all the landlords got together, plotting to take more money from people who already lived hand to mouth?

She had a lot to think about and it must be done soon.

But what?

3

The next day, the three librarians began more planning for summer activities.

'Some of the kids 'ave already gone 'op picking with their mums,' Mavis said. 'They go every year. Can't blame 'em. It's 'ard work but a change of scenery and the air smells a lot better than round 'ere.'

Jane nodded. 'That's right, three children who live next door went a week ago. The schools don't seem worried about them missing the last bit of term.' She paused. 'I hope that Mr Miller comes back to help with the scavenger hunt as he promised.'

Cordelia hoped he would come back too, and not only for his library suggestions. She had never felt as much as a tingle near any man since she and Robert, her lovely doctor boyfriend, began courting. Eugene had sparked some feelings in her body she had almost forgotten she had.

The librarians were interrupted by an unfamiliar man coming to the desk. In his late sixties, with a mop of white hair, he was dressed in a tweed suit and bottle-green velvet waistcoat despite it being a warm day. On his head was a matching velvet soft cap topped with a feather.

'Good morrow, fair ladies of this sanctuary of letters! I hope this fresh new day finds you as well as can be. I am new of this borough and would wish to join your good selves in this house of knowledge. Might that be possible?'

The women looked at him in amazement. Was he leading them on, trying to make fun of them?

Suppressing a smile, Cordelia stepped forward. 'Certainly, good sir. I'll give you an application form. You are welcome to sit over there. When you've completed it, bring it back and we will issue you with a library card.'

He bowed, holding his feathered hat which he swept almost to the floor. 'I will return anon,' he said with a toothy smile.

He returned in record time and handed his form back to Cordelia.

'I hear tell of the ample collection of literary works within these hallowed walls,' he said. 'I am an aficionado of the written word in all its forms. Pray, where might a lover of fiction start his peregrinations?'

Mavis almost choked in her attempts not to laugh at his flowery language and had no idea what peregrinations were. Luckily, Cordelia was ready to deal with this most unusual character. She looked at his form. 'Come with me, Mr Booker. We have works from Homer to Shakespeare and many others. Let me show you the way.'

He swept his hat off again as he looked at Jane and Mavis. 'Farewell, fair ladies, parting is such sweet sorrow.'

'Blimey,' Mavis said when he was out of earshot. "E's a rum 'un and no mistake. Must think 'e's Shakespeare or something.'

When Cordelia joined the other two again, she couldn't stop

smiling as she read his form. 'Just as I suspected – he's an actor. Retired, he said. I wonder if he ever did well.'

Jane looked up from the papers she was sorting. 'I've never heard of him and I didn't recognise him either. Mind you, if he was on the stage I'd never have seen him anyway.'

Cordelia held up her hands. 'Or he could have a stage name. But never mind that for now. We need to get back to what we were talking about. The scavenger hunt. The main problem is finding time to sort it out.'

Outside, a man with a barrel organ trundled by, the wheels of his cart squealing on the pavement. He was playing 'Roll Out the Barrel' and singing along. He had a fine baritone voice.

'We only need to prepare a week at a time and I'm sure Tom will help,' Jane mused. 'What would we do without him? We had no idea when he first volunteered here how valuable he'd be.'

'I've got an idea,' Mavis said with a cheeky grin on her face. ''Ow about asking...' – she dropped her voice – 'that Shakespeare bloke to do one, The Professor would do one, us three could do one each and Mr Miller could do that last one. That's most of the six-week holiday covered.'

Cordelia clapped her hands. As well as solving their time problem she knew she wanted to see Mr Miller – Eugene – again, although she would never have admitted it. 'Brilliant idea, Mavis. It will save us time and get library users involved. We'll ask them. We can do the first couple of weeks to give them time to prepare.'

Jane sighed. 'But we'll still need books for the little ones to take home and I'm worried we won't have enough choice.'

'Why, bless me, good ladies fair. May I interrupt your machinations?' Mr Booker was back, holding two books which he placed on the desk as he spoke. 'Might this lowly man be of some small aid to your most noble endeavour?'

Cordelia interrupted him, aware he was about to talk forever. 'Mr Booker, we welcome any suggestions you have.'

He lifted his cap and swept it to the floor again, almost dislodging the feather. 'I have the honour of knowing better than I can speak of, a luminary of literature. A very renowned writer named Stella Gibbons...'

Jane almost jumped up and down with excitement. 'The author of *Cold Comfort Farm*? You know her?'

Mr Booker nodded. 'She still resides in this bustling city as we speak and I wager her munificent spirit would cause her happiness to aid your endeavours. Shall I pen an entreaty for her assistance on behalf of this palace of learning?'

Cordelia almost hugged him. 'Mr Booker, I must verily say that would be of great help.' She stopped herself. Had she really said verily? Was his way of speaking catching?

'We'd need them double quick,' Mavis said. 'But we'd go and collect 'em if it's easier.'

Jane almost pushed her aside. 'I'll go!' Excitement made her voice higher than usual. 'I'd love to meet her.'

'I did overhear thy suggestion to involve me in thy most worthy activities for the children,' Mr Booker continued. 'I shall verily be honoured to participate. I shall be delighted to relish the opportunity to lend my pen to this most noble cause.'

Cordelia swallowed a laugh and replied, 'Prithee, good sir, let it be known that we shall be most delighted to have thy expert aid and counsel.'

When he'd gone Jane couldn't restrain a chuckle. 'You're not going to talk to us like that, are you, Cordelia? I'll need a translator!' She'd stamped the books he'd chosen. 'Okay, girls, what do you think he's just borrowed?'

'Proust? Shakespeare? *Canterbury Tales*?' Cordelia suggested.

'No idea,' Mavis said. 'Over my 'ead that one.'

By now Jane was having to put her hands over her mouth to stop herself laughing out loud. 'No... they were... they were... one romance and one Agatha Christie!'

When they'd stopped giggling, Cordelia said, 'But he's got a good idea there. Why don't we contact children's authors and ask if they'll give us any books? We can write to their publishers and ask them to forward them on. I'll do it, if you like. The publishers may have some unsold copies too.'

The door opened and Tom walked in using a stick. He was a conscientious objector but people thought he walked with a stick because of a war injury. When Cordelia agreed he could be involved with the library they'd discussed how he would explain his injury. It was from an accident, nothing to do with war. 'Please don't tell people you're a conscientious objector,' Cordelia asked. 'I don't mind but some others may feel differently. Plenty of people still remember that Great War. I don't want conflict in the library.'

Finally they agreed that Tom wouldn't lie, but he would dodge any difficult questions. It seemed to work.

'Tom!' Cordelia said. 'You're just the man we need. I must go to a meeting but Jane and Mavis will tell you what we were talking about. I bet you'll be of great help.'

Half an hour later they had a wealth of ideas but wondered how they would find the time to do them all. They made a list and allocated each task.

'Apply for a small grant from the Lord Mayor's war relief fund,' Tom suggested. 'I can make some posters asking for books and put them up here in the library. We can ask readers when they come in as well.'

'It don't seem much,' Mavis said. 'Let's hope our actor friend comes up with the goods.' She looked at Tom. 'Tom, would you do me a favour, please?'

Tom put aside the notebook where he had been writing the ideas. 'For you, anything, Mavis. What is it?'

'I want to have a meeting of tenants about the rent rises and lack of repairs. Get a strike going?'

Tom's jaw dropped open. 'A strike? A rent strike? Good grief. Won't the landlords just throw you all out?'

Mavis sighed. 'I've thought of that. For a start we can just refuse to move out. But I think if enough of us refuse to pay rent, we'll 'ave the benefit of numbers. The rich scoundrels will soon listen if they lose a whole lot of rent in one week.'

Jane had been listening and joined in. 'And you can get the newspapers involved, get some publicity.'

'So did you want me to make posters, Mavis? Is that the favour?'

She nodded and squeezed his arm. 'Yes, please. I 'ad a word with the vicar at St Marks on my way 'ere and we can use the church hall for the first meeting.' She pulled a face. 'I just 'ope I'm not rattling around there on me own.'

Tom laughed. 'If you are, there'll be no one to see your embarrassment.'

But would anyone come to the meeting?

4

As usual, the postman Gordon whistled as he walked along Bradfield Road. He was well past retirement age and often mentioned he was glad to be back at work. 'Stop me going off me nut with boredom,' he'd tell anyone who'd listen. 'Wish me knees were younger though.'

Their small home had no hallway so the post always dropped directly into the living room. Jane and her landlady Mrs S rarely had any letters and there was just one that morning. When Jane saw the handwriting on it her heart sank. It was from her mother-in-law Edith.

Mrs S saw her face drop. 'What's up, sweetheart? Is it bad news?'

Jane opened the envelope and unfolded the single sheet of paper inside. A fly flew in through the open window and landed on the letter like a harbinger of doom. Jane shook it off, wishing she could shake her mother-in-law off so easily.

'I'm coming to stay for a week from Saturday, love Edith,' she read. It was short and to the point. 'Yes, it's bad news. It's George's mother,' she said. She'd never mentioned her to Mrs S, there had never been a need to and Jane didn't like to even think about her. 'My mother-in-law. She says she's coming here for a week.' She paused and looked up at her kind landlady. 'She'll expect to stay here. I'm really sorry to ask, but can she? Helen can sleep with me and Edith can have the box room. She'll think it's a treat.'

Mrs S put down her gunmetal-grey knitting and stretched her arthritic hands. 'I don't mind, love, but you look as if you do.'

Jane folded the letter and put it back in the envelope as if putting it away might make it vanish. 'Edith's... shall we say... a difficult woman. She disapproves of everything and never stops moaning. And she likes a tipple a bit too much, if you know what I mean.' She unfolded the letter and read it again. 'She's coming next weekend.' Her pulse raced as she remembered the first time she'd met her mother-in-law.

George, her husband, had been a new boyfriend then, but had asked her to visit his mother in Bethnal Green with him. Although he lived not far away from his mother, he never seemed keen to visit despite her being widowed many years earlier.

'You don't have to come, love,' he'd said, squeezing Jane's hand tight. 'It won't be fun. Her favourite hobby is moaning about anything and everything. She wouldn't know happiness if it hit her in the face with a hundred-pound note.'

Hoping this new relationship would lead to something permanent with George, Jane agreed to join him. She was determined to make a good impression, putting on her best dress and spending ages getting her hair into a perfect victory roll. Her friend loaned her a handbag to match her red polka-dot dress, and with her scarlet lipstick she felt like the bee's knees. George grinned and wolf-whistled when he saw her, making her smile.

As they walked from the Tube station, Jane remembered his warnings and had to damp down her nerves. 'Do you really think she'll be that difficult?' she asked, glancing at her hand-some new beau. He shrugged, a non-committal expression on his face.

'I've never brought a girl home before so there's no way of knowing. But if she gets too bad, get behind me and I'll defend you with my life!'

To soften her up, Jane had brought a gift with her, a tiny bottle of Lily of the Valley perfume. She felt it in her bag. 'Everyone likes a gift,' she muttered to herself.

Edith, George's mother, had the bottom floor of a small terraced house, not unlike the one Jane had lived in with her parents. Like theirs, the front step was scrubbed shining white, and the net curtains were spotless too.

They had to knock three times before Edith opened the door, eyeing them up as if they were strangers come to sell her rotten fruit. The bitterness that radiated from her could almost be touched, like a cloud of noxious fumes that seemed to surround the very air around her. Jane found herself instinctively shrinking back, heart racing.

'You're late,' Edith said, taking longer than expected to stand aside and let them in. They were only five minutes later than arranged but Jane and George had already decided not to disagree with her about anything unless it was absolutely neces-sary. 'You'll be wanting a cuppa, I suppose,' Edith said, gesturing to the settee and filling up the kettle.

The room was tidy but sparse. Most women in Silvertown liked to make their homes cosy with ornaments or family photos. Not this room. It only had the bare essentials. The air was thick was stale cigarette smoke and Jane longed to open the window.

Having put the kettle on, Edith turned and looked at Jane. 'So you're the one he's mentioned.' She looked Jane up and down like a piece of pork on display in a butchers' shop. 'What do you do then? Got a job, 'ave you?' She nodded at George. 'Don't expect 'im to keep you. 'E'll never amount to anything, just like 'is dad.'

Jane had always been able to chat to most people, but this conversation was full of uncomfortable silences and she could feel George's tension, see his fists clenched beside her.

Bustling about, Edith made the tea and handed each of them a cup and saucer. 'You'll be wanting cake or biscuits. Well, you're out of luck. I'm a widow woman and this one 'ere,' she glared at George, ''e 'ardly ever sends me a penny.'

George spoke for the first time. 'Mum, you know I don't earn a lot yet and I've got rent to pay just like you. I send you money every fortnight.' As he spoke he glanced at the sideboard. There, beside a clock showing the wrong time, was a bottle of whisky and a half-full glass. 'Still liking your whisky then, Mum,' he said. 'Find the money for that then?'

Jane's breath caught in her throat as the atmosphere in the room, already cold, became frigid.

Without a word, Edith turned to the sideboard, topped up the glass and downed the whisky in two mouthfuls. Her eyes never left George as if defying him to say anything. ''Ow I spend my money is my business, so I'll thank you to keep your nose out of it.'

She spent the rest of the visit complaining about the damp in her bedroom, queues for food, the danger of war approaching, her bunions and the people upstairs being too noisy.

'But you can't complain, can you?' she finally said and Jane almost spluttered the remains of her tea all over the rug.

By the time they left, Jane's head was pounding.

'I'm sorry, love,' George said, holding her hand as they

walked down the road. 'She's always been difficult but that was worse than usual.'

They stopped to let two lads run past them playing cowboys and Indians. The boys had patched-up trousers and worn-out shoes but were oblivious to their poverty. Jane looked at them and then spoke to George. 'I've often noticed that if you're really poor, you don't feel poor if everyone around you is in the same boat.'

'You're right, love,' he said, stopping to put her arm through his. 'And my mum might be difficult but we mostly had food in our bellies.'

Continuing with her reverie, Jane shook her head, remembering how Edith had made snide comments to all and sundry at their wedding. Some were deliberately said loud enough for her to overhear. 'She's very plain, isn't she?' 'I can't think what George sees in her.' 'That dress doesn't fit very well.' 'She's got no bust to speak of, has she? Men like a woman with plenty on top.' 'This marriage won't last a year. You mark my words.'

Jane had tried to ignore Edith's horrible comments, to be as far away from her as possible, but the hall was small and Edith's voice carried. It didn't help that some people sidled up to Jane and told her what they'd overheard. They weren't trying to be mean, but she wished they hadn't repeated them.

Then worse still, Edith continued in her attempts to ruin their special day by demanding George take her home halfway through the little party afterwards. The mere memory of Edith's malicious murmurings to other guests filled her with a simmering resentment. She could still vividly picture the wedding – the way Edith's mouth became rigid like stone as she delivered her ultimatum. 'Take me home now. You're my son and you do what I say.' Her voice was loud enough for half the room to hear.

Jane's heart had frozen as she saw George's face fall, the colour draining from his cheeks. 'But, Mum, I'll pay for a taxi, that'll be a treat for you.' He'd pleaded in a desperate attempt to reason with his obstinate mother. 'You can't expect me to leave my own wedding party.'

But his mother was unmoved, her expression set in a stubborn scowl as she plonked herself down heavily on the nearest chair, still wearing her coat and hat, her handbag on her knee. Her presence loomed liked a giant disapproving shadow over what should have been a happy occasion.

George tried everything to get her to change her mind. He got her another drink, he walked away, he walked back and sat beside her holding her hand. Nothing worked, she remained unmoving.

As more people noticed what was going on, whispers spread throughout the room like ripples in a pond. Jane's cousin Charlie, well known for his plain speaking, went over and spoke in her ear, 'Throw the bitch out, Jane. I'll help ya!'

After ten minutes and against her better judgement Jane admitted defeat. 'You'd better take her,' she said to George, struggling not to cry. 'There's plenty of trains this time of day. You don't have to go in. Dump her at the door.'

As George escorted his mother out of the hall, the older woman turned to Jane and sneered at her in triumph, the entire debacle played out for all to witness.

Even this long after, Jane could still feel the burn of embarrassment and the sting of disappointment that her mother-in-law had felt she must ruin George's special day.

'I'm sorry, Mrs S,' she said, looking up from her memories to speak to her landlady. 'If she gets unbearable, I'll tell her to go.' She hesitated, wondering how much to tell her kind landlady, but there was no point in trying to hide things. 'She used to be a drinker. I haven't seen her for a while and I hope she's stopped.'

What she didn't say was Edith was likely to find ways to show them up if she was drunk.

Mrs S reached out and patted Jane's hand, her eyes full of understanding. 'Don't you worry, me dear, we'll manage. My brother, the oldest one, Harold, 'e was a drinker and nasty when 'e was in 'is cups. Me and my ma lost count of the times we 'ad to undress 'im and put 'im to bed. Killed 'im in the end. Blind drunk, 'e fell in the river and drowned.' She put down her knitting. 'Awful to say but 'e wasn't much missed.'

Jane felt a wave of sadness wash over her. 'That's so terrible, Mrs S. You've had a hard life.'

Her landlady gave a crooked smile. 'Not many around these parts what 'aven't.'

5

Cordelia looked up from her desk, her eyes catching the clock. It was almost three o'clock, and she knew Eugene would be arriving soon. She had tried all morning to avoid thinking of him but she'd been unsuccessful. They'd all been struck by how kind and friendly he was when he'd come in a few days earlier to register with the library.

He'd promised to show them a simple science trick they could demonstrate to the local children. When they'd told Tom about it his eyes lit up. 'That should keep them happy!' he said with a smile. 'I'll show them how it's done so they could impress all their family and friends.'

As if on cue, Cordelia heard Eugene's footsteps and stepped out of her office to meet him. He carried a small box under one arm, and greeted her with a wide smile. 'Morning, Miss Cordelia,' he said. He walked up to the desk, his eyes warm and inviting.

'Hi, Eugene,' she replied, her heart skipping a beat. She tried to deny it but she loved the way he said her name, the slow, gentle drawl that made it seem special. 'Tom should be here soon. He's our volunteer and really keen to learn this trick so he can show it to the children. How is your family history research going?'

He raised an eyebrow. 'One step forward and two steps back at the moment, but I'll get there.' He placed the box on the desk. 'I had to keep my promise to show this trick.' He lowered his voice. 'And, of course, I hoped you would be on duty.'

Cordelia busied herself with some papers to hide the blush creeping up her neck. She hardly knew how to answer and was saved by Tom walking in. He smiled when he saw them both. 'You must be Eugene,' he said with a smile. 'I'm looking forward to learning from you today. Let me just put my things away.'

Mavis, who had come to collect books that needed reshelving, greeted him warmly. 'Science today, is it?'

Tom and Eugene went into Cordelia's office and she followed them, glad she'd tidied up.

'Right, Tom,' Eugene said. 'Ready to see some magic? You'll probably know it, but hopefully younger ones won't.'

He'd found a sheet of red waterproof fabric at Rathbone market. It was second-hand and had seen better days but it would serve the purpose. He unpacked the box, explaining the experiment.

'We're going to make a baking soda and vinegar volcano. It's simple and makes so much mess the kids love it!'

Cordelia watched him, enjoying the way he was so engrossed in what he was doing.

'Okay, folks, all you need is this small bottle, some baking soda, vinegar and a bit of soap to make it bubble. But we'd better get this cloth down first to protect your desk.'

Cordelia's heart sank. 'Soap is really hard to come by these days.'

He opened a small bag next to him. 'I'd heard you guys have

a problem with that, so I got a few bars from the base. You can cut them up to share with the kids.'

'Their parents will be fighting for them,' Tom said with a grin.

Tom watched Eugene set up the materials and then he showed Tom how to make the simple trick fun and exciting. 'First,' he said, 'we put some baking soda in the bottle. About two tablespoons should do it.'

'Can we make half portions? There'll be plenty of complaints if the kids all use two tablespoons.'

Eugene slapped his head with his palm. 'You gotta forgive me, I keep forgetting how tough things are for you. Yes, half will be fine, it'll still work.'

Tom carefully scooped the baking soda into the bottle, then looked up. 'Which next?'

'You'll need to melt a few flakes from a bar of soap or washing flakes. I guessed you guys might not have any flakes, so I bought a packet from our stores. Add a small amount to the soda.'

They watched Tom do it as if he were ten years old instead of a grown man. 'And now, the vinegar?'

'Now the fun bit,' Eugene said with a wink. 'Prepare to stand back.' He paused and pretended to be a magician waving his arms around. 'Ready? Pour a small amount of vinegar into the bottle and watch out!'

Immediately the mixture began to fizz and bubble, overflowing and cascading down the sides. It did indeed look like a miniature volcano.

Cordelia clapped her hands, delighted. 'That's wonderful. I think you'll have to take them to do this in the alley at the back, or the library will be flooded.'

Cordelia watched as the two men cleared up the mess,

feeling a sense of warmth and contentment that drove away worries about the war and library budgets. Eugene's enthusiasm was infectious and she knew Tom would make the experiment exciting for the children. When they'd finished she walked Eugene to the door. He turned to her, his expression soft.

'I've really enjoyed this, and I'm going to be a regular in this lovely library.' He paused and looked into her eyes for a second or two longer than normal. 'I'm hoping I'll see you regularly too,' he almost whispered. 'Perhaps...' he started, but someone coming into the library pushed past him and he never finished his sentence. 'I hope I'll see you again soon, Miss Cordelia,' he said with a cheeky grin.

She walked back to her desk, her mind full of him, his smooth skin, his entrancing eyes, his cologne, his broad shoulders. She shook herself out of the trance-like state she was in. She wasn't looking for love. She already had it.

6

The few days before Edith arrived weighed heavily on Jane's shoulders and she wrote an urgent letter to George to see if he could get a day or two's leave if his mother got too bad. She guessed the awkward woman wouldn't go willingly at the end of the week as she'd said in her letter.

Preparing for her mother-in-law, she moved Helen's things into her own room and put clean bedding on the single bed. Then she looked around to make sure everything was okay. One thing was sure, if the room was as grand as a bedroom in Buckingham Palace, Edith would still find something to complain about.

Helen, sensing her mother's distress, tried to help, dusting and tidying her toys without being asked. Jane was proud of how sensible she was for a five-year-old.

When the dreaded Saturday arrived, Jane woke up with a knot in her stomach. She had the day off work and dressed herself and Helen with care. Mrs S, kind as ever, had cooked a few scones, making an aside that 'a bit of food might soak up the booze'.

The sound of a car pulling up outside the front door sent Jane's heart racing. To her surprise it was a taxi and Edith emerged with two large suitcases. Surely she wouldn't need all that for a one-week stay?

The moment Edith laid eyes on Mrs S sitting in her armchair in the living room, her demeanour was transformed dramatically. It was as if she'd been possessed by the spirit of a refined aristocrat. 'Oh, what a positively charming little abode you have here, Mrs Simmons!' she exclaimed, her voice dripping with a sudden posh accent that would have made the king himself raise an eyebrow. 'It's absolutely cosy and delightful. May I have the pleasure of calling you Mrs S, or would that be taking unforgivable liberties? You can, of course, call me Edith, darling.'

She glided forward, her movements surprisingly graceful for someone who was under the influence. She grasped Mrs S's hand between both of hers as if she were greeting royalty.

Jane watched this amazing spectacle unfold, her jaw dropping so low it nearly hit her chest. If she had been sipping tea, she would have sprayed it across the room like a startled llama. The fake posh accent, the sudden charm offensive – it was as if Edith had been replaced by someone from a parallel universe where manners and grace reigned supreme.

'I do hope we're going to be the best of friends, Mrs S,' Edith went on, her voice dripping with honey. 'You are so, so generous to extend such hospitality to me.'

Jane blinked rapidly, half-expecting to wake up from this bizarre dream at any moment. She pinched herself to make sure she wasn't hallucinating.

As Edith released the landlady's hand and turned to face Jane, Jane hastily rearranged her features into a forced smile, desperately trying to suppress the laugh caused by my Mrs S's look of disbelief behind Edith's back.

At least this visit was unlikely to be boring. She couldn't wait to see what other surprises Edith had in store.

'You go and unpack,' Mrs S said, leaning forward and, using her hands on the arms of her old chair, pushing herself up. 'I'll make us a cuppa. I expect you're thirsty after your journey.'

Edith look at Jane with a face so different from a second ago it was as if she'd had a face transplant. 'Where's my bedroom, sweetheart?' She moved towards the stairs then looked back at Jane. 'Well, you bringing my cases up or what?' The harsh words were said quietly enough to avoid being overheard.

Jane was exhausted by the time she'd lugged the heavy cases up the steep, narrow stairs. 'Come down when you're ready and have a cuppa. Mrs S has made some scones too.' Glad that Helen was out playing with her friends, Jane sat down and looked at her landlady who was buttering the scones.

'She's a charmer, ain't she? However I kept a straight face I'll never know,' Mrs S said. 'Will she be okay with your little one?'

Jane thought back over the years since Helen was born. 'I've just realised she hasn't seen her since she was a baby. George is never very keen to visit her, so he goes once or twice a year on his own. I've no idea how she'll be.'

'Well, we won't 'ave any booze in the 'ouse, that's for sure,' Mrs S said. 'If she gets drunk she'll 'ave to pay for it.'

Very quickly Edith was back with them, her smile fixed on again. 'Oh, scones,' she said as she sat down. 'How delightful.' She opened her handbag and poured something from a flask into her tea. 'Just to keep out the cold,' she said, presumably forgetting it was summer.

The painfully unnatural conversation went on a little longer until Jane was relieved it was time to collect Helen.

'Oh, my lovely granddaughter,' Edith said. 'May I come with

you? It's been so long.' She turned to Mrs S. 'So difficult when we live so far apart.'

Jane looked at Mrs S and raised an eyebrow. They both knew she only lived in a different part of the East End.

'You'll have trouble recognising her,' Jane said wickedly.

Edith's eyes narrowed and her jaw tightened, then the smile reappeared. 'Children grow so fast, don't they?'

They were less than a hundred yards away from the house when the real Edith appeared again. She was wearing high heels she tottered in, and clothes that Mrs S would say made her look like mutton dressed as lamb.

'Got yourself a cosy number there, ain't ya?' she said, all trace of what Jane was already thinking of as Lady Muck gone. 'How much rent do you pay?'

Jane was astonished at her rude question. 'I'd rather not say,' she replied.

'Well, why not? Cat got your tongue or something? You work in a library so you must earn a bomb.'

'My finances are my business. I don't expect to know yours.' The only response she got was a sneer, Edith's lipstick on her teeth showing vividly.

'So what's my granddaughter like then? Is she the image of me?' She patted her peroxide-blond hair. 'She'll be lucky if she is.'

Jane suppressed a snort. 'She's a lovely girl, very lively and always asking questions as they should at that age.'

Edith groaned. 'I remember George doing that. Drove me mad. I used to clip him round the ear.'

As they approached the church hall, Jane could hear the excited chatter of children and mothers. She took a deep breath, steeling herself for whatever embarrassment her mother-in-law was about to cause. When they stepped inside Helen came bounding towards them, her hair flying and her face smeared with chalk. 'Mummy!' she squealed. 'We did drawing. I drawed baby Jesus and a star.'

'That's wonderful,' Jane said, hugging her tight. But the moment was short-lived as Helen spotted Edith and became silent.

Edith flung open her arms, outstretched like a flamboyant opera singer. 'Helen, my darling,' she exclaimed, her voice carrying far and wide. 'Come and give your grandma a big, big hug!'

Helen, who couldn't remember seeing this strange woman before, promptly burst into tears and hid her face in Jane's skirt.

Affronted, Edith glared at Jane. 'Well, I never!' Her real voice was back but much quieter. 'Is this how you've raised her, Jane? To be afraid of her own grandmother? George will not be pleased when I tell him.'

Jane could have smacked her. 'She's just shy, Edith. She'll need a while to get to know you.'

Undeterred, Edith rummaged in her handbag and produced a gobstopper. 'Here, my little cherub,' she cooed, looking around to see if she had an audience. 'Have a sweetie from your grandma.'

Still clinging to Jane's skirt with one hand, Helen leaned forward as far as her arms would reach and grabbed the sweet. Then she ducked behind her mother again.

As they walked down the church path, Edith stopped to chat to every parent they met, regaling them with how wonderful her 'darling granddaughter' was. Jane could only look on in despair as Edith's behaviour had the opposite effect to that she antici- pated. One woman got too close and stepped back quickly, undoubtedly put off by the fumes on Edith's breath. Two mothers who knew Jane looked over her mother-in-law's head as she bent down to try to engage their terrified children. Jane gave the universal sign for crazy and they gave a knowing smile in return.

When Edith had exhausted every opportunity to show off she stopped abruptly outside the churchyard. 'I'll leave you now for a while. I must see if my old friends at the Duck and Drake remember me.'

'But they'll be closing before long,' Jane said, noticing the time on the clock tower.

'Don't be silly, Jane. You were always so naïve. I can't think what George sees in you.'

How long could Jane stand this before she did something she'd later regret?

7

The June sunlight bathed the densely built Silvertown streets as little Hetty Gregory tugged excitedly at her mother's hand. 'Come on, Mummy, come on!' she urged her mother. Though only six years old, she was the library's most dedicated young reader and couldn't wait to join the summer reading activities.

Her mother looked at her clutching her 'book bag' and thought back to the previous year when Hetty had had diphtheria. Her life had hung on a thread and Mrs Gregory had been terrified she would lose her. Even now she could remember that terror. She would never forget it. And despite the little girl being unaware of what was going on around her when she was ill, Mrs Gregory had sat by her bed reading her favourite stories to her – Peter Pan and Winnie the Pooh. She had almost collapsed with relief when Hetty began to pull through.

As the library clock struck eight thirty, they reached the steps into the library where several other youngsters waited. They were the usual mixture of local children, some with stunted growth, skin and hair and poor clothing showing the poverty of their lives. "Ere, can you read yet?' Willie, one of the kids with slight rickets, asked his mate, Fred.

'Nuh,' Fred said, turning down the corners of his mouth. 'Me dad can't and it ain't 'eld him back none.' If the librarians had heard the conversation they would have despaired. Many men in Silvertown worked on the docks. Although work was more available in wartime, it was a dangerous place to work with frequent accidents, some fatal. In peacetime they'd have to wait at the dock gates hoping to be picked for a day's work. Lack of education held many bright men, and women, from fulfilling their potential.

But Willie hadn't finished with his friend yet. 'Yeah, ain't only the docks your old man gets 'is readies from, is it?'

Fred glared at him. 'You keep your big gob shut. If my dad 'ears you you'll wish you'd never bin born.'

The little crowd were silent briefly as the heavy library door began to open with a familiar creak. They had decided to open half an hour earlier than usual on Saturdays for the club so that excited children wouldn't disturb adult readers.

Jane swung the door open, spotting Hetty practically jumping up and down trying to catch her eye. Jane gave her a special smile acknowledging that they knew each other well.

Relieved they had managed to secure additional books from various sources, Jane counted the children in. Although they were supposed to apply beforehand she predicted some would just turn up. She remembered being sent off to Sunday school by her mother. She hated it. Not because she didn't believe in God, although as a child she didn't really understand the Bible. No, it was because she was so bored. Now, as an adult, she realised her mother just wanted a bit of peace and quiet. She guessed that would be true for the mothers of some of these youngsters too.

'Come in, come in! We're really pleased to see you,' she

called out, delighted to see a dozen children pushing their way forward. Mavis was standing next to her.

'What're the chances of the little blighters behaving themselves?' she muttered.

'Come on, Mavis,' Jane replied. 'We'll keep them too busy to be naughty.'

Their own daughters Joyce and Helen were there with strict orders not to expect special treatment.

'Okay, everyone,' Jane called, clapping her hands. 'Sit yourselves down on the floor while I explain what's going to happen.'

There was the usual jostling and mutters as they sorted themselves out.

'Right, well done, everyone,' Jane continued. 'So, Mrs Kent here has some forms she'll put on the desk. We have two groups for the scavenger hunt competition – those under nine years old and those over nine years old. If you have already applied to be here, your form will be done. If not, stop behind at the end and we'll sort it out for you.'

'Do we get sweets?' Willie asked, rubbing his hands down his short trousers. 'I've only come 'ere for the sweets.'

'Told ya!' Mavis grumbled quietly.

'Willie, you'll have to wait and see. You will be given clues for things to look for in books in the library. They will be either here in the children's section or in the room at the back – the one with a big drawing of a book on the door.'

'Do we win sweets?' Jimmy asked louder this time.

'The prize is the fun of looking through books you might want to read... and maybe a sweet,' Jane started.

'What about them what can't read then, missus?' Fred asked. Willie kicked him hard in the shins.

Jane flicked the pages of one of the books. It was entirely pictures. 'Then you can have a picture book. And if you'd like help with your reading let us know. We have volunteers who will help you over the summer.'

'That's right,' Mavis chipped in. 'A lot of you missed schooling because of the bombing. It wasn't fair on you. We can 'elp you catch up.' She indicated the children's area. 'We've got a lot of books out ready for you to look at but if you 'ave something you're interested in but can't find we'll try to 'elp you find it. Your first task is to find books with an elephant in them. It can be a picture of an elephant or a story about one. You have ten minutes and, please, remember to keep the noise down. Remember the grown-ups here like things quiet when they come in.'

Surprisingly quickly some descended on the book table and shelves while others hurried to the door at the back. Watching them, the two librarians saw that the children who came regularly looked confident, but others like the two boys were hesitant, covering their uncertainty with wisecracks and nudges.

They were interrupted by a loud hammering on the door. Mavis looked at her watch. 'It ain't opening time yet. That can't be Bert.'

Jane shook her head. 'We'd better open it anyway or the noise will distract everyone.'

Struggling to contain her irritation, Mavis walked towards the door, muttering under her breath about impatient people. Her shoes, resoled with patches cut from a leaky hot-water bottle, moved silently.

'We're not open yet!' she shouted. But it did no good. The hammering continued. Sighing, she turned the big key and pulled the door towards her.

'Where is 'e?' A hulk of a man took a step forward. He wore a sleeveless vest that displayed inky tattoos on his arms and neck. He shouldered her aside so forcefully she almost fell over.

'Who—' But Mavis got no further with her question as the man strode towards the children. The younger ones shrunk at his approach, eyes wild. But he ignored them, zeroing in on Willie.

'There you are, you little bastard!' he boomed and, stepping none too gently between the children, he grabbed Willie by the ear and yanked him forward.

Willie yelped and tugged at his father's hand, but there was no letting go.

'Told you you got work to do this morning, didn't I?' his father said, ignoring everyone else in the room. 'None of this messin' about with sissy books. You turnin' into a girl or somethink?'

Mavis stepped forward. 'Excuse me, you're hurting—'

But this man wasn't listening. 'Come with me, you little bugger, or you'll regret it.'

Mavis stepped forward again. 'Let go of that boy's ear—' But her sentence was never finished.

The brute turned his head and glared at her. 'Keep your nose out of my business, you stupid old biddy!' The man's voice echoed throughout the whole library. Without pausing he dragged the unfortunate Willie out of the building by his ear.

The children had all stopped what they were doing while this was happening. Some looked frozen with fear, eyes wide and mouths dropped open. One or two took it in their stride as if this type of behaviour was normal.

'What'll we do?' Mavis whispered, but Jane was already speaking.

She held up her hands. 'I'm sorry about that, children, and I hope Willie will be able to come another day to find a book. But now, why don't you carry on looking for books with elephants.

Mrs Kent and I are ready to write down the names for you in case you want to borrow the book.'

When they had settled down to their task the two women took a few steps back and spoke in hushed tones.

'What can we do?' Jane asked. 'That man should be in prison. Poor Willie…'

Mavis's shoulders dropped and she wiped a tear from her eye. 'Nothing. The cops'll do nothing. They don't do nothing to blokes beating up their wives so they won't do anything about one doing the same to the kids. 'Appens to 'alf the kids around 'ere.'

Jane shook her head. 'Perhaps we should get one of the parents to sign a form saying they agree to their child coming. We'll talk to Cordelia about it.'

'I doubt Willie's dad will sign it. I don't think he can even read and write.' She shook her head. 'I've 'eard a lot about that man. Used to be a docker but got the push for turning up drunk and fighting. Put one bloke in 'ospital for a week they said. Got 'is finger in plenty of pies though. Makes a living somehow.'

8

Mrs S was reading a romance Jane had brought her from the library and Helen was happily engrossed drawing pictures of the farmyard animals she remembered from her time as an evacuee. Jane had just finished preparing vegetables when the front door burst open, revealing a dishevelled Edith. She stumbled into the front room with all the grace of a puppet with tangled strings. The smell of alcohol surrounded her like an invisible cloud.

'Hello, my darlings!' she slurred, her posh accent now a comical blend of King's English and a drunken sailor.

Helen looked up at her grandmother with wide, curious eyes. 'Grandma, you're walking all funny. Why are you walking funny?'

Edith walked over to her and pulled her up from the floor, twisting her round and catching her foot on a chair leg. 'I'm not walking funny, granddaughter mine. I'm dancing. Can't you tell?' She then proceeded to twirl, sway and move like a demented ballerina getting dangerously close to injuring herself or damaging the furniture in the small room. 'I saw some hunks in the pub,' she said, still dancing. 'Well-built Yanks, you know what I mean.' She wiggled her little finger suggestively. 'Black as the ace of spades they was. One of them said he comes into your library.' She looked at Jane slyly. 'Got yourself a fancy man while my boy's away, have you?' She stopped and patted Jane's face a little too hard. 'Now what was his name? Gene? Jude? John? Something like that. Ring any bells, daughter-in-law?'

Jane took a deep breath to stop herself lashing back. 'It sounds like Eugene. He comes into the library regularly.'

'Ha, told you so!' The comment was aimed at Mrs S. 'And now I've got to go to...' She collapsed into a chair, giggling like a schoolgirl. Within seconds she was snoring quietly, each out-breath making the front of her hair that had fallen forward rise and fall like a drunken yo-yo in slow motion.

'Mummy, Grandma's funny, isn't she?' Helen said, watching the hair moving up and down.

'That's one way to put it,' Mrs S muttered.

They had their tea, choosing not to wake Edith, then Jane took Helen to bed, reading her a bedtime story until she was ready to sleep. She kissed her gently on the forehead and went back downstairs.

Speaking quietly to avoid disturbing her mother-in-law, she sat near enough to Mrs S to avoid being overheard. 'I've got a confession to make. I just looked through her stuff. You know, those two big suitcases she brought with her? I think it might be pretty much everything she owns.'

Mrs S looked up in surprise. 'It can't be. Can it? What makes you think that?'

Jane recalled looking through Edith's stuff, careful to put everything back exactly where it was. As well as clothes she found important papers – a birth certificate, an insurance policy, her ration books and her rent book. It was the last item that alarmed her the most. It told a worrying story.

'I think she's been kicked out of her place. Her rent book is up there and I looked inside. She hasn't paid any rent for weeks and weeks. She must have been hiding behind the door when the rent man called.'

They both looked at the snoring woman. Then Mrs S spoke, horror in her eyes. 'You don't think she... expects to live 'ere, do you?'

'Over my dead body,' Jane said. 'She'd cause nothing but chaos and within a week we'd be ready to choke her.'

They both stopped talking when they heard footsteps on the stairs. Helen came in in her nightdress. 'I woked up, Mummy, and couldn't get back to sleep.' She went to sit on Jane's lap, looking at over at Edith. 'Has Grandma been asleep all this time? She must be very tired.'

Jane kissed her cheek. 'She is, she's had a very busy day moving here then going to see her old friends. Now, I'm going to give you half a cup of milk then it's back to bed for you.'

Outside they could hear the ARP warden doing her rounds, sometimes shouting, 'Close those curtains now!'

When Jane had gone back to bed the two women continued their discussion. 'The trouble is,' Jane said, 'if we try to raise it with her, she'll deny everything. I've never got to know her well, but George has told me more than enough to know how she operates.'

'Me mouth's as dry as a badger's arse!'

Edith's voice made them jump and they both looked at her as she struggled to sit upright. Her hair looked as if she'd seen a ghost, the cheek that had rested on the arm of the chair had a deep crease and she had dribbled, dribble that had dried on her chin.

'I think you need a glass of water and then get off to bed,'

Jane said. She saw her mother-in-law look at her as if to make a sarcastic retort, then notice Mrs S.

'I expect you're right, sweetheart,' she said, her words running into each other. 'I'll do that then have a wee and get up the old apples and pears.' She pushed herself upright then went over to Mrs S. 'Thank you again, kind lady, for allowing me to stay.' She forgot to close the toilet door and they could hear her groaning and muttering to herself as she urinated. Then she walked back into the living room and with a cheery 'Toodle-pip' she went upstairs.

'I wonder if she'll even get undressed,' Mrs S said. 'I hope she doesn't soil the bedding.'

But worse was to come.

9

'Did you have a nice day, Joyce?' Mavis asked her adopted daughter when she collected her from school. She didn't need to ask, Joyce looked tired, as she often was after school. Like many working mothers she was relieved the government had let a lot of schools open over the holidays. They didn't offer normal school lessons, but kept the children occupied while their mothers did valuable work.

Joyce's mouth turned down at the corners. 'We 'ad nasty fish paste sandwiches for our dinner. They were all dry and curled up. 'Orrible.' Her nose crinkled at the memory.

Mavis thought about how much money she had in her purse, counting how little she had to last until next payday. It had only been a few months since Joyce's adoption had become legal and she still felt a thrill every day when she saw her. But her money had to stretch further.

She thought back to the first day she'd met Joyce. Mavis and her soldier boyfriend Joe had hoped to have a romantic day together, but Hitler had put paid to that. They'd ended up helping the ARP people search through debris after yet another bombing. They both hoped to find people alive under all the demolished bricks and wood, but knew that more likely they'd find people dead or horribly injured.

They had just uncovered a woman's arm, sticking up from the rubble, as if pleading for help. The rest of the body was still hidden. A wedding ring and a watch glinted in the light. Mavis felt a lump in her throat and blinked back tears. This was yet another heartbreaking casualty of the Blitz, a horror that seemed to stretch on without end.

'Quick,' an ARP man said. 'She might just be alive under that lot!' But before they had time to start again, they heard a little voice.

'That's my mummy's watch,' a young voice said. 'Where's my mummy?'

Turning round they were both relieved and alarmed to see a little girl behind them looking confused and worried. They had no idea where she'd come from and she obviously didn't understand the implication of what she was seeing.

Mavis and Joe looked at each other aghast. 'I'll take care of her,' Mavis said, struggling to keep a sob out of her voice. 'You carry on here.'

She had stood up from their awful task and held out her hand, talking reassuringly to the little girl while they walked away from the scene. Looking back just before they turned a corner, she saw Joe looking at her and shaking his head. This little girl's mother would never hold her in her arms again.

Mavis had regularly visited Joyce in the children's home where she'd been placed, and had asked to adopt her soon after. It had been a long, nerve-wracking process. Then Joyce had taken a while to settle into her new home with Mavis and still woke up in the night crying sometimes, but Mavis knew that each day saw her more settled.

'Tell you what!' she said, pushing aside those memories and holding Joyce's hand. 'Why don't we get some jacket potatoes? There's a stall round the corner selling them.'

Old Bertie always had his chestnut stall in the same spot, not far from the school. He'd been there for as long as Mavis could remember and always wore the same clothes all year round. He stirred his wares and the homely, smoky smell of hot potatoes was as tempting as frying bacon.

Mavis held a few coins tightly in her hand, running her thumb over their worn edges as though trying to conjure up more money through touch alone. Her brow furrowed as she counted the meagre total, worrying her bottom lip. If this strike didn't work, if the landlords didn't budge on their demands, it would mean their life would be even harder. And Joyce didn't deserve that, not after what she'd already been through. Mavis glanced at the little girl, who was looking longingly at the potatoes. What if she, as a mother, couldn't even give her new daughter these few modest treats?

No, she'd fight with everything she had to stop the landlords' greed from winning. If they wouldn't see reason then, by God, she, Mavis, would make them. With new resolve stiffening her back, she smiled at the chestnut seller. The battle was just beginning. If Joe was here, she knew he'd be right beside her.

''Ello Mavis, gel,' the chestnut seller said with a cheeky smile. ''Ow are you today? And who's this pretty little girl?' Bertie bent down to Joyce's level and pinched her cheek. She brushed his hand away with a frown.

Mavis didn't want to get into conversation. She had more to do before she and Joyce headed for home. 'This is my daughter Joyce and we'd like two small potatoes, please.'

He picked up two pieces of newspaper and expertly twisted each to make cones to hold the nuts. ''Ere you are, sweet'eart.

Ready in a gif. Bob's yer uncle. That's tuppence to you.' He winked to let her know she'd got a special price.

'Oh, before I go,' Mavis said. 'I'm holding a meeting about a rent strike on Saturday. Five o'clock at St Marks' church hall. Will you spread the word?'

Old Bertie looked up, more alert than before. 'Cor, good on ya, girl. Them beggars, excuse my language, them landlords is a right lot of so-and-sos. I'll tell everyone I meet and come along meself too.' He stirred his potatoes. 'My daughter's place 'as got vermin. She's as clean as a new pin, but can't get rid of the buggers cos they comes through from next door. Holes in the walls the landlord won't do nothing about. And what they can 'ear the couple next door doing...' He looked at Joyce. 'Well, I don't need to spell it out, do I?'

'That's shameful,' Mavis said. 'I 'ear 'orror stories like that every day.'

Saying goodbye, they headed away from home towards the corner shop, walking past a group of children playing on a bomb site. They were scrambling over piles of rubble like a mountain range. Shouts and laughter echoed round the war-torn street as they tossed chunks of broken masonry, turning the wasted space into a happy but dangerous playground.

'Are we going to queue again?' Joyce asked wearily, her mouth full of a chestnut.

'No, love, I'm going to ask Mrs May to put up this poster.' Tom had made her half a dozen posters announcing the strike meeting. Yet again his artistic skills had proved invaluable. Strictly speaking, he was a library volunteer but he had kindly agreed to help her. There was the inevitable queue outside every shop they passed. 'Rent strike meeting, St Marks' church hall, Saturday at five o'clock!' She repeated the rallying cry again and again to everyone in the queue. Some people ignored her, minds fixed on other things. But others paused, nodding in solidarity.

A familiar woman called from the queue outside the butcher's shop. 'You tell 'em, Mavis. Them slum landlords need teaching a lesson or two!'

At each stop more familiar faces appeared, some of people she knew well, a few library regulars and others friends and neighbours. 'I'm with you, dear,' said old Mrs Foxon, leaning heavily on her stick, face drawn with pain, old before her time. 'My place hasn't had a spot of paint in ten years, but the ruddy landlord always wants more coin.'

'It's a disgrace, that's what is it,' added Tommy the coal man. 'Damp runs down the walls in our bedroom no matter how we try to sort it out.'

Bolstered by every favourable comment about her strike plan she was not put off by the few dissenters who worried about being thrown out of their homes if they didn't pay up. She was not to be deterred despite Joyce getting increasingly tired and irritable. She pasted two more posters on to lamp posts. People in Silvertown knew each other, at least by sight, and several more stopped and chatted to her as she worked. Each had their own story of poor or no repairs to their properties and the demands for more rent from their landlord.

'Can we go home now?' Joyce said. 'I'm tired and I want my tea and a wee.' She tugged on Mavis's sleeve. 'It's urgent, Mummy.'

Mavis stopped in her tracks, her heart squeezed tight with joy. *Mummy!* Joyce had called her mummy. It was the first time. She had never tried to get her to do so. She'd had a bigger copy made of the photo of Joyce's mother they'd found in her mother's locket. One copy stood on the mantelpiece and the other in the bedroom. She always wanted the memory of Joyce's mother to live on and had been happy to be called Auntie Mavis. But now that the girl had chosen to call her mother, she was thrilled and certainly wouldn't stop her.

She bent down and hugged Joyce so hard the little girl wriggled free. 'My love, we will go home right now. You've been a very good girl coming with me.'

'Why are you telling all these people?' Joyce asked.

'See, it's like this, Joyce. Sometimes, if things ain't fair, you 'ave to do something about it yourself if no one else does. I bet you see that 'appening sometimes at school, don't you?'

Joyce popped her last chestnut in her mouth and considered the question. 'Well, if that nasty Bobby Harris keeps punching me, I go and tell teacher. He punches other people too but they don't say anything.'

Mavis clapped her hands. 'Good job, Joyce. You gotta stand up for yourself in this world.'

Little did she know how hard doing that for the people of Silvertown would be.

10

Edith had gone missing for a few days but when she returned, she was in a state. She spilled her tea all over the rug, hiccupped and fell asleep in the chair in the living room. It wouldn't do. She had said she was coming for a week and it had already been longer than that. Jane had agreed with Mrs S that she would tackle Edith.

'Speak to 'er when I'm not around,' Mrs S said. 'She's more likely to be 'erself then, not put on them airs and graces she does for me.' She raised an eyebrow. 'And I'd be 'appy not to see 'er for a while after that last performance.'

After Jane had dropped Helen off at her school, she went back home, but there was no sign of Edith. Knocking gently, she opened the door to her bedroom and looked in. Edith was lying face down on her bed fully dressed. Jane stood for a minute wondering what was the best thing to do. If she woke her up, Edith would be in a terrible mood, but then she probably would even if she slept to teatime. A hangover is a hangover.

Jane decided she might as well get it over and done with. The room was dim and stuffy, the curtains still drawn tight against daylight. Jane opened them, then opened the window to let some fresh air into the stale room. The noise caused a slight stir in the rumpled mass that was her mother-in-law. Standing, waiting for Edith to come round, Jane took a deep breath, steeling herself for the inevitable confrontation.

'Edith, time to get up!' she said when there was no more sign of movement. She shook her mother-in-law's shoulder gently.

Edith groaned and turned her head slightly, squinting up at Jane through bloodshot eyes. 'What's the time?' she mumbled, her voice thick with sleep.

'Time to get up. Helen's gone to school and we need to talk.'

Edith muttered a few curses and dragged herself into a sitting position. 'Okay, okay, no need to go on, Missus high-and-mighty librarian. I'll be down in a minute.'

Mrs S was just going out the front door as Jane went back downstairs. 'I'll go and 'ave a cuppa with Lily next door while you talk to 'er. Good luck, ducks.'

Jane put on the kettle and stood thinking about Edith's situation. She knew enough about alcoholism to know it was a disease, but that didn't stop her feeling angry with the woman. From what George had told her, she'd been a drinker throughout his childhood too. That meant his home life had been chaotic as his mother had spent every penny she could on booze, never mind if the kids lived on bread and dripping. Jane tried to be sympathetic, understanding about addiction, but her strong belief that you always look after your children first made it difficult.

Then she thought about all the stories she'd heard in the library. Mostly they were about husbands spending all their wages on booze, leaving the wives and children with nothing to live on.

Her mind flashed back to a conversation she had had with

Mrs S a few months before. 'Do you remember Mrs Carter from round the corner, number twenty-seven?' Mrs S had asked, her voice filled with a mixture of pity and disgust. 'She drinks all day. Most of the kids round 'ere are poor, but their mums try to keep them respectable. Not 'er. 'Er kids run around smelly as anything, dirty clothes, no shoes and so hungry they steal off the stalls on the market.' She paused and shook her head. 'It's heart-breaking, that's what it is.'

Jane had seen the children and given them food from time to time. 'What happened to them?' she asked. 'I haven't seen them for ages.'

'Evacuated. She couldn't wait to get rid of them, then last I 'eard, she'd run off with some dodgy bloke. Never been seen since. Bet she won't tell the evacuation people where she's gone neither.'

Edith's heavy footsteps alerted Jane to her mother-in-law's imminent appearance. She walked into the living room, still bleary-eyed, although she had wiped her face and combed her hair. 'Make us a cuppa, won't you?' She plonked herself down on the chair she'd snored in before.

Thinking it might help to have a sensible conversation Jane made her some tea and toast, using some of their precious stock of jam on the toast. Then she sat opposite her.

'We need to talk,' she said, her nerves so on edge they were jangling.

'What about?' Edith didn't look at her as she spoke, too busy lighting a Woodbine. Then she blew the smoke Jane's way and took a bite of the toast.

Jane brushed the smoke away from her face. 'We need to speak because I think you've been kicked out of your house.' She stopped, waiting for a response, wondering how much to disclose. 'I... well, I saw your rent book and your other stuff. It looks as if you've got everything you own here.'

For a moment there was complete silence. Then rage twisted Edith's features as she absorbed what Jane had said. Her brows furrowed into a deep V. Her eyes blazed with indignation. Her mouth curled into a sneer and her nostrils flared. Her face turned blotchy red, a vein throbbing visibly in her temple. She sucked in a sharp breath.

'You... went... through... my... things?' she hissed, each word dripping with venom. Her voice was low and menacing, sending a shiver of fear down Jane's spine. Edith's body seemed to vibrate with barely contained fury, her hands clenching and unclenching as if she were trying to stop herself from striking out. 'How dare you!' Edith erupted, her voice so loud it seemed to shake the very walls. Jane instinctively took a step back, her eyes darting around the room, searching for something – anything – that would serve as a weapon if Edith turned violent. There was the poker not too far away, but Jane would probably never have the nerve to use it.

Her heart pounded in her chest, each beat echoing the rising tension. She could hear the distant hum of traffic outside, a car horn blaring briefly as if puncturing Edith's fury.

'Edith, please,' Jane interjected, struggling to steady her voice. 'I was wrong to invade your privacy and I apologise for doing that. But we really need to talk about this.'

Edith was having none of it. She stood up, pulled her body upright as she picked up her handbag. 'I told George he was making a mistake marrying you. You've just proved I was right.'

The air in the room felt thick and suffocating. Jane took another step back. But she needn't have bothered.

'Bitch!' Edith shouted. She turned round and rushed out the front door, slamming it so hard it rattled on its hinges.

Jane paced up and down the little room trying to calm herself, to stop her murderous thoughts and get herself back in control. This couldn't go on.

Still shaking, she went to the kitchen drawer and got out a sheet of writing paper, an envelope and a pen.

'Dear George...' she began.

Then she sat back and took a few minutes to calm herself. After all, if Edith had just become homeless her drinking might well be worse than usual. A few days wouldn't matter. Sighing again, she put the paper and envelope away. She tried to concentrate on cooking and housework but was too tense from the confrontation to think properly.

Fifteen minutes later Edith walked back in. She still looked rough but didn't appear to have drunk any more alcohol.

She stood in front of Jane in the living room but avoided her eyes. 'I'm sorry you're upset and I shouldn't have got drunk last night. It won't happen again. Okay?'

Jane didn't believe her for a second, but felt she should give her a chance. She stood up and held one of Edith's hands in hers. 'That's great, Edith. I'm sure it was just a slip-up and things will go better from now on.'

But she knew deep down that was never going to happen.

11

_____

'That one'll do me,' old Mr Archie said. 'Top banana. I knew I could count on you to find one for me.'

He tucked the book under his arm and watched as Tom picked up his walking stick.

'Get that on duty, did you? Where were you posted?'

'I don't like to talk about it,' he said, unwilling to say he was a conscientious objector. 'Is there anything else I can help you with?' He knew that many people who'd lived through the dreadful First World War refused to talk about it, so this answer was often accepted with little more than a shrug.

Mr Archie's question reminded him of the grim day he'd had to present himself to a tribunal to hear his case for being a conscientious objector. He'd already had to submit a formal application declaring his objection to military service. Not long after that he was summoned to appear before a local tribunal composed of a panel of civilians and, in this case, one military man. He'd looked at them, hoping to see understanding in their faces, but he was without luck. The military man glared at him and the others kept their faces blank, impossible to read.

'Our task here is to assess the sincerity and validity of your objection,' the tall, thin, upright chairman said. 'You may now present your case, explaining why you object to helping us win this war.'

Hearing those words Tom felt his case was hopeless. The way the question was phrased implied they wouldn't believe him and assumed he was a coward. However, he forced himself to stand upright, using his stick, and read his prepared statement. 'In addition to my moral objections, I have a deformed right leg due to an automobile accident.'

He was told to sit down and faced a barrage of questions about his beliefs – partly developed during his time in India where he had volunteered to work among the poor and learned about Buddhism. The questioning seemed to go on forever and throughout he tried to read the faces of the questioners. Some nodded as if understanding points he made, but he realised that didn't mean they agreed with him.

Finally it was over and the chairman stood again. 'Thank you. We will write to you with our decision within a few days.'

Those days had seemed endless, counting the hours, unable to sleep. He'd hoped that if they didn't give him a full exemption they would give him suitable work to do. And they had. As well as the library work, he worked for the Red Cross.

As he watched Mr Archie go to the desk to get his books stamped, Tom shook aside those stressful memories and turned back to what he'd been doing.

He rubbed his aching leg, noticing dust motes highlighted by the sun coming through one of the library windows. Then as he stood up again, something on a stack opposite caught his eye. The shelf was where rarely borrowed books were kept, not one he went to much, but for some reason he found himself taking the two or three steps to the stack and reaching out. He had no idea precisely what the book was, yet his heart beat faster and his breath caught in his throat.

As Tom's fingers traced the worn leather binding, a shiver ran down his spine and the murmurs of the library users seemed to fade away. Holding his find closer, he squinted to make out the faded gold lettering on the cover, holding it this way and that to illuminate it with the dim sunlight coming through the window. He gasped when he made it out. It was a book he had hoped to find since those days when he first worked in a bookshop years earlier. His heart pounded in his ears as he carefully pulled the book closer, almost afraid it would crumble in his hands.

With trembling fingers, Tom gently opened the cover, his eyes widening as he carefully turned the delicate pages. The musty, papery scent filled his nostrils, instantly transporting him to his days working in that old bookshop. He inhaled deeply, savouring the familiar smell. He admired the typography, the craftsmanship that had gone into producing this volume long before. He could scarcely dare to believe what he had found. Had it been missed when the library was renovated for the visit of the king and queen the previous winter? There was every like- lihood that a decorator would not understand its value and simply put it back on a shelf.

Glancing up, he scanned the room quickly, half expecting someone to have noticed his discovery and rush over to snatch it from him. But the library patrons remained oblivious, absorbed in their own pursuits. A faint smile tugged at the corners of his mouth as he carefully closed the book, running his thumb along the aged cover one last time. He was certain it was genuine – no false edition could match the weight of history he held in his hands.

How he longed to keep the find to himself. He knew it would be worth a lot of money, but to him the value would be owning such a precious volume. His breathing became shallower as he struggled with his inner demons – surely he deserved to keep the book. He'd found and recognised it. Without his expertise it would probably have mouldered away on the shelf for many more decades.

It would be easy to hide it, to never mention its existence. But even as the thought formed, a wave of conscience flowed over him. He couldn't steal from this library, this place that had become a sanctuary. But the temptation – it was almost unbearable. He had to hand it over to his boss.

Didn't he?

He clutched the secret of the book for more than an hour, his internal turmoil over what to do rendering him inattentive. Two readers had to ask him for advice more than once and several times he found himself staring into space. The book, safely tucked in his jacket pocket, seemed to pulse with a life of its own. Should he share his discovery with Cordelia? If he did, it might condemn it to obscurity. Or should he keep it? Wouldn't that amount to the same thing?

He imagined himself sitting in the heat of an Indian summer talking to Guru Anand under a banyan tree as he had done so often during his stay there. The air had been thick with the scent of jasmine and the distant echo of a temple bell. Under the sprawling canopy of the tree, he visualised Guru Anand's serene face, eyes closed in meditation, the ancient wisdom of his words resonating in the stillness.

There had been many chats between them as Tom learned more about Buddhists' beliefs. He could imagine what Guru Anand might say. 'In moments of inner conflict, remember what you have learned, my son. The book you have found is a material attachment. Attachments can cloud our judgement and lead to suffering. Reflect on this truth: "To hold on to possessions and secrets is to burden the heart; to let go is to find freedom.""

Remembering his guru's kind face and tranquil nature brought clarity to Tom's mind. Of course he couldn't keep the book. If he did so he would be as bad as a rich man who would buy it at auction and keep it locked away from sight forever.

As he stood remembering, the library's high windows cast a long shadow across the dusty wooden floor, creating a patchwork of light and dark.

His decision was made. He would show the book to Cordelia.

But before he could do so he heard raised voices from nearby stacks.

'I had this book first!' a young man was protesting, his face flushed. 'I need it for my homework assignment.'

A woman was struggling to get it out of his grip. 'And I need it for my book club meeting. That's just as important. Give it to me now!'

Tom walked over to them, the inner peace he'd just found fractured by their loud argument. 'Let me see if I can help,' he said, taking the book from the student. 'Let's sit down and look at the dates each of you need the book for. Also, I'll see if we have another copy somewhere or if I can get one from Canning Town Library. How does that sound?'

It took a few minutes to sort out their disagreement, but eventually they went away satisfied. Their conflict had momentarily distracted him from his dilemma about the book, but now the decision he'd made came back to him.

He had to speak to his boss.

* * *

Cordelia finished helping the patrons who needed her help, a frown creasing her brow as she watch Tom waiting to speak to her. He was pale, clutching a book to his chest like a lifeline.

'Are you okay, Tom? You look as if you've seen a ghost.'

He just stared at her, eyes wide. He half showed her what he was holding.

'What is it?' she asked, her mind still on working out the summer rotas for herself, Mavis and Jane.

'It's... it's a first edition of *Sense and Sensibility*!' he gasped, first looking round to make sure he couldn't be overheard. 'It must be worth a fortune!'

Cordelia's eyes opened wide. With her library qualifications and experience, she knew she was looking at a fortune in Tom's hands if he was right. 'Come into the office,' she said, giving Mavis a nod to ask her to take over the desk.

Once inside she closed the door and invited Tom to sit down. Only then did she reach out for the book. He half held out his hand and then clasped it to his chest yet again. 'I... I...'

Cordelia smiled. 'You can't carry it around for life, Tom. Come on, let's have a look together. If you're right it could be the answer to the library's money worries!'

But what if he was wrong and it was just another old book?

12

Mavis and little Joyce walked up the worn stone steps of St Mark's Parish hall, their footsteps echoing in the gentle hubbub of the early evening. Mavis paused at the heavy wooden door, her hand resting on the old brass handle.

'What's wrong, Mummy?' Joyce asked. 'Ain't we going in?'

Mavis smiled at her. This evening she not only hoped to convince the people of Silvertown to have a rent strike, but she wanted to be a role model for her new daughter. Show her how to be strong and stand up for herself and others who are less fortunate. She was disappointed Miss Unwin couldn't be there but promised to let her know what happened.

'Come on, love, push the door with me.'

They pushed together and the door opened with a creak. Taking a deep breath, Mavis stepped inside, holding Joyce's hand.

'Coo, there's no one 'ere,' Joyce said, clutching a book and her favourite doll. The one with brown hair and button eyes.

'I hope there will be soon,' Mavis said, looking around. There were rows of mismatched chairs standing silent and expectant.

She'd been to the room many times, and Joyce attended Sunday school there as she had as a child, but this time it was different. The very air seemed loaded with anticipation. Important decisions would soon be made here.

Joyce sat down on a seat at the back and looked at her book while Mavis walked about. Her footsteps sounded unnaturally loud against the worn floorboards and her heart beat faster in anticipation of what was to come.

What if no one turned up? What if people laughed at her? What if they shouted abuse? Would she be able to cope? She'd spent countless hours preparing for this evening, and had got help and support from the other librarians. Surprisingly, help too from The Professor, who had experience of public speaking on his side. He'd outlined how to tackle the meeting and she could have kissed him when she'd finished writing down all his valuable advice.

Reaching the small stage, really too small to have that title, Mavis ran her hands along the smooth surface of the wooden podium. She imagined herself standing there very soon looking out at a sea of faces, some familiar, others not. Could she convince them her idea was a way to help themselves and force the landlords to behave as they should?

What would Joe say if he was here? 'Sock it to them, girl!' That's what he'd say.

She closed her eyes, struggling to calm the butterflies in her stomach. She'd heard so many stories of hardships from local people over the years, and especially since she'd called this meeting. She thought of families, children, elderly people living in small, unsanitary places, some with damp walls and insects everywhere. People already living day to day, struggling to find enough money to eat. With the recent rent rises that many had suffered, life was even harder.

She looked at the back of the room. Joyce was engrossed in her book, her doll tucked under her arm. Behind her on the wall was a wooden cross. Although never sure about her beliefs it somehow gave Mavis strength. Yes, she was doing the right thing, fighting for what was right.

She could hear the distant sounds of life outside the church-yard. Children playing, the horns of the ships in the docks, the hooters of the factories changing shifts. Listening to the familiar sounds, she grew calmer, her resolve strengthening.

The tenants would be here soon, and she hoped they would be ready to stand with her and demand a fair rent and decent repairs.

Ten minutes before the meeting was due to start she remembered a piece of paper Tom had given her as she was leaving the library. 'It's a list of landlords,' he'd said. 'It might not be complete, but that's all I could find out.'

She quickly ran her eyes down the list of names, not paying much attention. She was sure she wouldn't know any of these people. They certainly wouldn't live in Silvertown. But then one name leaped out at her. Carmichael. She froze as she read it again. The handwriting was difficult to read. Maybe she'd read it wrong.

But no. She was right. The name made her heart thunder at the implications.

It couldn't be.

She looked yet again, squinting to make sure she was reading correctly.

She was.

A cold dread gripped her. Cordelia's father... owned a whole street in Silvertown.

He was one of the negligent, greedy landlords. Cordelia had mentioned that her father owned some property in the village near their home, but Mavis felt sure she didn't know her father owned any in Silvertown.

The truth slammed into her like a body blow. Dazed, she gripped the lectern to steady herself, the damning list still clutched in her fingers. Fragmented memories flashed into her mind of one tense day when Lord Carmichael had come into the library. He'd stormed through the doors, shouting Cordelia's name, completely ignoring anyone else present. His face was puce with rage. Poor Cordelia, blushing with embarrassment, hastily ushered him outside before he disrupted the patrons further. Mavis gathered he was furious about something Churchill refused to do. It seemed to her that Cordelia was the nearest punchbag to unload his anger on.

She knew instantly that she would be caught in an impossible situation. Her fondness for Cordelia would probably conflict with the actions she was going to take against people like her boss's father. She hoped this news wouldn't ruin the close relationship she valued so much.

She took two deep breaths. How could she confront this terrible news and keep her focus on the meeting? She had to. Steadying herself, she folded the paper and tucked it under her notes. 'Come on, girl,' she chided herself. 'Deal with one thing at a time like you always do.'

Steadying herself, she checked the clock and hurried over to Joyce. 'Do you need a wee before the meeting starts, love?'

Without looking up from her book, Joyce shook her head, her fingers tracing the words she was reading. Mavis was so proud of her. She had no idea if Joyce's mother had encouraged reading and guessed there wasn't a lot of choice in the children's home she had lived in after her mother's death. Despite that, she'd taken to it like a duck to water, encouraged by Mavis's thoughtful choice of books.

The sound of voices and footsteps approaching signalled the arrival of the first tenants, making Mavis's heart pound. This was really going to happen! She opened the door. 'Welcome! Come on in!' She greeted each person warmly as they stepped inside.

She recognised many of the faces. Bert and The Professor from the library were there along with Mrs Gregory and little Hetty, who was trying to keep her baby brother amused. There were several people from her street and at least half a dozen who were regular library users, and many others she didn't know. To her surprise there was also the couple who lived in the rooms above her, Nellie and Jim. They had to walk past her to get in and out of the house but they tended to keep themselves to themselves.

It was only when the numbers coming in dwindled and she couldn't see anyone else walking along the church path that she went back into the hall. She was astounded.

There wasn't a single empty seat. There were even about ten people standing against the walls, smoking and chatting to people near them.

Her heart pounding so much she thought she might faint, Mavis walked towards the front of the hall, smiling to people she knew who caught her eye. The atmosphere in the room was of palpable anticipation. The earlier murmurs of conversations gradually faded as she walked, replaced by a hushed silence broken only by the occasional creak of a wooden chair being moved or a child chattering.

All eyes were fixed on her as she turned to face them. Some had expressions of hope, others looked suspicious, their brows creased in doubt and their arms crossed defensively across their chests.

She would have to win them all round. Could she?

Taking a deep breath, Mavis cleared her throat, then took a

sip of water she had at the ready. 'Thank you all for coming,' she began, her voice weak initially, but quickly gaining strength.

She quickly looked at the back of the hall and was relieved to see Joyce was still engrossed in her book, ignoring everything around her. She remembered doing the same thing as a child, her mother getting impatient when she'd asked her to do something and she was so lost in the story she was reading she didn't hear.

She took another deep breath.

'Friends, fellow tenants,' she began, her voice reaching every corner of the room. 'I've called this meeting because we are sick and tired. Sick of leaking roofs and mouldy walls, tired of being treated like inferior beings, not worthy of somewhere decent to live.'

She paused and looked around, giving time for her words to sink in. She was relieved to see many people nodding in agreement.

'But we do matter! I matter, my little girl Joyce matters, and you all matter. We are the very lifeblood of Silvertown. I've spoken to many of you and the common things I hear are lack of repairs and rent increases...'

To her surprise The Professor stood up and interrupted her. He looked every inch a lawyer, the sort of man people would listen to. 'And that's illegal. At the beginning of the war the government passed a law that rents couldn't be increased without good reason.' He paused and looked around. 'I can't think of one good reason. Can you? We have the law on our side!'

As he sat down again people applauded him and several people shouted, 'Hear! Hear!'

But one man, sat at the front with folded arms, stood up and turned to face the room.

'Don't listen to a bloody word, you lot. They're all commies.

You stop paying rent and you'll be chucked out on your ear, mark my words.'

Mavis could have throttled him and was relieved when a few people shouted him down.

'Let Mavis speak!'

'Landlords paying you, are they?'

He sat down again with a thud, resuming his aggressive posture.

Mavis held up her hand, waiting for the hubbub to quieten. 'This... gentleman has a point and a valid one, one that many of you 'ave already expressed to me.'

The room went very still. Their homes may have been substandard, but they were all they had.

'If we stick together, if we all stop paying rent at the same time and show we mean business, our money-grabbing landlords will 'ave to take us seriously. Their incomes, gained from our 'ard work, will suddenly stop. That'll make them take notice!'

She looked around, relieved that most people were still looking interested.

'And we'll get the newspapers involved. They'll show these landlords up for what they are and they won't like that!' She paused and stood more upright. 'It won't be easy, but us people in Silvertown have lived through the Blitz and still face regular bombings. We're living with fear and shortages, hardship and heartbreak, but we still 'ave our fighting spirit and no one can take that away from us!'

The room erupted with excitement and determination, applause long and loud. For the first time in her life Mavis experienced a surge of energy coursing through her entire body, realising that she had the power to motivate people. Her, Mavis Kent. All these people had listened to her! She could see determination on almost every face, determination to fight for their rights, for a decent place to live and their dignity, no matter what the cost.

She felt a huge sense of pride at the faces before her. Her people, her neighbours, her friends, people from the close-knit and downtrodden community that was Silvertown. She knew this was just the beginning of a long and probably unpleasant battle. But the power she felt at that moment was not her own, it was the power of every person in that room.

She held up her hands again. 'Now that I know you are with me, I will soon, very soon, be putting up posters to let you know when to start. And we'll have a march through Silvertown so get ready to make some banners. Bring along your kiddies, prams and all. The more noise we make, the better! We will win!'

The man in front of her muttered 'Bloody commie!' again, but no one took any notice of him as they stood to leave. Every single person wanted to shake Mavis's hand and say a word of encouragement.

When they'd finally gone she collapsed into a seat next to Joyce, exhausted.

'Have I told you you are a fantastic little girl?' she said, putting her arm around Joyce's shoulder, her pulse slowly getting back to normal.

Joyce looked at her with her head on one side. 'Is it teatime yet? I'm 'ungry.'

But Mavis wasn't to get her tea just yet.

13

Mavis was thinking everyone had left the meeting but then noted one man was still there. He was well dressed in grey trousers and a white shirt with a hand-knitted sleeveless jumper over the top.

'I wonder if I can join you for a moment?' he asked Mavis. His accent gave away that he wasn't from the East End. 'I've been watching you and I am so impressed with what you are doing.'

Mavis frowned. Surely this well-spoken man wasn't living in one of the run-down houses. 'My daughter is keen to get 'ome to her tea. Will this take long?' She had an apple in her bag and gave it to Joyce to keep her happy a few minutes longer.

The man introduced himself as Paul Wheeler. 'I'm a lecturer at East London College. Although I'm not a communist myself, I've been working closely with a group of communists to help improve housing in London. We have a lot of ideas that will help your campaign. Do you have time to talk about it?'

Mavis was taken aback. Her, talking to a college lecturer? The nearest she'd ever come to that was talking to The Professor at the library. Her own education was as short as most girls in the

East End, although she'd always been a keen reader and given herself an informal education.

'Well, Mr Wheeler, I'd love to talk. 'Ow about you walk with me and Joyce to our place. I can give 'er something to eat and offer you a cup of tea while we chat. That sound okay?'

He checked his watch then nodded. 'That sounds perfect. I've got another appointment later but I've got time now.' He bent down to Joyce's level. 'Do you mind if I walk with you? You'll get your tea quicker if I do.'

Joyce merely nodded, too engrossed in crunching her apple to be interested. Mavis helped her put her book in a bag and gave her another hug. When she was growing up hugs had been in short supply. Her dad was rarely to be seen and a great believer that kids should be kept out of his way when he was around. Her mum didn't seem to know how to hug or cuddle her children, not even the little ones.

The three of them walked past familiar Silvertown sights: war posters urging 'Keep mum', 'Come into the factories' and 'Grow your own vegetables'; past a baby asleep in a pram on the pavement outside a house. The pram was tied to the door knocker with a bit of string to stop it drifting off if the wind got up.

'Look, Mummy, a baby,' Joyce said, standing on tiptoe to peer into the battered pram. The baby was sound asleep wrapped up in a hand-knitted cover.

Mavis smiled. 'That's little Doris,' she said. 'She's got six sisters.'

Joyce looked up at her longingly. 'Can I have a sister?' she asked, her bottom lip out.

'I'm afraid not,' Mavis said. She had helped deliver baby Doris as she had two of her sisters. Each street or batch of streets in the East End had its own 'auntie' – a woman people turned to for all sorts of help when they didn't know what to do or hadn't enough money for professional services. Mavis was one such auntie. She helped with childbirth, she laid out the departed, wrote letters for the less literate, and frequently fought battles for individuals.

One battle she'd helped with was for baby Doris's mother, Gladys. She'd been about six months gone when she knocked on Mavis's door, exhaustion making her look years older than she was. Pale and thinner than she should be with limp hair and an aching back, she stepped inside and sat down as if her legs wouldn't hold her up another minute.

'Can you 'elp me, Mavis?' Gladys asked as Mavis put on the kettle. Mavis was glad Joyce was out playing with her friends. She guessed this was going to be a conversation not for little ears.

She went to the small kitchen, calling over her shoulder, 'What's the problem then, love?'

Gladys groaned, rubbing her bump as the baby inside her shifted about. 'It's me old man, Jonny. You know 'im, don't you?'

Jonny's reputation was well known throughout Silvertown. He was a docker but in his spare time was either gambling or chasing girls. It was like he didn't care he was married and had a family to support.

She came back in with a tray of cups and a plate of bread and jam slices which she pushed towards her visitor. 'What's 'e bin up to this time?'

They sat either side of the modest table, nudging aside some drawings Joyce had been doing.

Gladys looked down at her hands, her nails bitten to the quick. 'It's... well, you'll guess, it's Jonny. 'E wants a boy, see, and every time I 'ave another girl 'e says it's my fault. Gets nasty. Never as much as looks at 'em.' She looked up at Mavis, her strained face showing her desperation. 'As soon as I 'ave a girl, he's on top of me again... you know what I mean... trying to make a boy. The rest of the time 'e's 'ardly ever to be seen.'

Mavis leaned over and held her hands. 'And I'm guessing from the state of you 'e don't give you much for your 'ouse-keeping neither.'

Outside they heard the rag-and-bone man's shout. 'Any old rags? Rags and bones!' With every day that passed he got less for his cart. Bones were put in stock to give thin stews a bit of good-ness and rags were used for rag rugs and all manner of things. Women like Gladys wore clothes that were barely more than rags.

'So what would you like me to do?' Mavis asked, squeezing Gladys's hands. 'You know I'll 'elp if I can.'

Gladys pulled her hands away and wrung them together, the knuckles going white. 'It's... well... I don't know what to do. I can't 'ave another nipper. The last one nearly killed me. You know, you was there. And I ain't got enough money to feed the ones I got.'

'But Jonny 'as enough to go to the pub though,' Mavis added.

'Yeah. Anyway I don't know 'ow to stop 'im when 'e wants to... you know what... I just can't 'ave another one... This one's got to be me last.' She was a strong woman. She had to be to look after all her daughters on the pittance Jonny gave her. That didn't stop tears slowly trickling down her pinched cheeks though. 'Can you 'elp?'

Mavis sighed and sat back on her chair, arms folded. She had an idea what to do but didn't want to make promises she might not be able to keep. 'You leave it with me,' she said, sounding more confident than she felt. 'I'll see if I can do anything. But I can't make any promises nor nothing.'

She'd ended up having a word with a local man, Peter. Her

mum, who'd been an auntie before her, had delivered Peter and they'd both known him and his family all their lives. Peter did a bit of bare-knuckle fighting at weekends. Mavis told him the problem and before she'd even finished he nodded. 'Just tell me the pub he goes to and leave it to me.'

'Nothing too much!' Mavis said, worried Peter might end up on the wrong end of the law if he did too much damage to the errant husband.

The determined way he spoke left her feeling sure he would help. 'Understood,' Peter said and shook her hand. 'I'll deal with it. He won't be the first.' Mavis never asked him what he had done, but he put a note through her door saying, 'It's all sorted.' Sometimes it was better to be in ignorance.

Gladys's front door opened now as the three walked past, breaking Mavis's reverie. Gladys was still too thin, still wearing a threadbare dress and wrap-around apron, but with a wide smile as she looked at Mavis.

'I don't know what you did, Mavis. But thank you.' She didn't need to be explicit in front of Joyce and Mr Wheeler.

Mavis's heart lifted. 'Glad to 'elp,' she said with a grin. 'Won't stop now, but see you soon.'

She, Joyce and Mr Wheeler carried on their walk, past a repair gang doing their best to patch up a bombed house, past women queueing outside a butcher's shop, and three women standing on their doorsteps catching up on the day's news.

'I 'eard that lovely lad John from Arthur Street copped it on the docks.'

'He'll get a surprise when he comes back from war and finds a new baby. 'E's bin away a year or more.'

'That Mildred's old man, he's losing 'is marbles, we'll 'ave to 'elp her.'

14

Mavis was pleased to notice that Mr Wheeler didn't seem at all put out by everyday life in Silvertown. Poverty didn't mean these tough matriarchs couldn't have pride in their run-down homes.

Mavis was sure her visitor lived somewhere much posher. Still, it sounded as if he'd been working in areas like hers for a while.

They stopped off at two houses on their walk to Mavis's home. The first was the home of Mrs Patel. Very elderly, she had outlived most of her family and her only son was away fighting.

Mavis had begun to discuss with her getting a rota of people to do her shopping.

'Thanks for coming, my Jaan,' Mrs Patel said. 'It's so good to see you. Your smile always brings me happiness.' She looked at Paul. 'Who's this handsome young man you've got here?'

The flicker of a gas lamp in the room cast long shadows, barely illuminating the small space.

'I'm Mr Wheeler. Paul. I'm hoping to help Mavis with her campaign to get better treatment for tenants. It looks as if you don't have electricity yet.'

The muffled conversation of neighbours drifted through the thin walls, a constant reminder of the close quarters they shared. 'No, no electricity. I've asked and asked, but nothing ever happens.' Mrs Patel looked from one to the other, offering tea.

'I'm afraid we don't have time for tea at the moment,' Paul said, 'but do you mind if I ask you a few questions about your situation or is that being too personal?'

Mrs Patel pulled her hand-knitted cardigan closer around herself. 'I ain't got no secrets. Couldn't 'ave with walls as thin as these!'

Paul got out a small notebook and pencil. 'Would I be right in guessing you get a widow's pension?'

She nodded. 'That's right, don't know what I'd do without it. Thirty-two shillings a week don't go far when me rent is eleven shilling a week. Prices keep going up all the time too, don't they? Mind you, them nice people at the Widows and Orphans people come round once in a while with a bag of this or that. It all helps. I used to do charring but me knees and me back ain't up to it any more.'

Shaking his head, Paul asked one more question. 'What exactly needs fixing in your home?'

'What doesn't!' She scoffed. 'Them stairs are so dangerous it's a wonder I 'aven't fallen through them and broken me neck. The plumbing only works when it feels like it and it's impossible to get warm in winter.'

'That's a disgrace,' Paul said, horror showing on his face. 'I'm hoping we'll be able to do something about it, but we can't make any promises.'

'But here is that book you asked me to get from the library,' Mavis said. 'I've checked it out for you.' It was *And Then There Were None* by Agatha Christie.

'Lovely,' Mrs Patel said. 'I never guess who did it no matter how many of her books I read.'

The next stop was to the mother of one of Joyce's friends, Pamela. They sometimes babysat for each other. It was a quick doorstep conversation to confirm details of their next babysitting. Pamela had babysat when Joe had got an unexpected twenty-four-hour pass and they'd wanted to do something special. She smiled at the memory. He wouldn't tell her what he'd got planned but looked very pleased with himself all morning. She lost track of the conversation with Paul as she remembered it. A walk along the Thames, eating fish and chips out of newspaper on benches, then afternoon tea, followed by a variety show at the Hippodrome. A memory she would keep forever.

Paul repeating what he was saying brought her out of her reverie.

'It seems as if you know everyone around here,' Paul said as they walked. 'My grandmother lived in Canning Town in a property very like these. She died before her time, probably because of the poor living conditions.'

'So that's why you're so keen to help?' Mavis asked.

He nodded, his face more sombre than before. 'That's right. She died when I was too young to remember her, but my mother missed her very much.'

At home when Joyce was eating her tea, Mavis placed a cup of tea in front of Paul. 'Now, how can you help us?'

He picked up his cup. 'First let me say how impressed I am with what you've achieved so far. It must have taken a lot of organisation and indeed courage.'

Mavis raised an eyebrow. 'It's surprising 'ow much energy you find when you're angry enough. Now, you said you could 'elp us.'

Stirring his tea, Paul began. 'The key is solidarity. Our experience in other parts of London is that the bosses, the landlords, they'll all try to divide you. They'll offer deals to some, threats to others.'

A knock on the door interrupted him. Mavis recognised that knock. 'It's my neighbour come to see what's happening. Give me a mo.'

She answered the door and sure enough there was Mrs O'Connor in her slippers and rags in her hair. 'Got any spare tea, love? Just a twist'll do,' she asked, craning her neck trying to see who Mavis's visitor was.

Mavis never let go of the door. 'I'm busy just now, love. I'll drop some off in a while. Must go now.'

'Is that the nosey old bat?' Joyce asked when the door was closed, making Mavis go pink. She decided to ignore the comment and sat down opposite her visitor again.

'You were saying about solidarity.'

He nodded. 'I was. It's really important not to let them break your unity. What they fear is exactly that. That you'll all stick together and they'll be out of pocket because the rent money isn't coming in.'

'Some are worried in case they get thrown out or the police work with the landlords and cause more trouble.' As Mavis spoke, the realisation of responsibility for what she'd started weighed heavier and heavier. Her palms felt clammy as she clenched them on her lap.

Paul ran his fingers through his thick brown hair. 'That's where we can help. We've got connections, resources. We can organise whatever you and your people need. You don't have to do this alone.'

Joyce, growing restless, pushed her plate away and picked up her book. 'Will you read me a story, Mummy?' she asked.

Mavis, still thrilled to be called mummy, smiled at the child she loved so much. 'A bit later, love. Let me finish talking to this man first. Would you like to go out and play with Maggie next door?'

Her face lighting up, Joyce put on her cardigan and scampered towards the door, then looked back. 'Where's my skipping rope, Mummy?'

Mavis opened a door in her sideboard and got the rope out. 'Here, sweetheart. Remember to watch out for cars and stay in this street.' Turning back to her visitor she turned the implications of his offer in her mind. 'The thing is, we don't want to be beholden to any political party. This strike is about us, our community, not them.' She ran her fingers around the edge of her table feeling the bumps and bruises of its history.

Paul twisted his empty cup on the saucer. 'I can understand that, Mrs Kent. But I mentioned I'm not a member of the communist party, or any other, come to that. I just think the ways things are is unfair and want to do what I can to help. You can use the help that's offered in whatever way you want. If it comes to it we even have a sympathetic solicitor who will write to the landlords. That usually gets them worried.'

Mavis sat back in her chair, mulling over his words. The sincerity in his voice and manner was overcoming her initial suspicion and cautiousness. Perhaps this unexpected ally could give the support they all so desperately needed. And that support would help her to feel it wasn't all down to her. She knew the road ahead would be long and fraught with problems, but with the right people by their side, they must surely have a better chance of winning.

She looked at him as she poured another cup from the old blue-and-white striped teapot. 'You've convinced me, Mr Wheeler,' she said, a determined glint in her eye. 'Let's work out 'ow we can work together. The fight is just beginning. And please, call me Mavis.'

The sounds of Joyce and her friends outside continued and without really being aware, Mavis caught a skipping rhyme she'd said as a child.

> *'Apples, peaches, pears and plums,*
> *'Tell me when your birthday comes.*
> *'January, February, March...'*

Over all these years it had never occurred to her until now that the chant was an excellent way for children to learn the months of the year.

'Sorry,' she said, turning back to Paul. 'Got distracted by them little ones.'

Paul leaned back in his chair, his expression thoughtful as he considered all the steps the community would need to take. 'One of the most important things we've found in other communities is the formation of a tenants' union.' He tapped his fingers against the worn table. 'We can help you do that, if you like. By organising yourselves into a cohesive body, you'll have a much stronger voice and more leverage when you start negotiating with those landlords.'

Quickly running through the people involved in the meeting earlier, Mavis identified several who would help such a move. 'Yes. I can see that makes sense,' she said, putting milk in her tea. She sat back and looked at him.

'I teach history and especially the history of this part of the country. Every day I'm talking about the unfairness of life in the East End. Not many of my students come from around here, yet I know there will be plenty who are bright enough to study at university. They just don't get the opportunities.'

What he said about the lack of opportunities was true, as Mavis knew well. This man, who she'd only just met, who had privilege and education, was willing to stand alongside her community. It gave her more hope for their success.

'You've convinced me, Paul,' she said, her voice filled with renewed enthusiasm. 'Let's do this. Let's build a tenants' union and show these damn landlords we won't be pushed around no more. They'll 'ave to listen to us then.'

Paul produced a sheet of crumpled paper from his pocket and a pencil. 'I'll make a list of things you can be getting on with. How about we meet in a few days' time and see what steps to take next?'

Before Mavis could answer, Joyce rushed in the door. 'Mummy, Maggie's got a new kitten and she wants me to go and see it. Can I? Can I, Mummy?'

'Of course you can but be sure to be home before it gets dark.'

Paul stood and picked up his things. 'Excellent. I'll speak to my colleagues and we'll begin a plan. If you're happy with it we can move ahead. Of course, you can agree to it or not. It's your campaign, not ours.'

When he'd gone Mavis sat back in her old armchair, excitement coursing through her veins. Change was coming to the East End, and she would be at the forefront, leading the change. The landlords and the higher-ups with money might have had the power, but her people had something far better – the unbreakable spirit of a community with a sense of purpose.

15

'I can't believe how many books we've gathered,' Jane said, her voice echoing in the small, rarely used room at the back of the building. The musty smell of old paper and dust filled the air, and cobwebs hung across the corners like grubby lace. Piles of books towered around them, proof of the success of their book drive. It had been Jane's idea. 'We'll need more books if we're going to keep getting new readers at the rate we've been doing,' she'd suggested in one of their weekly meetings.

Cordelia nodded. 'The irony is we've got a little money to buy some more books but they're hard to find. That huge fire in Paternoster Row put paid to that idea. Five million books turned to ashes. It still gives me nightmares.'

It wasn't only that devastating fire that was a problem. Since paper rationing was introduced at the beginning of the war, it was increasingly difficult to find any for anything considered non-essential. Luckily, amongst the piles of miscellaneous things in the basement, they had found a pile of paper. Old, a little wrinkled, but useable. There was also a roll of wallpaper which was a godsend, as it could be cut to any length.

For some time they had been talking about having a mobile library. A van that would enable them to bring books to the many factory workers in the area. Time had been tight to plan their book drive but they were keen to build up their stock before the mobile library started. By putting their heads together they had been ready in record time.

With Tom's artistic help they had made eye-catching posters publicising the drive, and taken it in turns to visit WVS centres, cafés and anywhere else they could think of where people congregated, to make their plea.

Jane, who had been timid when Cordelia first took the job managing the library, astounded them all. She had confidently stood outside the library, head held high, voice firm. She had changed her hairstyle to a fashionable pompadour style and a few attractive wisps of hair framed her pretty face. Her eyes, that had once betrayed her inner fears, were now bright and alert. She looked at passers-by, calling in a clear, unwavering voice, 'Bring us your unwanted books! We urgently need your unwanted books.' Then, even more surprising, she did the same outside the new British restaurant nearby which was busy every hour it was open.

The restaurant stood out amongst the war-torn buildings, its freshly painted exterior like a beacon of hope. The facade was a warm, welcoming blue, reminiscent of the sky on a summer's day. Large windows, showing its previous life as a huge shop, were criss-crossed with blast tape but still let plenty of daylight in. Over the doorway, in bold white letters it declared itself 'The British Restaurant'.

As Jane stood there shouting for book donations her mouth watered from the delicious smells of the food on offer inside. She knew all about it and had promised to take her daughter Helen there one day soon. Just inside the entrance she could see some of the menu – Toad in the hole 8d; Fish and potato pie 7d; Bread pudding 3d; Tea 1d. Then at the bottom she read, 'Only one slice of bread with each meal.' Her stomach rumbled at the thought of her favourite toad in the hole.

Most people had been too busy to do more than glance at Jane's poster board but one man thought it was an invitation to get fresh.

'What'll I get in return for a book or two, sweetheart?' he asked, undressing her with his eyes and licking his lips suggestively.

She was so surprised she just gaped at him.

'Come on, girly,' he went on. 'You look like you're just begging for it.'

Without a second's thought she swung her board and swiped him in the head with it – a good clump. It wasn't hard but enough for him to rub his head and look at her as if he couldn't believe this woman would do such a thing.

'Frigid bitch!' he muttered and stormed off cursing the whole time. 'Needs a good seeing to!'

A young woman who had seen what had happened approached Jane. 'Nice swing. You got him really good,' she said. 'I hope he has a nasty headache.' She looked properly at Jane's poster board and nodded. 'I'll see if me and my mum have any books to spare. Perhaps see you in the library one day.'

Although most people had walked past Jane, apparently ignoring her and the poster beside her, it must have had some effect. The librarians were surprised when a steady flow of books began to appear. Some were dropped off by people coming into the library – regular users, but sometimes people who had never stepped foot in the building before came in. Some carried a single dog-eared book while others staggered in under the weight of a dozen or more. Sometimes they would even arrive in the morning to find a small parcel of books on the doorstep.

After a few days they had enough to sort out. Tom was on the front desk while they hunted through the pile, yet again proving his worth.

As they sorted, each of them found a book that meant something personal. Jane found a copy of *Wind in the Willows* and smiled as she remembered reading it to Helen when she'd first returned home from being evacuated. There had been difficult times trying to get the little girl to settle back in the run-down city after all the excitement of being on the farm, but the one time of day when they cosied up was bedtime reading. That book helped them to bond again. She stroked the copy in her hand. It was in better condition than the one they still had at home, and she decided she would swap one for the other.

Mavis found *The Fortnight in September* by R. C. Sherriff. 'I'd forgotten this one,' she cried. 'I read it again and again and wished we could afford holidays at the seaside. A day trip to Southend was the most we ever managed when I was a kid. Not even a proper beach there, but us kids didn't care. It was an exciting day out.' She shuffled through the books. 'I wonder what Joe would like? He's not a big reader, but I keep trying to convert him.'

Cordelia passed her a book. 'How about *The Thirty-Nine Steps*? The main character is a man and it's very exciting.'

'Perfect!' Mavis said, putting it to one side. 'If that don't get him reading, nothing will!' She looked at Cordelia. 'Found anything special for you?'

Cordelia shuffled through a small pile she had set aside, trying to choose her favourite. In the end she chose *A Room of One's Own* by Virginia Woolf. 'Among other things this one's about women's need for financial independence.'

It reminded her of her time as an undergraduate at the University of Cambridge. Her mind drifted back to her days at Girton College in the late 1930s. She remembered the ivy-covered walls, the portraits of female college masters on the dining room walls and the beautiful spreading gardens. She and the other students had spent endless hours in the college library, poring over books and later engaging in lively debates about what they'd learned.

Those years, so different from her parents' expectations of what a 'nice girl like her' should be doing, undoubtedly shaped her. It had been a struggle, but she refused to be forced into marriage with a 'suitable' man. She was determined she would make her own choices in life, not just follow what was expected of her 'set'. Yes, the college library had fostered her love of books and literature that would never end.

'Not much female financial independence around here,' Jane said, bringing Cordelia out of her reverie. 'Most women are waiting at the factory gates on payday hoping to get their housekeeping before their other half spends it in the pub.'

'Too right,' Mavis said. 'Loads of kids go 'ungry otherwise.' She looked over at Cordelia. 'Is it right you spent all that time at that college and never got a degree?'

Her question made Cordelia remember the many discussions they had about it at Girton. Every male student in other colleges, as long as they at least scraped through the exams, would be awarded a degree. But even the most brilliant female student could not.

She shook her head. 'That's nothing. Not that long ago the tutors could decide whether to let girls in the room at all. Some would, others made them stay behind a screen and others still wouldn't let them in at all. I've read an old diary about a student who used to open the door just a crack to listen, but she could never see what was written on the board. If she was lucky the tutor wouldn't have rubbed it off. In that case she'd sneak in when everyone had gone and copy it. But it was hard luck if it had been rubbed off.'

'Bloody hell,' Mavis said, red in the face with anger. 'So they get a degree just because they've got a... a... tadger! You must've wanted to kill some of 'em.'

Cordelia laughed. 'You're not wrong there. We wanted to string some of them up, especially the ones who didn't do any work.'

16

It was one of the library IIP days, when staff and volunteers helped people to locate their missing loved ones after the bombings.

'I don't know why they don't call it the missing persons' office, or something,' Mavis said. 'Still, people seem to know about them.'

Jane was moving chairs and small tables preparing for the IIP people when they arrived. She paused for a moment wiping her brow. Even this early it was already hot outside. 'Well, thank goodness there's less bombing now, though that one last week was terrible. I wonder how many people were killed or injured. I expect it'll be busy this morning. Imagine going from pillar to post looking for your husband or wife or brother or whoever. You could spend ages doing that and get nowhere.'

They'd just finished preparing the area when they heard a knock at the rear door, one never used by normal library users. Jane hurried over and opened it to find the two IIP workers waiting.

'All ready for you,' she said. 'Can I get you a cuppa before you start?'

One of the workers, Miss Nelson, nodded. 'That would be lovely, just what we need.' She seemed weighed down by an inner burden. 'It's going to be hard today. There have been more deaths since the last bombing. The doctors do all they can, but...' She wiped a tear from her eye. 'Will this wretched war never end?'

Her companion put an arm around her. 'It's got to end one day. We'll beat the damn Germans, especially now the Americans are helping us.'

Mavis joined in. 'Let's 'ope we all live long enough to see that day. Imagine the celebrations there'll be!' She paused. 'I wonder what they'll do about all the German prisoners of war. There's loads of them. Will they get sent back? Some of them, so I heard, quite like it 'ere prisoners or not. After all, they work in the fields and some get to know local people.'

Miss Nelson grunted. 'I've heard some girls even go out with them. Nazi whores I call them! Their mothers must be so ashamed.'

Mavis was about to challenge her for her awful comment but Bert knocking at the front door let them know it was time to open up. Jane and Mavis were relieved to get away from the conversation.

'I'll be over with the tea in a minute,' Jane said as she walked towards the door. Bert rushed in to read the newspapers as usual and there were a dozen or more people queuing for the IIP session. 'Good luck,' Jane whispered as they walked past her.

A bus pulled up at a stop opposite as she let people in. A newspaper boy was calling out the latest news, 'Blackout regulations tighten!' War was awful, she thought, but nothing seemed so bad on a sunny day. Then she saw Edith walking by on the other side of the road, and her good mood evaporated like steam from a cooling kettle. Where was she off to now? It wasn't like her to be up and about this early, she'd still been fast asleep when Jane left the house.

Mavis had joined her and saw where she was looking. 'Who's that you're looking at? You look worried.'

They walked back to the circulation desk, then to the little kitchen area to put on the kettle. Before Jane had time to answer Mavis attended to someone who came into the library with a query about books on how to learn first aid, then she joined her colleague again.

'So what's going on then? You look right hacked off.'

Keeping an eye on the desk, they made the tea, spooning tea leaves into the old brown teapot that had been a part of the library longer than anyone could remember. 'Hang on a moment while I take the IIP women their tea and I'll tell you all about it.' Jane loaded cups, saucers, spoons and a small amount of sugar onto a tray.

When she came back Mavis was stacking returned books onto the trolley. She looked at the clock. 'Tom'll be 'ere in a minute. 'E can put them back on the shelves if his leg isn't too painful. Come on then, girl, tell Auntie what's wrong.'

Jane looked around, reluctant to share anything if any library users could overhear. Fortunately there weren't many people present, and fewer near them.

'It's Edith,' Jane said with a sigh, feeling guilty about talking about her mother-in-law. 'You know, George's mother. She said she was coming for a week but that's been and gone and she's being...'

'A right pain in the butt. You've been a bit quiet about 'er but I can read between the lines. What's she been up to?'

Two more readers came up to the desk to get their books

stamped and talk about the price of everything in the shops – a common complaint.

'Them two 'ave always got something to moan about,' Mavis said. 'I know them. Pretend they 'aven't got two pennies to rub together when I 'appen to know they're better off than most in the East End.' She tidied a pile of books before continuing, 'So what's old Edith been up to then?'

When they'd gone Jane looked around again to be sure they could speak privately. She thought back over the last few days. 'She's never nice to me, but as posh as posh can be to my land-lady, who saw through her in seconds.' She laughed. 'It's hard to keep up that sort of accent, especially when you're in your cups.'

'Still drinking then, is she?' A solitary magpie tapped on the window as if asking to be let in. Mavis looked at it. 'I remember when I was a kid we 'ad a rhyme about them. Now what was it... I know. One for sorrow, two for joy, three for a funeral, four for a birth, five for heaven, six for hell, seven for the devil, his own self.' She laughed. 'What a load of old tosh. Now, we were talking about your mother-in-law still drinking.'

'Always, some days worse than others.' Jane's face tightened with frustration. She took a deep breath before continuing. 'Let's see, so far she's done a load of things. Mrs S is sure she's taken some money out of her purse. She found the half-bottle of sherry left over from Christmas that Mrs S had hidden, and drunk the lot. Then she was rude to the rent man calling him a bloodsucker when he's just doing his job. One night she brought a bloke back with her.'

'What!' Mavis said aghast. 'In your tiny house? Everyone would have heard what was going on.'

A steely glint shone in Jane's eyes. 'I wasn't about to let that happen. I'd just gone to bed and was reading when I heard them coming up the stairs. Trying to tiptoe and whisper they were, but drunks aren't so good at that.'

Mavis was looking at her open-mouthed. Was this the same timid Jane she'd first met who wouldn't say boo to a goose? 'So did you do something?'

'Do something? Do something? I put on my dressing gown and caught them just about to go into Edith's room – which is really Helen's room. "Where do you think you two are going?" I said. They looked like a couple of naughty schoolkids who'd been caught stealing sweets. Edith spluttered that I was a nosey cow but the bloke swore at her for wasting his time when he'd bought her several drinks and expected something in return. Then, cursing loud enough to wake the household, he ran back downstairs and out of the house.'

Through the open window they heard the rhythmic clatter of a horse-drawn coal cart passing by.

'Bloody hell, Jane,' Mavis said. 'Good for you, that was brave.'

Jane's expression softened slightly, but her frustration was still obvious. 'You get brave if you're really angry. I've had enough. I've dropped so many hints about her leaving it's a wonder she doesn't fall over them and break her damn neck. I've left newspapers in her room where I've circled rooms to let and the same with jobs. I'm wasting my time. Something's got to be done before I choke her.'

17

'Is that my dress?' Jane said as Edith was about to leave the house. She stood up to get a better look. 'It is, isn't it? Take it off immediately.'

Edith responded with a rude gesture, her face twisted in a scowl, then she walked out of the house slamming the door hard, the sound echoing through the room.

So angry she could hardly breathe, Jane took a deep breath to calm herself, but her heart was still beating fast when she turned back to Mrs S. 'How I haven't throttled her yet I don't understand.'

Mrs S put down her knitting mid-stitch and nodded. 'I know she's George's mum...' Her gaze drifted toward the door. The silence stretched out between them. 'But she'll have to go if she doesn't buck her ideas up. I think I've been patient but...'

'You have! You've been an angel, Mrs S,' Jane said. 'I'm so sorry. I never thought she'd be this bad.'

'She's been up to things. Things I haven't told you about.' Mrs S's voice was strained as if she were picking her words with care.

Jane sat forward. 'What has she been up to?'

'Those that drink are often trouble, one way or another. You're usually at work or doing something with Helen. You don't see what I see.'

Jane's spirits plummeted. 'Oh no, what else has she been up to?'

Mrs S moved around in her chair, grimacing as her arthritis pained her. She looked toward the kitchen as if remembering something unpleasant. 'For starters, she leaves the kitchen in a right mess when she's had her breakfast. Greasy plates often with fag ends stubbed out on them. Often leaves them in cold water too. It's a right sod to get them clean.' She shook her head, her face a picture of disgust and weariness.

'I'm so sorry, Mrs S. I didn't know she was doing all this. That's horrible. If she does it again, leave the dishes on the side and I'll wash them when I get home.'

'And how am I going to make myself a bite to eat about dinner time then? That kitchen's so small, there's hardly room to move. You know that.'

They were silent again apart from the ticking of the clock and the footsteps of people walking past outside. Jane's brow furrowed with worry. There had to be a way round this. Edith was a nightmare, but she almost certainly had nowhere else to go. But then, a voice whispered in her ear, where does she go when she vanishes for days on end?

Finally she spoke. 'What if I prepare some meals in advance and leave them for you while I'm at work?' It wouldn't take her long to make some sandwiches.

Mrs S shook her head, her face sad, reluctant to speak. 'It's not just the meals and the kitchen, dear, it's... everything.'

Jane couldn't believe there was more. 'Oh dear, what else has she been doing?'

'Yesterday I found her rummaging through my chest of drawers. I think she was hoping to find something valuable she could sell.' She gave a bitter laugh. 'If she thinks I've got anything valuable she doesn't know me very well.'

'That's just awful,' Jane said, feeling as if the air were being squeezed out of her body. 'I had no idea it was this bad. I should have paid more attention. But with working and everything...'

Mrs S looked up sharply. 'Jane. This is not your fault. It is hers. And there's other things. She'd burned a cigarette hole in her sheets and they're so dirty it will take a month of Sundays to get them clean.' She reached over and patted Jane's hand. 'None of this is your fault, my dear. But...' She paused, long enough to take a deep breath. 'I hate to say it, but she will have to go.'

No one would blame her. It was her house and Edith had never contributed a penny since she'd arrived. The words hung heavily in the air, bulging with finality. Jane knew Mrs S was right, but getting Edith to go would be a fight.

18

Twenty-five people! Mavis was thrilled that so many people had responded to her posters asking if tenants would be involved in the rent strike campaign. Although her meeting had gone well, asking people to give up their time was another matter altogether. Most people had families to look after and worked from dawn till dusk just keeping their heads above water.

They were in a smaller back room in St Marks' church and she had managed to persuade the very busy WVS workers to provide tea and biscuits. To her delight two had expressed a wish to be involved in the protest movement.

Mavis looked around as people settled themselves. It was early evening and most people would be getting their tea at home, but she was glad to see four people who she knew worked in the factories, seven older people who would no longer be in paid work, Mrs Gregory whose daughter Hetty was a regular at the library, Jane and her landlady known as Mrs S who walked in heavily leaning on a stick. Seeing their expectant faces gave her a warm feeling and the courage she would need to continue with the campaign.

Waiting until everyone had their tea and biscuit she stepped to the front of the room. Even though she knew each person in the room was on her side, on the side of right against unscrupulous landlords, she still felt nervous. Paul, the college lecturer who was advising her, told her the success of the strike would rely on getting the commitment and involvement of as many people as possible.

Taking a deep breath and rubbing her damp palms on her skirt, she began to speak. 'Thank you all for coming tonight. It's wonderful to see so many of you here, ready to take a stand against these landlords who 'ave been taking advantage of us for so long.' While she spoke, she made sure she looked at every person, catching their eye.

'Too damn right,' an elderly man with only one arm said. 'I lost this arm in the last war. Homes fit for heroes they promised. Hah! Fit for nothing but chickens and rats!'

Several people muttered, 'Hear! Hear!'

'You are absolutely right, Mr Badstock,' Mavis said. She'd known the man since she was a nipper and he'd sometimes put a farthing into her hand when they met. She'd clutched it tight all the way to the sweet shop, knowing it wouldn't buy much, perhaps a few aniseed balls or a tiny bag of broken biscuits. 'Well, you 'ad a hard fight in the trenches, a terrible fight. I'm not saying what we're doing will be that bad, of course I'm not, but it's a fight nonetheless.'

The door opened and she was delighted to see Paul Wheeler come in. He gestured that he would sit in the back of the room so she continued.

'Just as men fought together in the last war, and fight together in this one, we have to fight together to get a home fit not just for heroes but for all of us...' She paused to let her words sink in. 'Let's face it, it's not just the brave boys fighting who are heroes, it's us lot, the people of the East End who are struggling with bombing, rationing and of course terrible 'ousing. Yet we manage to bring up our children and carry on.'

She was surprised that her words raised a round of applause. Uncharacteristically she blushed at the response but held up her hand for silence.

'What we need is to get you to split up into groups. Each group can tackle one aspect of the fight.' She indicated Paul at the back. 'Mr Wheeler here has experience of helping this type of fight and will advise us.'

She stopped and unrolled a piece of old wallpaper she'd found in the library basement. On it she had written the group tasks.

'Awareness raising,' she read. 'That's about speaking to as many people as possible. Get their commitment, reassure them about any fears they have, try to get them involved, that sort of thing.'

She bent down and produced some smaller posters, artistically made by Tom.

'What with paper rationing we can't 'ave notes to put through everyone's door as I'd like to. But I thought that in the tenements, there could be one on each landing. Then put more everywhere you can think of.'

'I can pin one up in the factory,' a burly, tattooed man shouted.

'Excellent!' Mavis said and, with a wide grin, walked over and gave him one. 'Now, before we get any more volunteers, and I 'ope plenty of you will, let me tell you what else we need.'

She turned back to the big poster but was interrupted by the door opening again. Her heart sank when she saw who had walked in.

Two thuggish-looking men. Mavis knew they were Mr

Stanstead's henchmen. They slowly walked to the side of the room and leaned against the wall without a word. One was smoking a cigarette, its ash an inch long. The other rolled a toothpick around in his mouth but still managed to look at the group with a sneer. They exuded an intimidating air, with their burly frames and menacing presence. Their thickset shoulders and muscular arms showed evidence of physical strength and scars were proof of street brawls. Dressed in worn-out leather jackets and trousers, it was clear they expected no opposition.

Every single person turned around and looked at them, the atmosphere in the room changing in a heartbeat. Everyone knew who they were. Mr Stanstead was the biggest property owner in the area and well known for having no hesitation to get his own way.

'Can I 'elp you gentlemen?' Mavis asked, struggling to keep her voice steady.

'Nah,' the smoker said. 'Just looking around, checking who's here.' He slowly looked around the room, brought his hand into a gun shape and pretended to shoot people.

The nervous silence in the room was broken by Mrs Gregory. 'I know you two,' she said. 'You been trouble since you was in short trousers with your backsides hanging out. And I know how to deal with you an' all.' She reached into her handbag and produced a police whistle which she blew long and hard. The effect was electrifying, everyone suddenly as still as statues. Except her. 'The cops'll be 'ere in a minute. They walk round 'ere regular as clockwork. If they ain't ones in the pay of your boss, you'll be for it.'

As if to reinforce her words she blew the whistle again, long and hard, its shrill sound filling the room once more.

Two of the factory workers, big, burly men with bulging muscles, stood up. They glanced at each other then slowly walked towards the henchmen, never taking their eyes off them.

The henchmen sneered again, but the smoker dropped his fag on the floor and made a theatrical play of treading it into the floorboards. He looked as if he wished he was crushing every person there. The other one spat his toothpick out. Point made, they strolled out of the room, arms swinging widely.

It was as if everyone in the room had been holding their breath. As soon as the door closed behind the thugs the atmosphere in the room changed again, this time filled with a mixture of relief and determination. Mavis took two deep breaths to get her beating heart under control. Her voice still trembled slightly as she held up her hand for silence.

'Let's not be intimidated by these thugs. They're just trying to scare us, but we won't back down, will we? We'll fight for our rights!'

The room erupted in loud applause and encouraging cheers. Looking around, Mavis's confidence surged, fuelled by the solidarity and strength of the people gathered there.

She continued the meeting outlining the remaining tasks, including organising peaceful protests, gathering evidence of landlord neglect, seeking legal advice (Paul offered to do that), and reaching out to community groups for support. The energy in the room was palpable, each person eager to help, to contribute their skills. Often they would be using skills they had never used before but not one person appeared daunted. They were all eager to make sure they won.

By the end of the meeting, Mavis felt a renewed sense of hope. These people, many of whom had never even attended a meeting before, never taken action against wrongdoing, never realised they could be in charge of their own destiny, were inspired to act.

With plans in motion, Mavis was confident the strike campaign would gather momentum. The fight had hardly begun and she knew it would be long and hard, but they wouldn't rest until justice was served. Together the people of Silvertown would show they wouldn't be bowed down, they would defy the odds and create a better future for themselves and their community.

When they'd gone Paul helped Mavis tidy the room. 'I was so impressed by the way you and the others handled those thugs,' he said. 'I have to admit I was a bit scared.' He stacked the last chair and wiped his hands on his handkerchief. 'You're doing all the right things, Mavis, but get in touch if you need more help.'

19

Eugene's friends often teased him about how much time he spent in Silvertown Library. 'There's a bigger one in Canning Town!' they'd mock him. 'But perhaps the broad who works there ain't so cute!'

Used to their teasing, he just ignored it and went to the library anyway. He had a good excuse, he was doing family history research. So far he'd had little time to devote to this but on this particular Saturday morning he arrived at opening time. He'd be in luck if it was Cordelia's weekend on duty, but even if she wasn't he'd find out more about his ancestors.

He walked in and grinned immediately. He was in luck. She was at the desk, stamping an elderly woman's books, chatting about the weather and the woman's bunions. He had time to watch her without her being aware. He'd read somewhere that the most beautiful people always had symmetrical faces. She almost did, but her generous lips went up one side more than the other when she smiled. He thought it was endearing.

Then, as the older woman walked away, Cordelia looked up

and saw him. Her smile was as big as his. 'Eugene!' she cried. 'Have you come to teach us some more science?'

He walked to the desk, taking in her clear skin and the faint trace of her flowery perfume. 'I've been in several times since then, but I've never managed to see you.' He pretended to cry and she play-punched him.

'What can we do for you today? Are you still looking into your family history?'

He reached into his pocket and took out a letter. 'I got a letter from my ma. She says our ancestors used to be performers and she's convinced they sang and danced here. Vaudeville or something.' He hesitated, wrinkling the letter between his fingers. 'It's probably just an old family story.'

Her eyes twinkled as she looked into his. 'Never ignore those. There's usually at least some truth in them. Just last year we had someone come in convinced there was someone with a title in his background.'

Eugene laughed. 'I guess he was hoping he was due a country estate and a ton of money.'

'He was but he was out of luck. It took him ages looking through the records and he did find someone who was a very minor lord. But that line of the family had died out. He was so disappointed I thought he would cry.'

Eugene smoothed his letter, folded it up and put it back in his pocket. 'Well, let's hope I have more luck and with someone as special as you helping me, my chances have got to be good.'

Cordelia chewed her lip thoughtfully, her gaze drifting away from Eugene's hopeful smile. 'I suppose I can spare a few minutes,' she conceded, wondering if she was doing the right thing.

She looked around, knowing that both Tom and Jane were on duty. She could be spared. The inevitable paperwork could wait. But she knew Eugene's request wasn't entirely innocent. The powerful attraction between them couldn't be denied. She looked anywhere but into his eyes, at his strong forearms showing below his rolled-up shirt sleeves, at the triangle of chest hair below his neck. Anywhere where she might keep her emotions under control.

But it was a lost cause. 'Come with me, Eugene. Your best bet is to look through old newspapers. You might not find articles but look for adverts – probably something about a coloured musician or exotic music, that sort of thing. Do you have any name?'

He sighed. 'Bessie Johnson. It might not even be her real name, but that's all I know. She was supposed to be a singer.'

Cordelia wanted nothing more than to sit beside him, feeling his masculine closeness as she helped him trawl through old newspapers. But she couldn't justify it and in any case Jane and Mavis would never let her live it down. They didn't miss a thing.

She led him to the reference room and showed him where the old newspapers were. 'Any idea what year we'd be looking for?'

He frowned trying to remember what he'd been told. 'I suppose about sixty years ago.'

Knowing she should be doing a million and one other things, she helped him find the right bundle of papers. Once they reached for the same paper and their fingers touched lightly. They both left them there a second or two longer than normal but then she pulled her hand away, aware of the electricity between them.

'Shall we make a list of terms to look out for?' she asked, deliberately delaying going back to her work.

They sat side by side, far too aware of each other, making a list. It was surprisingly long: coloured, negro, exotic, oriental, entertainer, performer, musician, vaudeville artist, variety show, music hall – the list seemed endless.

The door opened and Mavis entered. "Ave you forgotten you've got a meeting with your boss soon?' she asked. She tried unsuccessfully to look innocent with her comment but the way her eyes moved from one of them to the other showed she was aware there was something going on between them.

Guilt fought with panic in Cordelia's mind and she stood up so quickly she almost knocked over her chair. 'Oh, thank goodness you reminded me. We got lost in family research.' She smoothed her skirt and looked at Eugene. 'I'll leave you to it. I hope to see you another day.'

He stood up and shook her hand formally. 'I sure hope so. My ma would love it if I found something. Let's hope I do before the war gets in the way.'

20

She'd been awake long into the night making notes about the upcoming rent strike, how it would work, who would need to be involved in the planning and resources they would need. Paul Wheeler advised that to have maximum impact she must get people from nearby boroughs to join in – Canning Town, West Ham, East Ham, Poplar and Barking. After some thought she decided contacting their libraries for help would be the best way to start that process.

But the nagging fear of telling Cordelia her father was one of the horrible landlords kept intruding, making her lose concentration.

How could she do it? Tell her boss, who she knew would never behave as her father did. Who would never agree with his actions. But he was her father. She was sure to be conflicted. This was different to giving bad news about putting some figures in the wrong column or damaging a book.

It was with a heavy heart she opened the rear door to the library and stepped inside. But hammering on the door stopped her thoughts as Bert waited to get in to read his papers.

Although he smelled a lot better these days and was even polite sometimes, other days he was as grumpy as ever. 'You're two minutes late!' he grumbled, back to his old self. They felt less irritated with him since they'd learned he was caring for his elderly, infirm mother. Life must be hard for him. Perhaps coming to the library gave him some breathing space.

Mavis struggled with the best thing to do. Delay telling Cordelia about her dad? But Tom had spotted Lord Carmichael's name on the list and maybe others would start looking too. In fact, she sighed, she would have to say something.

The morning was busier than usual. Several times people came in to talk to Mavis about the strike and it was hard to get her work done. Mrs Morris, an elderly Jewish lady, came over to her but coughed for some time before she could speak. 'Sorry,' she gasped when the coughing stopped. 'The doc says me cough is caused by all the mould in my place. The walls are black with it. I wipe them every day, but it always comes straight back. And the damp runs down the walls.' She reached out and took Mavis's hands in hers. 'Tell me, bubbeleh, do you think your strike will work? Will the landlord sort things out for me? It's killing me.'

Each conversation left Mavis in more of a quandary, not least because Mrs Morris lived in a property owned by Lord Carmichael. As the hours ticked away, she grew increasingly nervous about having to tell Cordelia about her father.

In the end she knocked on Cordelia's door while Tom was on the desk and Jane was restocking the stacks with returned books.

Cordelia looked up from a list of improvements to the library she was planning if they were lucky with the book sale. She looked tired and Mavis hated to be the bearer of bad news.

'Cordelia…' she said, hesitating. ''Ave you got a minute?'

'Of course, sit down,' Cordelia said. 'You look very serious.'

Pulling out a chair, Mavis hesitated again. 'I've come in to tell you about... it's... well... it's difficult.'

Cordelia frowned. 'Is something wrong? Is Joyce okay? Has something happened to Joe?'

'Yes, but it's not them. Tom gave me a list of Silvertown landlords 'e'd managed to find somehow. And... well, it's about your father...'

The colour drained from Cordelia's face, her eyes widening with shock. 'My father? Has something happened to him?'

Mavis unfolded the paper she had been clutching, her hands damp with sweat. She took a deep breath, willing herself to stay calm. 'No, I'm sorry if I put that worry in your 'ead. The thing is, 'e owns several properties around 'ere. They're in pretty bad condition, Tom thinks. I've been putting off telling you.'

Cordelia stared at her, struggling to absorb the full meaning of Mavis's words. When she understood, she slumped back in her chair, eyes filled with tears. 'Are you sure, Mavis? My father owns some of those slums?'

Mavis twisted the hem of her blouse in her fingers. 'I'm afraid so. And there's more, I'm afraid. 'E's one of the landlords who 'ave increased rents since the war started.'

Cordelia got up from her chair and walked to the window, not seeing the scene outside. The silence between the friends stretched heavy and oppressive. Finally, Cordelia spoke, her voice barely above a whisper. 'I'm ashamed to say this but I can believe it. He owns several cottages in the village near our place and he doesn't look after those either.'

Outside, a pigeon fluttered on the windowsill, its beady eye seeming to see Cordelia's heartbreak.

She turned around. 'It feels as if everything I've done is tainted now. How can I ask people to fight against landlords when my own father is one of them?'

Seeing her distress, Mavis walked towards her. 'We all know it's not you, love. You'd never do something like that. I'm afraid there's worse news. As The Professor told us, in nineteen thirty-nine the government brought in an act forbidding rent rises unless there was a good cause. Your father, along with other landlords, is breaking the law. 'E might not know. 'E's probably got an agent dealing with these things for 'im.'

Cordelia wiped the tears from her cheeks with the back of her hand. She'd known for years that her father held different views on life from hers and more recently her mother's. She and the other librarians struggled daily to help improve the lives of the people of Silvertown. But now she felt all her good work was tainted by association with the man she thought she loved, despite their differences.

Catching her breath, she walked back to her desk and looked at Mavis, recognising concern and sympathy in her friend's eyes. She realised how difficult it must have been to deliver this news. Especially difficult when she was involved in trying to improve the housing in the area.

'I don't know what to say...' Cordelia looked down, shuffling the papers in front of her without seeing them. She stood up again and walked up and down behind her desk. Her thoughts were a jumble of confusion, anger and a deep sense of betrayal. How could her father, who pretended to believe in fair play, be responsible for such dreadful living conditions? How could he live in such comfort with a clear conscience? Eventually she turned to the still-silent Mavis. 'There's nothing I can do about this at the moment, but rest assured I will speak to my father about this very soon. I have to find a way to make this right.'

She squared her shoulders, dreading the conversation with her father, knowing he would be defensive and angry. But then she remembered that her mother had grown in confidence and gradually developed beliefs much like Cordelia's own. Perhaps they could speak to him together. It was certainly something to consider.

'Thank you for telling me, Mavis. That must have been difficult.' She reached out and squeezed her friend's hand. 'I promise you, I'll do my best to get things sorted out.' With that, she slumped back in her chair. How on earth could she sort out this mess?

21

'Jane, sweetheart,' Mrs S said, her voice more hesitant than usual. 'Have you already told Edith I need her to go?'

Jane was busy cutting up vegetables for a Victory Stew, at least that's what the government liked to call it. But it was really just vegetables and whatever else you could lay your hands on. The smell of boiling cabbage and turnips mingled with the earthy aroma of pearl barley. She'd got a bone from the butcher that had some scraps of meat still on it. They'd come off during the cooking and gave it some flavour.

Her thoughts were miles away, wondering how to stretch her money to the end of the week. 'Sorry, Mrs S, what did you say?'

'Have you told Edith she can't stay here?'

Jane put down her knife, wiped her hands on her apron and went into the living room, perching on the arm of the settee. 'No, I haven't seen her for days. You know what she's like, goes missing for ages then turns up again like a bad penny. Why do you ask?'

Mrs S rubbed her sore knees and flinched. 'I looked in her

room this morning. I'm not sure but I think some of her stuff's gone. Not all of it though.'

'I wonder where she goes when she vanishes for days on end like she does?' Jane didn't like to add that she guessed there would be a man involved. One who would pay for everything. But she told herself to be more generous. Maybe she was visiting friends from where she used to live.

'I'll never understand that woman as long as I live,' Mrs S said. 'And she's not a good influence on your little one either, is she?'

Maybe the gods somewhere had heard their conversation. An hour later there was a sharp knocking on the door. Jane's heart leapt as it always did with unexpected visitors. Everyone feared the dreadful knock that heralded the telegram boy bringing bad news.

It was bad news, but not to do with George.

'Mrs Wilkins?' the young policeman standing at the door asked. 'Is that you?'

She nodded, her throat constricted with fear. George was stationed in England but he could still have been injured somehow.

'It's Mrs Wilkins,' the policeman said. He appeared far too young for his job and looked like he wanted to be anywhere but there then.

'Yes, that's me,' Jane said. Had they sent her a deaf officer?

'No...' He went pink. 'I'm sorry, I didn't mean you. It's the other Mrs Wilkins.' He paused then looked at his small note-book. 'Mrs Edith Wilkins. She's in hospital, I'm afraid.'

'Hospital? Edith?' Jane gasped, struggling to make sense of his words. 'What do you mean?'

'She's in St Andrews Hospital, the one in Bromley. She had

an accident a couple of days ago but I understand she's only now been able to provide any information about herself.'

There was a rustling from the living room and Mrs S came to the door. 'Is she going to die?' She sounded hopeful, and cruel though it was, Jane had to suppress a smile.

'Do you know what time visiting is?' she asked the policeman who had been about to turn away.

'It's usually six thirty to seven thirty and one afternoon, but I don't know which one.' He was about to leave when he turned back. 'My mum was in there ages ago. I remember they were very strict about visiting hours and didn't like children going.'

When he'd gone Jane and Mrs S went back into the living room. 'Did Granny bang her head like I did when that nasty boy pushed me over?' Helen asked, looking up from her book about princesses.

'I don't know what happened, love, but I'll go to see her this evening and find out.' Jane looked over at Mrs S. 'Do you mind keeping an eye on Helen?'

Mrs S smiled as she always did when she thought about spending time with Helen. 'Little ones keep me young,' she often said, although her arthritis didn't seem to know about it.

The visitors to Victoria Ward were all kept waiting, one or two anxiously looking through the glass panel in the doors. They had ten minutes to wait. 'No good trying to get in sooner,' one young woman said. 'What do they think will happen? We'll all become mass murderers like Al Capone and murder everyone in their beds?'

'They say it's too tiring for the patients,' another said, her face scornful. 'I think it's just them trying to have power over us visitors. What difference would five or ten minutes make, that's what I want to know.'

A plump middle-aged woman snorted. 'It's more important

that the ward is tidy and the bed corners perfect than what's good for the patients.'

Jane sighed. There was a lot of talk about the British fighting spirit in the newspapers, but the truth was people moaned about everything – rationing, shortages, bombing, ARP wardens and hospital visiting times.

When the doors were eventually opened by a ward sister wearing a uniform so starched it crackled as she walked, people rushed in as if someone had let off a firing pistol.

Jane walked up and down the ward twice looking for Edith. She passed women of all ages, some sitting in an armchair by their bed, others sitting in theirs obviously in pain, yet more apparently asleep. Finally Jane found her. Edith was lying on one side and had a large bandage on her head, but her eyes were open. 'Hello, Edith,' Jane said. 'I managed to find some fruit for you.' As she put the fruit on the small bedside cabinet she heard rustling from the bed and when she looked again Edith had turned over.

Had she not seen or heard Jane? Confused, Jane went round to the other side of the bed and leaned forward so her face was level with Edith's.

'Edith? It's me, Jane. I only just found out about your accident. I brought you some fruit.'

Her lips tightening, Edith closed her eyes and no matter what Jane said or did, she never opened them again. Jane sat beside her hoping she would at least acknowledge her presence. The only movement was a flickering of her eyelids and an occasional facial twitch. Jane felt sorry for her but had to swallow her fury. She'd done a lot to help her mother-in-law and now she was being very deliberately ignored.

After ten minutes she said, 'I'm going now. I'll come back tomorrow and hope you're feeling better by then.'

There was no response.

Jane's eyes flashed with irritation and she bit her lower lip hard enough to leave marks. She drummed her fingers on her handbag, her entire body almost vibrating with pent-up exasperation.

As she walked back towards the door she passed the sister's desk. Her name plate said 'Sister Norman'. Wanting to find out more about Edith's accident and health she stood in front of it for a few seconds before the sister stopped what she was writing and looked up. 'Can I help you?'

So irritated she struggled to form her words, Jane answered. 'I'm Mrs Wilkins. Edith Wilkins's daughter-in-law. I didn't know what happened to her until this afternoon. I still don't. All I know is she had an accident. And she won't speak to me. She's just pretending I'm not there.'

'Sit down here,' the sister said, sympathy in her face. 'I'll speak quietly so we're not overheard. As I understand it, your mother-in-law was run over by a horse and cart during the blackout. It was several hours before anyone found her.'

Jane immediately felt guilty for being irritated with Edith. What an awful thing to happen and to just lie there by the side of the road alone with no one to help. 'I know it's hard to see things in the dark, but I'm surprised no one found her sooner,' she said.

The sister took a deep breath. 'It was late at night so not many people about. And I'm afraid...' She paused as if wondering how to continue. 'I'm afraid she was quite drunk. A blessing really because she probably didn't feel the pain. Alcohol can act as an anaesthetic.' She leaned forward and looked Jane in the eyes. 'I'm afraid she needs help. She has withdrawal symptoms. Not unusual for alcoholics. Has she tried to stop drinking in the past?'

Jane thought back to everything she knew about her mother-in-law. George had told her she had always been a drinker, but never said if she'd tried to stop. 'I just don't know. Since George and I married he's visited her on her own because... well, she can be difficult. But I'm sure he'd have told me.'

A nurse came through the door and placed a file on the sister's desk without a word. The sister acknowledged her with a nod and simply turned it upside down. 'Mrs Wilkins is in a poor way,' she continued. 'Probably because of the drinking. At the moment she's still quite unwell and the head injury is making her confused some of the time.'

'Is there nothing that can be done?' Jane asked.

'I'm afraid facilities are few and far between, but if she agrees to seek help we will do our very best to get her into some sort of rehab. But it's too early to arrange that yet. She'll be with us a while longer.'

22

The streets of the East End were no stranger to hardship, but on that sunny August day in 1942, a different kind of struggle was brewing. The three librarians, with fire in their hearts and determination etched on their faces, stood at the head of the growing crowd before the war memorial. They held handmade banners high, the words 'Fair Rent now!' and 'Repairs now!' painted in bold, uneven letters.

The Blitz may have finished but the people of the East End were ready for this next battle. For too long they had tolerated dreadful living conditions and increasing rents. They were determined things had to change. And change now.

As more people joined the crowd, the air crackled with a sense of purpose, of determination.

Their faces flushed with excitement and resolve, the three friends looked out over the sea of people, recognising neighbours, library users, friends and strangers who had all come together for this moment. All had pledged not to pay their rent for the current week.

Mavis turned to Cordelia and Jane, her eyes sparkling with

anticipation. 'Ready?' she asked, her voice barely heard over the hubbub of the crowd. 'Remember the route? Down North Woolwich Road first.'

Her friends grinned back, their smile wide and infectious. 'Right, let's go!'

'I hope it doesn't rain again,' Jane said. 'I've got a hole in my shoe.'

With a nod, they raised their banners higher, the painted slogans catching the sunlight. As they took their first steps forward, they began to chant, their voices loud and clear.

'What do we want? Fair rents! When do we want it? Now!'

Within seconds, the crowd joined in, their voices becoming a powerful chorus that echoed through the war-damaged streets. The chant grew louder with each repetition, as if the very strength of their words could shake the foundations of the crumbling buildings around them.

They were the usual diverse tapestry of East Enders. Mothers pushing babies in prams, their faces weary but determined as they marched for a better future for their children. Older men, some leaning heavily on walking sticks, hobbled along with the procession, their weathered faces bearing the deep lines of a lifetime of hardship. Children skipping and chasing each other, their laughter mingling with the chants.

Mavis and Cordelia changed them.

'No more slums! No more greed! Proper housing is what we need!'

As the procession wound its way through the narrow streets, curious onlookers emerged from doorways or peered out of windows. Some put on coats and joined the march without hesitation. Others weren't so sure. What if the strike backfired and they were thrown out of their homes? Their fear stopped them joining in even if they agreed with the sentiment.

It was a perfect day for a march, earlier rain had stopped and the streets, usually grubby with horse droppings and debris from the factories, shone in the sunshine. It was sunny, but not too hot and the crowd were in good spirits. For the first time in years many of them felt in charge of their destiny. They had put up with too much bad treatment from their landlords.

They were delighted to see two newspaper reporters making notes about the march, their photographers busy snapping the proceedings.

They funnelled the river of people from the broad road to the narrow streets and lanes of the side streets. Their voices brought more people to their doors, several more joining in.

The Indian man who ran the corner shop came out and cheered them on as did many of the women queueing outside the butcher's next door. Their smiles cheered the librarians and put a spring in their step.

'Look how many people are on our side!' Mavis said with a wide smile, holding her banner higher. 'They know we've got right on our side.' If only Joe could be here, she thought. He'd be joining in, proudly waving a banner and shouting the chants along with everyone else. She missed him so much and was glad her work, Joyce and this campaign took her mind off her longing for him to come back.

But trouble was to come. Turning into the next street they came face to face with the well-known landlord Albert Stanstead. A tall, broad, imposing man, he stood firmly in the middle of the street, arms on his hips and a deep scowl etched on his face. He was flanked by two equally burly men. Although they adopted his stance, they looked less confident when they saw the size of the crowd in front of them.

'Well, well, well,' he said, sneering, his voice dripping with disdain. 'I heard you lot were coming this way. Bloody East End troublemakers from the library and your pathetic followers.' He stopped and spat on the floor. 'Do you seriously think this little parade will change anything?'

The three friends had halted the march, their chants fading into an uneasy murmur. They looked at each other and without hesitation stepped forward.

'It ain't us who are the troublemakers,' Mavis said. Her voice was calm but loud enough to be heard by the crowd. 'We're 'ard-working people who deserve fair treatment. A fair rent and proper repairs.'

Stanstead shook his head as if weary of them already. 'If you lot can't pay your rent, you can go somewhere else!'

He would have known, as everyone did, that even before the war accommodation was difficult to find. With so many properties bombed it was much, much harder – families living in cramped, often insanitary, rooms.

'We all live 'ere, many of us 'ave for generations. Without our rents you won't be able to enjoy your comfortable life, will you?'

But he hadn't finished. 'You lot would have signed leases...'

'What leases?' someone a few rows back shouted. 'I never 'ad no lease.'

'Nor did I,' several more people shouted.

The crowd were growing agitated, muttering and swearing loud enough to be heard by the landlord and his thugs.

'Mr Stanstead, we usually pay our rent but for this week and maybe future weeks, we will not be paying until there are changes.'

He sneered again. 'Changes? I don't think you're in a strong position to make any demands for changes.'

Cordelia put on her best posh voice. 'Mr Stanstead, I am Lady Cordelia Carmichael and I know that you and the other landlords who have increased rents are breaking the law.

Furthermore, any landlord with an ounce of decency would repair these homes to provide a decent standard of living.'

He grinned and looked her up and down as if mentally undressing her. 'Having a la-de-da voice don't count for much with me, girly. Nor a title. My men and I are going now but this isn't over. If you lot...' He waved his hand to include the crowd. 'If you don't pay your rent you'll be out on your ear. Never doubt it.'

The atmosphere amongst the marchers was electric as they overheard many of the comments.

'Bastard!'

'We'll get thrown out!'

'Better pay up.'

'I'm not giving in.'

The three friends stood their ground, their faces resolute despite the intimidating presence of Albert Stanstead and his henchmen. Soon the murmurs of fear and worry among the crowd were drowned by a surge of defiance.

Stepping forward, Mavis spoke, her voice filled with determination. 'We've 'ad enough of you and your like taking advantage of us 'ard-working people,' she declared, her voice firm with conviction. 'I'm telling you now, we won't be silenced any more. We deserve fair treatment, a fair rent and decent living conditions. I'll bet you wouldn't want to live in one of these properties you own.'

The onlookers, encouraged by the bravery of the three women, rallied behind them. Voices rose in protest again, this time louder and more insistent. 'Fair rent! Decent homes! Fair rent! Decent homes!'

The atmosphere crackled with energy as the determination of the crowd surged. Albert Stanstead seemed taken aback, but only for a moment. Soon his sneer appeared once more. 'You lot think you can defy me? Just wait and see what happens if you do. You'll soon change your bloody tune!'

He gestured to his henchmen and the three of them strode off, pushing people aside as if they were insects.

When they'd gone the crowd seemed to lose energy although several called out, 'Bloody good riddance,' and similar comments.

Mavis and Cordelia were worried they were losing the cohesion of the crowd. 'We gotta keep them riled up,' Mavis said to Cordelia. 'Leave it to me!'

She, who knew almost everyone and often their families as well, stood on a doorstep and faced them.

'If we stick together they'll 'ave to back down.' She pointed to the reporters who were busy scribbling on their notepads. 'The press 'eard what that... sorry excuse for a man... 'ad to say and I'm sure they'll be sympathetic to our cause. Not least...' – she smiled at the nearest reporter – 'because I delivered your little boy. Lovely lad 'e is too. 'Is proud mum brings 'im to the library regular as clockwork. Now, people of Silvertown, my warriors, my soldiers for right, are we going to win this fight?'

A loud cheer gave her her answer and she and Cordelia began the march again. 'You were amazing, Mavis,' Cordelia said, linking their arms together.

The chanting began again. This time it was, 'What do we want? Fair rents! When do we want them? Now!'

'You were a force of nature back there,' Cordelia said, her eyes alight with admiration. 'Ever thought of trading our library shelves for the political stage?'

Mavis snorted. 'Political? You gotta be kidding. Too many 'orrible men talking non-stop but never saying a sensible word for my liking. They'd never listen to a woman anyway. I'd spend all my time wanting to punch them.'

The determined march continued through the streets, their chants echoing off the war-damaged buildings. Several people behind the librarians chatted to them, excited to be taking action at last. The brief conversations lifted their spirits. They knew this was the beginning of a hard battle, one they hoped wouldn't last too long. Mr Wheeler had told Mavis that whilst all the strikes he'd heard of had succeeded, they'd taken varying lengths of time.

Yes, this was the beginning and they were determined to see it through.

As they turned into the next street, they saw a familiar sight, children playing in the rubble of a bombed-out house. All were poorly dressed, two lads had no shoes. Inevitably they were playing war games. Sticks became rifles, bricks became grenades. They'd divided themselves into two teams, some playing the roles of brave British soldiers, while others took on the part of the enemy. Loving every minute, they shouted commands at each other.

'Take that!'

'Die, you German swine!'

Some 'collapsed', pretending to be shot and making the most of long, painful apparent deaths. Others continued making explosive sounds, mimicking the sounds of gunfire and grenades.

Mavis sighed. 'Poor kids. Growing up thinking war is normal, but the poor blighters probably can't remember anything else. Still, reminds us what we're fighting for, don't it?'

The march continued on its winding route back to the war memorial.

Some people had fallen by the wayside but others had joined in and the two women felt energised by their commitment.

Once a bus passed them and the driver hooted his horn. Her horn.

'Isn't that your friend, what's 'er name?' Mavis said.

'Rosalind, you're right. I haven't seen her for ages but we're having a night out soon.' Cordelia was looking forward to it. Rosalind always led a much more exciting life than she did, even now she had volunteered to be a bus driver, something Cordelia never believed she would do. They would have a great time. Rosalind always knew the best places to go.

Thinking of it made her feel guilty anticipating a fun evening out when her boyfriend Robert was stuck in the heat and flies in North Africa. But she knew he would say she couldn't put her life on hold.

Finally, they gathered around where they had started – the war memorial. Mavis, encouraged by Cordelia, climbed on a nearby bench and looked around at the people, her people, who deserved so much better than they had.

'My friends,' she began, her voice loud and clear. 'Today we've made a great start – *you've* made a great start. We're going to show those rotten landlords and the authorities that we won't take any more. We want fair rents and decent housing...'

She paused and the crowd cheered, echoing her words.

She held up her hand. 'But this is only the beginning. Mark my words, it won't be easy but us East Enders are used to struggle, we face it every day of our lives.'

She waved her arm around and wished she hadn't spotted Mr Stanstead and his thugs standing in a shop doorway watching her. He was leaning against a doorpost, arms folded, a toothpick in his mouth and a scowl on his face. Unnerved for a second, she almost stopped but remembered their goal, took a deep breath and straightened her back. Fair rents, decent housing.

'Look around you,' she said to the crowd, her voice ringing down the street. 'These are your friends, your neighbours, your workmates, your children. That's what we're fighting for – a better future for every single person in Silvertown!'

As she finished the crowd erupted with cheers and shouts of, 'For she's a jolly good fellow.'

While most people drifted off, several came to speak to them, fired with enthusiasm for the action and offering their help. They gave Mavis their names and addresses and she thanked them wholeheartedly. 'There'll be plenty for you to do,' she said, smiling so hard her cheeks ached.

When they'd all gone, the two women collapsed onto the bench and grinned at each other.

'I reckon we've earned a shandy at the pub, what says you?' Mavis said.

They stepped carefully around the edges of a bomb crater as they walked towards The Ship, the recent rain making the earth soft and treacherous.

'Do you know what we're doing reminds me of?' Cordelia said, her voice tinged with memories of old frustrations.

'What's that then?' Mavis asked, her brow furrowed as the navigated a particularly muddy patch knowing she had card-board inside her shoes that would quickly go soggy.

Cordelia waved her hand as if she wished she could dismiss the memories. 'You know I went to the university in Cambridge. Well, after years of struggle, they finally allowed women to study there. But they refused to give them degrees.'

Mavis stopped so abruptly that a lock of her hair fell out of her old straw hat.

'Yes! You did all that for nothing!' She brushed the hair away, her movements sharp with indignation. 'Them 'igher-ups in that university must be as bad as these landlords. What're they frightened of, that's what I'd like to know.'

'A number of things, I suppose. Some secretly worried we'd do better than them. Others thought that if we got degrees theirs would somehow be less valuable. Some were just plain against women doing anything but cooking their dinners and having babies.'

They walked on, their steps synchronising as they moved through the streets where jagged gaps between buildings showed what Silvertown had already been through.

Mavis shook her head, unable to believe what she was hearing. 'You get used to us women being treated like we're not worth much 'ere in the East End, but I'd always thought things'd be different for you posher folks.'

Cordelia laughed. 'I wish you were right, but it's the same everywhere, Mavis. Until recently my mother always did what my father told her and thought nothing of it.'

'Really?' Mavis asked. 'That's interesting. What made her change then?' She nodded to the man selling fruit on the corner of the street who gave her a smiling salute in return.

'I think I told you a large part of our home was taken over by the army for a convalescent home.'

Mavis snorted. 'Yeah, I remember your dad was right upset about that.'

'He was. He came into the library one day if you remember, fuming because Mr Churchill wouldn't do what he wanted.' She paused and looked before crossing the street. 'Anyway, my mother began volunteering with the soldiers who were convalescing. She wrote letters for them, or read to them if they'd been blinded. It opened her eyes to another world.'

''Ow the other 'alf lives, I suppose.' Mavis pulled Cordelia back. 'Careful, you nearly got run over then.'

Cordelia jumped back, almost tipping backwards. 'Yes, it's changed her a lot. She finally realises that not everyone has the same chances our family had.'

They'd reached the pub and Mavis opened the door, letting Cordelia go first. 'What'll it be?' she asked.

'Let me get them,' Cordelia said, indicating seats they could take. 'Shandy?'

'Better 'ad,' Mavis said. 'I'll 'ave to collect Joyce soon and I can't go there three sheets to the wind.'

It seemed like Mavis knew half the people in the pub. A couple had been at the meeting and came over to congratulate her, others just smiled a greeting. She looked around and noticed all the people she'd helped. The Johnson family with a letter to the council about getting a bigger place because they lived with their six children in two rooms. Mrs Kite about understanding a letter she'd received from her landlord. Miss Smithon, one of the surplus women whose fiancé had died during the First World War, who'd come to cry on her shoulder when her only brother got the Big C and there wasn't much hope for him. So many stories in such a small area.

She was brought back to the moment by Cordelia sitting near to her, nearly spilling the shandy on her shoes.

'You never finished telling me about what 'appened at your university. Did you win?'

Cordelia shook her head. 'We did everything you're doing now. Meetings, groups to cover different aspects of the protests, marches. It did no good. They're still not giving degrees. I think they must be one of the last, if not the last university in the country.'

Mavis took a sip of her shandy then wiped her mouth. 'So you didn't win after all that effort. Even clever posh people lose sometimes. Let's hope we do better. One up for the down-trodden.'

23

Several days later Rosalind knocked on Cordelia's door, the sharp triple tap she always used.

'Cooee, anyone in?' she sung before Cordelia had time to get to the door. 'Your very best friend is out here waiting!'

Cordelia had just got out of the bath with its regulation five inches of water. Not enough to encourage her to enjoy soaking in it reading a book as she did before the war. Throwing her dressing gown round herself she hurried to let her friend in. She flung open the door and the two women hugged.

'It's been ages,' Cordelia said, pulling Rosalind inside and looking at how she was dressed. 'Looks like you've just finished work too.'

Rosalind looked down at her bus driver uniform, dusting off some bits of fluff. 'I thought I'd never get away. Even though there's not so much bombing, the routes still keep changing as buildings collapse or roads are reopened. It's enough to give anyone a headache.' She picked up her bag and headed for the bedroom. 'Okay if I have a quick wash before I get changed? You can come in and talk to me.'

Cordelia sat on her bed, talking to Rosalind through the open bathroom door. 'Rainbow Corner tonight, is it? Or have you thought of any other plans?'

Rosalind walked in and opened her small case, getting out a dress and shoes. She shook the dress and hung it over the wardrobe. 'I was thinking we could start there. Trouble is, they don't serve any alcohol. But never fear...' She opened up her bag and like a magician produced a silver whisky flask with a flourish. 'I've thought of everything. We can top up our drinks with this.'

'One thing I've always known about you, Rosalind, is you never miss a trick! And I expect you're hoping to find a rich Yank too,' Cordelia said, struggling to do up her dress.

'Turn around,' Rosalind said. 'Let me help.' She tugged at the zip which had caught in some fabric. 'A rich Yank would be nice. From what we see on the flicks, everything there is wonderful.'

'That's impossible,' Cordelia said, turning round and checking herself in the mirror. 'Just Hollywood trying to sell films. There's got to be poor people too.'

Undoing her uniform tie and shirt, Rosalind nodded. 'I bet some poor English girls will marry a Yank thinking she's going to live in luxury and get a nasty shock when she gets off the ship.' Outside, they heard a boat's siren, and a car backfiring. 'Let's get going or we'll miss half the fun,' Rosalind said, pulling an expensive royal-blue dress with gold trimmings over her slim body.

Forty-five minutes later they walked towards Rainbow Corner on the corner of Shaftesbury Avenue. There was one similarity between this part of London and the East End. Two women stood near the building the friends were to enter. The women wore low-cut white blouses and very tight short skirts, their high heels clicking against the pavement as they approached the GIs who walked by. The prostitutes' laughter was loud and brash and their bartering not much quieter.

'Men will pay for women everywhere,' Rosalind said. 'You've got to feel sorry for them. I can't imagine anyone would... you know... for money if they didn't have to.'

Relieved that fortune was kinder to them, the friends stepped into Rainbow Corner. The entrance area was framed with photos of film stars lining the corridor and felt like walking into a movie scene. A cheerful hostess in a smart royal-blue uniform greeted them, asking if they'd been there before. 'I can see you're Brits too,' she said with a knowing smile. Two soldiers came in behind them and immediately began talking to the hostess. Before she answered them, she turned to Cordelia and Rosalind. 'I'll leave you to it. Have a terrific evening, y'all.'

With an unexpected tingle, Cordelia wondered if Eugene would be there. 'Something to eat first?' she asked. 'Not too much or we'll be too full to dance.'

Rosalind laughed. 'It's only here you could get that much to eat!'

They went to a restaurant on the second floor. The sign over the door read 'Red, White and Blue' and the name definitely reflected the décor. American flags and Union Jacks provided a riot of colours against the plain white walls. Alongside them were plenty of saucy pin-ups. All the girls had voluptuous figures and were dressed in revealing outfits with a minimal army theme that left little to the imagination. As well as tables and chairs in the middle of the huge space there were some more intimate booths where the lighting was dimmer.

A long counter stretched along one side of the café where waitresses dressed in smart red uniforms with blue and white accents bustled here and there, taking orders and serving up heaped plates of food.

'The smells in here make my mouth water,' Rosalind said, looking at the menu. She licked her lips as she read – cheeseburgers, fries, meat loaf and mashed potatoes, and even good old British staples like fish and chips.

They gave their orders and looked around. Most of the tables had two or more people on them. Some only had GIs enjoying a meal together, but others were mixed with English girls dressed to the nines fluttering their eyelashes at their dates.

They both chose cheeseburger and fries – the days when anyone could get both minced beef and cheese in a single dish were long gone since rationing but here it was an everyday option. Soon they had eaten their fill and sat back with cups of coffee. 'I can't remember the last time I had real coffee,' Rosalind said, inhaling the delicious smell and groaning with pleasure.

As Cordelia listened to Rosalind recount a funny story from her work, her gaze wandered around. Suddenly, she froze, her heart skipping a beat. There, across the room, was the man she had half hoped to see. Eugene was seated at a table with three other black soldiers, his deep laughter carrying occasionally across the room. He was sideways on to her and hadn't spotted her.

'Cordelia, are you even listening?' Rosalind said with a grin, noticing her friend's distraction.

'Sorry,' Cordelia said, her cheeks flushed. 'But he's here, the man I told you about.'

Rosalind followed her gaze and spotted Eugene. 'The handsome Yank who joined the library? Well, why don't you go and say hello?' She had a mischievous grin as she spoke. 'Go on, make yourself known. I'll be here enjoying another cup of coffee.'

Cordelia hesitated, biting her lower lip as she considered Rosalind's suggestion. The energy between her and Eugene was undeniable, an electric current that hummed in the air whenever they were near each other. But... But... What about Robert? They may not have been engaged but had been going out for a long time and wrote each other loving letters frequently. If she let whatever it was with Eugene progress, she would be unfaithful to a man who was serving his country in awful conditions in North Africa.

Rosalind watched her hesitation. 'Oh, for goodness' sake, girl. Just go over there or I will myself!'

With a stomach full of frantic butterflies Cordelia stood and took the first step towards his table. It took all her courage. As she neared him, he spotted her from the corner of his eye and turned towards her. His eyes widened in pleasant surprise.

'Cordelia!' he exclaimed, standing up to greet her. 'What a wonderful surprise.' He gestured to the three soldiers seated with him. 'Guys, this is Cordelia, the head librarian at Silvertown Library. Cordelia, meet my friends, Marcus, Jamal and Tyrone.' He pulled out a chair. 'Do you have time to join us?' He turned and saw Rosalind looking their way. She gave him a cute wave. 'Bring your friend too!'

Tyrone pulled out another chair and the two women joined the group.

'I think I've seen some of you around Silvertown from my bus,' Rosalind said with a flirty smile, her eyes moving from one man to the other.

'What, you're a bus driver?' Tyrone said. 'We never get bus drivers as cute as you in Ohio.' His smile showed a set of perfect white teeth, the like of which was rarely seen in the East End where people had no spare money for dentists.

'We're all working on repairs in Silvertown,' Eugene said, indicating his friends. 'Back home in the good old US of A, Tyrone here is a plumber, Marcus is a bricklayer and Jamal is a bookkeeper. But when we're doing repairs we just do whatever we're told.'

'People in Silvertown sure are poor,' Jamal said. 'The houses are in a worse state than where I live. The ones that are still standing, of course.'

'It's a disgrace,' Cordelia said, anger in her eyes. 'At our library we do everything we can to help the community but it's never enough.'

'Oh?' Jamal said, raising an eyebrow. 'How so?'

Before long Cordelia told them about Mavis's strike and everything they were doing to get improvements to the run-down properties. The men were fascinated at the way the local people were fighting for themselves.

'We'd be happy to help in any way we can,' Marcus said, his voice full of sincerity. 'I don't know if you are aware that there's a scheme for you Brits to offer hospitality to us Yanks. I had a terrific meal with a family in Canning Town last week. They were sharing even when they had so little.'

Cordelia smiled at him. 'I bet you were kind enough to take some sort of gift with you.'

'Sure did. Some stockings, a tin of bully beef and some chocolate. They were over the moon.'

Jamal chipped in. 'I'd be happy to help with any book-keeping or figure work. Until this war really gets going for us, it's good to help. At home we never understood what you folks have been going through.'

Their food and drinks arrived. The men took the delicious food for granted unlike Cordelia and Rosalind.

'When I had that meal with the family in Canning Town,' Marcus said, cutting into a juicy steak. 'They explained how your rationing works. Not just food but clothes and everything. You folks have had it tough for such a long time. Back home we don't know the half of it.'

'And that's not counting all the dead and injured,' Tyrone said.

Eugene put down his knife and fork. 'You know at their library they don't just distribute books. They have a room where they help people find their missing loved ones. We weren't here when the bombing was at its worst, in the Blitz, but thousands died and often survivors had no idea what had happened to their families and friends.'

He picked up his knife and fork again, shaking his head at the thought of what the East Enders had been through.

'Everything okay?' a waitress asked, appearing as if from nowhere.

'Perfect, miss, just like you,' Marcus said, patting her bottom. She ignored him.

Eugene looked at Cordelia as if to apologise for the crudeness of his friend. She raised her eyebrows and briefly put her hand over his. Instantly she felt that strong tingle and quickly removed her hand before she found herself pulling even closer to him.

'Are you girls dancing here this evening?' he asked.

Cordelia looked into his eyes, hoping that his words meant they would spend the evening together. She was to be disappointed.

Rosalind answered for both of them. 'We are, we've got on our dancing shoes and plan to dance the night away. Are you guys going to join us?'

Eugene's mouth turned down at the corners. 'I wish we could but we've got to go to a regimental function.' He looked at his watch, then at his friends. 'We'd better get going or we'll be late.'

'I'll see you in the library soon.'

24

'A tin of corned beef? Got your coupons?'

Like all women, Cordelia was adept at using her coupons sparingly, and the government regularly issued recipes for meals made with coupon-free or low coupon ingredients. The recipe she'd chosen from the latest leaflet was for mock fishcakes. The original recipe didn't have any fish but she'd managed to get a tiny bit of haddock from the chip shop.

She checked her list before paying Mr Cook who had run the corner shop for as long as anyone could remember. He always wore a brown cotton coat and had a pencil stuck behind his ear.

The recipe called for potatoes, an onion, parsley, grated cheese, flour, salt and pepper and fat for frying. Yes, she had everything and when she got out her purse to pay she became aware of footsteps behind her and murmurs from two other women who were waiting to be served.

'A darkie!' one exclaimed loud enough for the man to hear. She had her arms crossed under her generous bosom and her eyes were narrowed.

'Yes, ma'am,' the man said in an accent straight out of an

American film. 'I'm a darkie like you said and I hope to be of some use to you folks. Our Red Cross has given us orders to help with repairs to your buildings around here. You sure could use the help. This here's my first day and I hoped to buy some smokes before I quit for the night.' He looked around open-mouthed at all the goods on display. 'You sure sell a lot of things in your little shop, sir,' he said to Mr Cook. 'It must be difficult with supplies being so low.'

Cordelia took in his work clothes – a denim shirt and work trousers, sturdy work shoes and a thick leather belt. She felt admiration for the way he had handled the woman's comment.

The two women avoided his eyes and went about asking for their shopping, but Cordelia couldn't leave the shop without saying something. 'I had heard we would be getting some help with repairs,' she said. 'You'll have seen how badly we've been bombed and we are grateful for help, although it will take some time for people to get used to having you around.'

He grinned. 'It'll take some time for me to get used to it too,' he said, getting a selection of coins out of his pocket. 'I can see from the shelf how much the smokes are but your money has me flat confused. Can you help me find the right amount?' He held out his hand showing a mixture of coins.

The two women tutted as if he'd asked Cordelia to strip naked in front of everyone. Ignoring them she helped him find the right money and smiled at the man again before saying goodbye and leaving the shop. She was a hundred yards down the road before the implication of what he'd said struck her. If the work group were here, surely Eugene would be too. Her heart beat faster and she felt her face heat up at the thought. If he was here, he would call into the library again, she was sure of it.

It was a lovely evening even though the smell from the factories was ever-present. There had been no bombing for a few days so the air was clearer than usual and birds were singing in the trees. She smiled as she spotted a squirrel running up a tree trunk with breathtaking speed, a dog running after it.

The sound of laughter caught her attention. It was coming from the Cricketers pub on the next corner. As she got closer she realised it was a group of Americans, no doubt all part of the same work detail as the man in the shop. They hadn't noticed her and she had time to focus on their varied accents. She had no idea where each accent came from though. For the first time she understood how difficult it must be for them to understand all the different accents they found in London. London was full of people from all over the country, indeed all over the world. Even she didn't understand some accents from Scotland herself.

She continued along the bustling street, her footsteps matching the rhythm of her racing heart as she recognised one of the men in the group. He had his back to her but she just knew it was Eugene, the way he held his body, his infectious laugh. He was part of a group of men relaxing after a day's hard work and as she neared them she could hear them complaining about the beer.

'Don't they have cold beer here?'

'I've drunk piss that tastes better than this!'

'I'm gonna try a Guinness, anything Irish has got to be better than this.'

She smiled. Before the Americans arrived, there had been leaflets warning people about the differences in their cultures. Americans talked openly about money and their accomplishments, they appeared to be bragging, their food was better, everything in England was so small, so worn out. She had grinned when she read the leaflet. America would have been worn out if it had been subjected to the Blitz for weeks on end too.

Had the GIs been given similar teaching, she wondered. She tried to imagine what it would say, but only had what she'd seen in films to guide her. Obviously the British pounds, shillings and pence, perhaps queuing, slang, driving on the left, tea and cakes, fish and chips, so many differences.

Getting closer, her breath caught in her throat as a mix of anticipation and nervousness washed over her. They hadn't seen her and she paused for a moment to gather her thoughts, debating whether to make herself known or cross the road and continue on her way. But the wicked desire to see Eugene grew irresistible. With a surge of courage she knew she shouldn't have, she took a deep breath and walked closer.

He spotted her, his smile widening when he recognised her. 'Cordelia, hi!' he called out. 'Come and join us.' He turned to his friends. 'This is Cordelia, Miss Carmichael. She's the head librarian here in Silvertown.'

The others, all black GIs in work gear, greeted her warmly. They were different men from the ones she'd met in the Rainbow Corner.

'Say,' one of them said, 'are you the broad... sorry, mustn't say that over here, the lady with the title? I never met anyone with one of those before.'

Cordelia put down her bags and grinned teasingly. 'Yet you haven't bowed in my presence!'

The man looked aghast. 'Oh, should I have done? Is that the etiquette over here?'

She smiled again. 'I'm joshing you. Isn't that what you say? I'm teasing you, but you can buy me half a shandy to make up for it.'

Eugene took her bag and put it next to the wall where it

wouldn't get crushed by the men's feet. 'So what are you doing here, Cordelia?'

Before she answered, the pub door opened and a middle-aged man almost fell out. Blind drunk, he looked like a comical cartoon character, a cloud of alcohol fumes surrounding him. His legs barely held him up and he staggered into one of the GIs. 'Shorry,' he muttered, then seemed to take in the scene. 'Hi, lads,' he said, unable to focus on any of them. 'You lot need a wash.'

With that he staggered off, careered from one side of the pavement to the other, and narrowly missed falling into the road.

One of the men held up his glass and looked at the half-drunk contents. 'I don't know what he was drinking, but I'd have to have a tanker full of this stuff to be half as blotto as him!'

His colleague came out with Cordelia's shandy.

'Say, that's got to be even weaker than this stuff!' the man said, holding up his glass again.

'Shall we see you in the library again soon?' Cordelia asked Eugene.

He touched her arm lightly, sending little shocks down her body that she shouldn't be feeling.

'Sure you'll see me. I'm going to come in on Saturday to see that man you call The Professor. He's going to give me more tips about researching my family history.'

'You doing that?' the man next to him said. He looked at Cordelia. 'My name's Gordon and I'd like to look up my ancestors too. Do you run classes at the library?'

His question took her aback. They didn't but it was a good idea and one to discuss with the others.

She stayed another ten minutes and although on the face of it she was chatting to several of the men about their time in London, she was constantly aware of Eugene's presence. Aware of their stolen glances as they apparently carried on chatting to the others but were acutely aware only of each other. But she told herself off. The attraction was too strong for someone like her with a long-term relationship and it simply had to end.

'Oh,' she said, looking at her watch. 'I must go. I'm sorry, I have to meet someone and I'll be late.' She turned to Eugene. 'I hope to see you and the others in the library soon.'

All the way home she felt guilty about her attraction to this man. *But I've only chatted to him and his friends. That's nothing to feel guilty about*, she told herself. That guilt got worse when she found a letter from her boyfriend Robert waiting for her. He'd been in the North Africa theatre of war for ages, working in often makeshift hospitals treating the ill and injured in terrible conditions.

It was with trepidation that she put the letter on one side while she put on the kettle. The wireless blared news of the Battle of El Alamein and she was terrified for him every day. Memories of Robert flooded her mind, each one a precious fragment of their shared history. She sat back and closed her eyes, the once vivid image of his face materialising before her, fainter than it used to be but still etched with tenderness. She remembered his smile, just a little lopsided, tugging at her heartstrings.

She remembered his cologne too with its hints of sandalwood, mingling with the faintest trace of antiseptic that he never seemed able to completely wash away.

Time was eroding even these most cherished memories. The edges of his face blurred, details fading like an old photograph left out in the sun. She struggled to hold on to them, but they were slipping away like grains of sand falling through her fingers.

Would she be able to resist her attraction to Eugene which he obviously reciprocated? When Robert returned from war would he still be the same man she knew? Would they be able to continue their relationship, building it stronger and stronger?

As she waited for the kettle to boil she thought how glad she was to have a free evening. She planned to spend it relaxing and reading the latest book she had borrowed from the library. For some time she had volunteered to pack Red Cross boxes for the troops two or three evenings a week. It was a job that didn't require much attention, just putting things in boxes, making sure every soldier got their fair share. But this was one of her free evenings.

She had plenty of things to occupy her mind at the library and the evenings packing boxes had become simply times to chat with whichever volunteers were on at the same time as her. Some of the stories she'd heard from the girls were enough to make her hair curl and she regularly thought she should write a book herself.

All these thoughts went through her head as she made the fishcakes and drank her tea. Yet although she tried to distract herself, she found herself glancing at Robert's letter frequently. Until she'd met Eugene her heart had skipped with happiness when she saw a letter from her boyfriend, but now she felt uncertainty and guilt even though she had done nothing wrong.

Was she going to be faced with tough choices in the future?

_____

25

Cordelia's family home looked less like itself every time she visited. As her taxi dropped her off after a long, tiresome train journey, she looked around. It was a glorious late summer day. The sight of the grand, ivy-covered manor, with its towering chimneys and tall windows, filled her with a bittersweet mixture of nostalgia and apprehension. Memories of running around the grounds with her brother Jasper made her smile, even if he did sometimes pinch her or pull her hair. Sadly, Fred, the old gardener, had gone to heaven in the first few days of war. Jasper had always tried to cadge a cigarette from him. But canny Fred always gave the same answer – 'When you're twenty-one!'

Even though a lot had changed, the building itself, now so different, was also similar to those days. The front of the house where horse and carriages once brought elegant wealthy people to visit was now alive with invalids. More than two thirds of the building had been requisitioned by the government for use as a convalescent home for injured soldiers. There were several tables with chairs around them. Each chair was full of men enjoying the summer sun. Some had bandaged heads or eyes, others had walking sticks or frames next to them. Yet more walked slowly around the area, often supported by a nurse.

The sight of these brave soldiers, some with visible injuries, others with haunted eyes, was a poignant reminder of the sacrifices made during this never-ending war. Cordelia felt a pang of guilt, knowing that while these men had given so much for their country, her own father had been profiting from the suffering of people in the nearby village and Silvertown.

The once meticulously manicured garden on either side of the drive had been transformed into practical plots for growing vegetables and fruit. Cordelia smiled with satisfaction. This was exactly how it should be. But she knew her father felt differently. He had even tried to speak to the prime minister, Mr Churchill, whom he had gone to Harrow School with. He still fumed that Mr Churchill would not even see him, much less do as he demanded.

As she walked round to the side entrance that the family and staff now used, dread of the upcoming conversation with her father felt like a heavy weight in her stomach. It was with great relief that the first person she saw was her mother.

Before the convalescent hospital had moved to their stately home she had been a typical upper-class wife and mother. She did what was expected of her by her class and her husband. She ran the household staff, held dinner parties, opened fetes and organised village women to do charitable activities.

However, volunteering to help the injured soldiers write letters home had opened her eyes to a wider range of experiences, a wider range of people. She learned to her surprise that enlisted men, whom she would once upon a time have looked down upon quietly, were often very bright. They simply lacked opportunities to improve their lives. As a result, she was much more open-minded about many of the issues Cordelia felt passionate about.

Inside what she rarely thought of as her home any more, Cordelia was greeted by the familiar smell of polished wood and roses picked from the small section of the garden rescued from the vegetable beds. She put down her bag and gas mask, smiling when she saw a 'Make do and mend' leaflet with a pile of letters on a small side table. Her parents had never mended anything in their lives. That was what staff were for.

Lady Carmichael hugged her daughter warmly, itself a change. Cordelia and her brother had been brought up largely by nannies and tutors. They saw their parents for an hour a day at most and hugs and kisses were frowned upon. Having a stiff upper lip was paramount and Cordelia's father believed physical affection made children weak-willed.

As they walked towards the drawing room, Lady Carmichael looked at her daughter. 'What is it, Cordelia? You said on the telephone that you had a problem to discuss with your father. Are you in some sort of trouble?'

Cordelia sighed. 'Let's sit down and have some tea and I'll tell you all about it.'

The household once had a generous complement of staff but the men had mostly gone off to war and most young girls preferred the better pay and shorter hours offered by factories. But there was still a skeleton staff and Maisie, a maid of all works, appeared with a tray of tea and biscuits. As they waited they made small talk.

'What news of that man of yours? Do you hear from him often?'

Cordelia had told her mother about Robert but not where he was stationed. She wasn't supposed to know but they'd invented a simple code so he could let her know in his first letter. He was in North Africa. He couldn't say much in his letters because they were always censored, so mostly she'd had to rely on the wireless and Pathé News at the cinema. And everyone knew the newspapers were edited too.

She'd learned that the last few weeks had been the worst yet for his area. First in the Battle of Gela, the Germans had pushed the British army back to the Egyptian border. Then Tobruk was lost, but finally two more bloody battles secured the region for the British.

Bad news of military men was by telegram, often delivered by youngsters in short trousers. Every time she saw one of them on their post office bikes her heart did a dreadful jump. So far, though, it seemed Robert had been lucky. As a doctor treating the troops he was near the front line but not on it.

'He's fine as far as I know, Mother,' she replied. 'You know what it's like. I wait ages for a letter then three arrive the same day.'

They were in the smallest living room and Cordelia's favourite. It was her mother's study. Warm honey-coloured wood panelling lined the walls, while a plush deep-blue carpet cushioned the floor. Against one wall stood her mother's small desk with a vase of roses on top.

'So, Cordelia, tell me what the problem is,' her mother said, handing her a cup of tea.

As Cordelia took the cup and saucer she wondered how to approach the subject. Her mother no longer automatically agreed with everything her husband said, but she still deferred to him on most things.

'It's difficult, Mother,' Cordelia began, stirring a spoon of sugar into her tea. 'You'll remember that you and I have tried to get Father to improve the cottages he owns in the village...'

Her mother shook her head. 'I hate to speak ill of your father,

Cordelia, but the only work he has ordered is roof repairs. And so much more is needed.'

It was the opening Cordelia needed. 'I wanted to talk to you about something similar. As you know, many of the properties in Silvertown are in a much worse state. I've been hearing a lot about them. Even my staff, Mavis and Jane, live in houses that are badly in need of repair.'

'That's dreadful, my dear,' her mother said. 'Can't something be done about it?'

Outside they could hear patients singing 'Boogie Woogie Bugle Boy', a song to lift any spirits.

'They always have choir practice outside when the weather is good enough,' her mother said. 'I quite like it, but it drives your father mad. Luckily his study is at the back of the house.'

'You asked if something can be done about the properties in Silvertown, Mother. Mavis is calling a rent strike...'

Her mother gasped. 'A strike! Isn't that somewhat drastic?'

Cordelia nodded. Perhaps this conversation was going to be harder than she'd hoped. 'Nothing else has worked to get the land-lords to do the repairs needed. On top of that many of them have increased the rent and that is illegal.' She paused and stirred her cup, even though it only contained the dregs of her tea. 'The thing is, Father owns several properties in Silvertown. People are living in dreadful conditions and he has done nothing to improve them.'

Her mother's face fell and she put down her cup and saucer with a bang, making herself start. 'Oh, Cordelia, I don't know what to say, my dear. Your father has always been more inter-ested in profit than people. I never imagined he would be quite so... so...'

'Heartless? Money-grabbing?' Cordelia closed her mouth, wishing the harsh words had never escaped. Surely they would turn her mother against what she was saying. But instead her mother took her snowy-white handkerchief out of her bag and wiped her eyes.

'I'm so ashamed,' she said, holding back tears. 'I should never speak ill of your father but of late I've been ashamed to be his wife.' She stood up and walked to the window where a small group of men were doing physical exercises. A little further down the garden others were picking vegetables or pulling up weeds. 'What can we do about it, Cordelia?' she asked, keeping her back to her not to face her daughter.

Cordelia went to stand beside her, putting her arm through her mother's. Even this small gesture would have been unthinkable before her mother had learned so much about life from volunteering with the patients convalescing in the bulk of their home.

'I'm going to speak to him, try to get him to do something. Will you come with me, Mother, or would you prefer I speak to Father alone?'

* * *

Cordelia stood before her father's study door, her hand raised to knock. However, the simple act of asking permission to enter brought back a flood of childhood memories, recalling the same nervousness and uncertainty she had experienced all those years before. The formality of this ritual harshly reminded her of the emotional distance that had always existed between the two of them.

As she rapped her knuckles against the sturdy oak door, Cordelia couldn't help but wonder what mood her father would be in. He could be a kind and generous man, albeit in an emotionally detached way. But he could also be impatient and brusque.

After waiting a short time she rapped again, harder this time. A full half-minute later she heard a muffled 'Enter!' Taking a deep breath to steady her nerves she turned the brass handle and stepped inside.

The study was dimly lit despite the bright, sunny day outside, a desk lamp being the only source of light. Lord Carmichael sat at his imposing mahogany desk, so different from his wife's. Moreover he didn't look up as Cordelia entered, his pen continuing to scratch across the page.

Cordelia stood just inside the door for a short while, gathering her courage. The silence in the room was heavy, broken only by the ticking of an old grandfather clock. Finally, she took a few nervous steps forward, coming to stand directly beside her father's desk.

'Father...' she began, her voice sounding small and uncertain even to her own ears. She clasped her hands tightly in front of her, bracing herself for the difficult conversation about to happen.

Her father held up his hand, silencing her. The gesture, so often directed at her throughout her life, immediately sparked anger in her chest.

Nevertheless she told herself to calm down, to take deep breaths. Angry, she wouldn't put her case across well.

A minute later he looked up, surprised to see her, as if she had never spoken. 'Oh, Cordelia, I didn't know you were home.' Even though he was acknowledging her, he seemed to have little interest or pleasure in her return.

She nodded. 'I've just been having tea with Mother, but I have something I'd like to discuss with you.'

He sighed and shuffled papers on his desk. 'Is it something

your mother can deal with? I'm very busy.' He looked down at his papers and dismissed her with a wave of his hand.

But she was having none of that. She leaned forward and put her hand over the document he was looking at. He pushed her hand aside and she pushed it back sharply. 'Father, I said I need to speak to you. Now.'

He looked up at her, sat back in his chair and folded his arms. 'What is it? There's a war on and I'm very busy doing war work.'

She stood upright and attempted to calm her churning emotions. But she had learned her tenacity from him years earlier. 'Father, I have a very difficult matter to discuss with you.'

'Difficult?' he looked down at his papers again, already losing interest in her and her words. 'Have you been sleeping around? Are you pregnant?'

She put her hands on her hips. 'How dare you! I. Am. Not. Pregnant. I have discovered that you are the owner of several very run-down properties in Silvertown, where I work and live...'

He held up his hand again. She could see that he was surprised at her knowledge but wasn't going to budge. 'Cordelia, I fail to see how the condition of those properties is any concern of yours. I have much more pressing issues to deal with.'

Cordelia took another deep breath to calm herself. 'It does concern me. I see these people every day. Their homes are squalid, not because they are dirty but because of lack of repairs. And their health is definitely affected by dampness and infestations.'

'My dear girl,' he said, steepling his fingers in front of his chest. 'You're letting your emotions run away with you. These are business matters, not books to be placed on shelves. Those properties are investments, nothing more. I've never even seen them.

My agent deals with such matters. You'd do well to leave them to people who know about these things.'

She was stunned at his insulting and uncaring response and bit her bottom lip to stop herself saying something she would regret. 'Father, I've seen some of your properties myself. The living conditions are deplorable, and not only that but you've put up the rent which is illegal. You are breaking the law, Father.'

Lord Carmichael's chair scraped against the floor as he stood abruptly. 'Illegal? Nonsense. If the tenants are unhappy, they are free to find somewhere else to live. I'm not running a charity here, Cordelia. I'm running a business.'

'But, Father, surely you must see that...'

'Enough!' He slammed his hand on the desk, cutting her off. 'I am a busy man, and will not be lectured by my own daughter on matters she can barely understand.'

Cordelia's voice rose to match his. 'Are you implying I am stupid, Father? I understand perfectly well. I've seen the suffering first-hand. Illness caused by damp walls, infestations... How can you be so blind to...'

'I said enough!' Lord Carmichael's face reddened, his eyes narrowing. 'This discussion is over. I have more pressing matters to attend to than the complaints of a few ungrateful tenants.'

'But what about being lectured to by your wife?'

Cordelia and her father turned towards the door abruptly. Neither had heard Lady Carmichael come in.

'I agree with Cordelia, my dear. I have not visited Silvertown but I have spoken to soldiers recovering from dreadful injuries received while fighting for king and country. Many of them live in exactly the conditions Cordelia is talking about.'

Her father looked from one to the other, his breathing fast and his face turning red. 'I will not be spoken to in this way. I am the master of this house and what I decide to do with those properties is none of your business. My decision on this is final.'

He made to sit down again and look at his papers, but Cordelia had not finished, especially as her mother now came to stand beside her.

'Your decision may be final, Father, but I will not stand by and watch as our family profits from the suffering of others. That has been happening with the village properties for years and years.'

Cordelia's hands trembled as she clenched them into fists at her sides. Her heart pounded in her chest, and she felt the heat rising in her face. She took another step forward, her voice shaking with barely contained fury.

'If you won't take action,' she said, her words measured and cold, 'then I will.' With that she stamped her foot, the childish gesture a stark contrast to the determination in her eyes.

Her father's reactions reflected many occasions during her childhood when he hadn't listened to her. Like many parents of his class and period, he believed children should be raised by their nannies and seen but not heard. As a child, Cordelia's eyes would sometimes wander beyond the window, to the gardeners looking up to spot their children running towards them after a day at school. She watched as rough hands, soiled from their day's work, lifted their child and spun them round, laughing, delighted to see them. To Cordelia, their warmth felt as distant as the stars.

The longing for such an embrace, such closeness, never really left her. She had, for years, craved the comfort of her mother's hug or her father's praise at some small thing she had achieved.

Her closest childhood friend had been Mrs Taylor, the family cook, who gave her little treats – a biscuit or a sweet along with smiles and hugs. And along with old Fred she'd helped Cordelia make a tiny vegetable garden just outside the kitchen.

Many times Cordelia had tried to get her father to come to admire her latest triumph – some beans growing up sticks or a small cluster of freshly pulled potatoes.

But he never came. He never considered her important enough to give up his time for.

On her way home that evening she was saddened by the memories, even more determined to help Mavis with her fight for a rent strike. They would win and she would, somehow or other, get her father to repair his properties both in Silvertown and their village.

26

As Cordelia walked towards home later she pushed her father's intransigence from her mind. Instead, she considered the latest news from the North Africa campaign. The broadsheets were praising Montgomery's forces for checking Rommel at El Alamein, but she had no idea what that meant for her beloved Robert out there in the desert trying to save lives. She hoped there would be a letter from him waiting when she got home. She certainly had plenty to write to him about: Mavis's strike, the prospect of the auction of the first edition, and the scavenger hunts. She knew reading about these would please him, taking him away from the hardship he faced every day. She hadn't so far decided whether to tell him about her father owning some of the properties in Silvertown.

Although she disliked much of what her father did, she didn't want to poison Robert's mind against him before they'd even met. Nonetheless she was deeply ashamed of her father and it caused her mental conflict every time she thought about him.

But first, she had to find something for her dinner. Like most people she had some old newspaper in her bag. Since paper rationing many shops expected housewives to have their own wrapping paper. But since paper rationing newspapers had got smaller and had fewer pages. Even throwing away a small scrap of paper was considered unpatriotic.

The East End streets rang with the cries of vendors hawking their wares. One old man Cordelia regularly bought from greeted her like a long-lost friend. "Ow you doing, miss?' His firm voice belied his wrinkled face and bald head, but his smile was genuine. 'Got some new apples in today from me cousin's farm. Want to try one?'

'I'd love to,' she said with a grin. He expertly cut one in half and handed half to her while taking a bite out of the other half despite having several missing teeth. The apple was tasty and juicy, delicious. 'I'll have four, please,' she said, getting out her purse.

'Got a bag, love?' he asked.

She took a string bag out of her pocket. She hated it, it always seemed to bash against her leg, but needs must.

'Thank you, miss,' the man said when she'd handed over the money. 'See you soon.' He immediately turned away and shouted his usual story. 'Apples and pears. Get your fresh fruit 'ere!'

His voice competed with the sound of clattering hooves and cartwheels as Cordelia wove her way towards the shops. All around her the everyday crowd of people were going about their business, children were fighting or playing. Two girls sat on the pavement playing jacks. Judging from their identical ginger hair and freckles, they must have been sisters. The taller one snatched the jacks from the younger one who howled her protest. They looked up at Cordelia with surprise. "Ay, miss, are you a film star?'

She laughed. 'I wish I was. What makes you think I might be?'

The young one spoke up, showing the gap in her front teeth. 'Well, you looks like a right toff, don't you?'

Cordelia laughed again. 'Well, you're wrong about that, but I am toff enough to have two sixpences in my purse. Would you like them?'

The girls sprung up from the floor like jack-in-the-boxes and held out their hands. She pressed the money into each grubby palm.

'Have fun spending it, girls.'

Although they were poor, Cordelia felt a sudden sense of envy. She had never had a sister to play with and Jasper, her brother, always wanted to play war or cowboys and Indians. But she chastised herself, those girls already faced many more difficulties with poverty and war than she ever did as a child. But they still managed to have fun and laugh. And be cheeky too.

As she walked the air was full of what she thought of as quintessential East End aromas. Cooking smells from a dozen different nationalities.

Passing the Royal Oak pub Cordelia noticed children hanging about outside while their parents enjoyed a drink inside. A small group of children huddled together against one of the windows, sharing a glass of lemonade, their faces flushed with excitement. Through the open door she caught a glimpse of the patrons inside. A group of men were huddled around a table, their pints apparently forgotten as they argued heatedly about the latest news from the front. They were so loud that she heard one man, a burly docker with muscular arms and a thick cockney accent, slam his fist on the table, demanding attention. 'I'm telling you, lads, Montgomery's got Rommel on the run sure as eggs is eggs. It's only a matter of time now!'

Cordelia sighed as she heard him. If what he said was true, then Robert would be home before long. However, she'd read the newspaper reports in fine detail and didn't think that particular theatre of war would be over very soon. And when it did, would she and Robert be able to pick up where they'd left off, their feelings the same? Would her attraction to Eugene prove very fleeting, a schoolgirl crush, or would her feelings deepen? Eugene wouldn't be staying in the area long, nor indeed in England. That fact would surely help influence her thoughts to some extent. Those questions kept her awake at night until she fell into an uneasy sleep.

As she passed one of the small terraced houses she heard the beginning of the seven o'clock news on a wireless and decided she was too tired to cook. She had bread and cheese at home, they would have to do. When she opened her door she kicked off her shoes and rubbed her eyes, trying to find the energy to even prepare her simple meal.

Maybe Robert's letter would settle her feelings one way or the other. His letters were still something to be cherished and she put this latest one on her small table while she went to get herself a drink. The anticipation of opening it and reading his news was part of the pleasure.

As she made herself a sandwich she turned on the wireless and was relaxing to some music until it was interrupted and a sombre voice announced: 'It is with deep regret that we must let you know of the death of His Royal Highness, Prince George, Duke of Kent. He was killed yesterday in a plane crash while on a military mission to Iceland.'

Cordelia sat down heavily, hardly able to believe what she'd heard. The Duke of Kent had been controversial with rumours about his private life, but he was well regarded by the people. Everyone remembered his beautiful wedding to Princess Marina of Greece. The wedding was shown on Pathé News at the cinema and many brides wore copycat versions of her breathtaking dress soon after. Now she was yet another war widow.

As Cordelia ate, she ran her hands over the precious envelope, enjoying the anticipation but also worried that Robert's news might be bad.

Finally, with slightly trembling hands, she opened his letter. As usual he had used tiny script to cram in as much as he could.

My darling Cordelia,

I hope this letter finds you well. We probably don't hear half of what you are going through over there, but still it sounds terrifying and I worry about you every single day. I hope you are able to find enough to eat and have not been bombed out again. You are so precious to me.

You will probably want to know news from here. This posting is undeniably challenging, both physically and emotionally. The days and nights are filled with relentless duties caring for the wounded soldiers suffering from the unimaginable injuries of war. We can hear the battlefield noises from here, the sounds of the gunfire and sometimes, horribly, the cries of the wounded. But as always I am impressed by the courage and devotion of the staff here and the resilience of the injured we treat. They support each other and sometimes support us too. I only wish we could do more for them.

But all is not gloomy. Sometimes we have a sing-song and even had a visiting ENSA show recently. They bravely tour so many theatres of war entertaining the troops. The show wasn't first class but we haven't laughed so much for ages and the singers and comedians were a treat. It's often said that ENSA stands for Every Night Something Awful rather than Entertainment National Service Association. But we enjoyed the show immensely and admired their courage coming to dangerous locations when they are not forced to do so.

I often reminisce about our time together, the moments of pure joy and the dreams we shared. In the most difficult times, the memories sustain me in a way nothing else could. I can't wait to hold you in my arms again and send you my love as always,

Robert x

Cordelia's heart swelled with pride as she read about Robert's life, the way he was healing the sick despite very difficult circumstances. It made her everyday worries feel insignificant. It also made her more determined than ever to help the people of Silvertown who had suffered so much.

27

Cordelia and Mavis stood outside the bustling office of *The London Gazette*, one of the city's most prominent newspapers. They clutched a folder filled with documents – survey results, personal testimonies, evidence of the dire living conditions in Silvertown and reports of their actions to date. Frustrated with the lack of response from landlords so far they decided that a newspaper with a wider reach would give their work more prominence. And by getting directly involved Cordelia was doing what she could to get her father to mend his ways.

Located in a grand Victorian building in the heart of the city it had so far evaded being bombed like so many buildings in the area. The facade boasted ornate architectural details, though the years and smoke had weathered its once pristine appearance. The stone exterior, adorned with intricate carvings, bore the marks of time and the occasional pit holes and scorch marks from bombings nearby. Despite the scars, the building stood tall, a witness to the spirit of newspapers and the capital.

Taking a deep breath, Mavis pushed open the large door and they stepped into the reception area. They were greeted by a distinct aroma of ink and the rhythmic sounds of typewriters and printing machines. A receptionist sat behind a white-painted desk on which there were two telephones and a typewriter. Every minute or two someone would enter or leave the building, always with an air of urgency.

'Can I help you, ladies?' the receptionist asked, looking up from her typewriter. She was no more than seventeen and obviously a film fan, with her shiny brown curls reminiscent of Judy Garland.

'We're here to see the editor, please,' Cordelia said. 'I'm Lady Cordelia Carmichael and we have a story he will be interested in.'

'Have you made an appointment?' she asked.

'We haven't but I'm sure he'll want to see us when he knows about serious issues in the East End at the moment.' Cordelia was using her poshest voice which was really her normal one.

The receptionist shook her head. 'Oh, is this to do with the rent strike? My uncle lives in Silvertown. He has nasty creepy-crawlies climbing up his walls but the landlord won't do a thing.' She looked from one of them to the other. 'Are you something to do with it? He's very excited about it. Someone getting something done at last he says.'

The two friends grinned. 'Yes, Mavis here is leading the strike, and if anyone can get things moving it's her. Do you think the editor will see us? We need all the publicity we can get.'

'I'll call his secretary, but I can't promise he'll see you. He's always extremely busy. But if he's a bit awkward I'll explain to his secretary. She can twist him round her little finger.'

Cordelia stepped closer to the desk. 'I hate to name-drop but sometimes telling someone I have a title makes a difference. Will you be sure to tell him, please? It is about a scandalous situation in the East End his readers will be interested in.'

The receptionist indicated they should sit in some chairs to the side of the door while she phoned ahead. As they waited, the area was a constant hive of activity. Some young women hurried through, dressed very smartly and with immaculate make-up. Judging from their conversation they had just come back from their lunch break.

'It's a pity Jane couldn't come with us today,' Mavis said, tugging at her jacket. 'Still, someone 'as to keep things going at the library.'

The receptionist tried to make the call for them but was several times interrupted by people coming in with queries of one sort or another. Finally, ten minutes later, she hurried over to them. 'You're in luck, he says he can spare you ten minutes.' She grinned. 'You were right, it was your title that did it!' She gave instructions on how to find his room and wished them well.

Walking through the newsroom was thrilling, like something out of a film. Rows of desks, cluttered with wire baskets full of papers, typewriters, notebooks and coffee-stained mugs stretched ahead of them as they walked. Some desks were empty while others had journalists tapping away frantically on their typewriters. To one side one of the women who had just walked in was filing papers in a battered grey metal filing cabinet. The room buzzed with urgency and excitement like a beehive, the reporters working as hard as worker bees. The room was an assault on their senses, with the smell of ink mixed with smoke and the clacking of typewriters.

'Blimey,' Mavis said as they walked. 'Why don't they open some windows? The ciggie smoke in 'ere is enough to choke you. A lick of paint wouldn't go amiss neither.' The room was indeed grubby, walls stained with cigarette smoke and patches showing where notices or photos had once been displayed.

Finally they arrived at the editor's office, a small room right at the far end of the newsroom. There was a large sign on the door: 'Gregory Harmer – BOSS!' They looked at it and exchanged a nervous glance before Cordelia knocked on the door.

There was a long pause during which they could hear the editor cursing and then slamming down his phone. 'Come in if you must!' he called.

They stepped into his office, unable to believe it was even more untidy than the desks they had just passed. A wobbly pile of paper and an overflowing ashtray fought for space on the grubby desk. Piles of newspapers and manuscripts were scattered about the room.

'Who are you?' he asked, a deep frown on his brow.

Cordelia took a further step forward. 'I believe the receptionist announced we were coming.' She held out her hand to shake his. 'I'm Lady Cordelia Carmichael and this is my colleague Mavis Kent. We—'

'Yes, yes, I know who you are. Now, what's this fabulous and scandalous story you've got for me?' His phone rang again. Without looking he picked it up and immediately slammed it back down in its cradle.

Gritting her teeth and determined not to be afraid of this man, Mavis stepped forward. She fidgeted with the folder they had prepared, her mind racing. She couldn't shake the feeling that something was going to go wrong. Even though this man was impatient, it seemed too easy. She glanced at Cordelia, looking for signs that she felt the same. She placed a folder of information on his desk, struggling to know where to put it. 'It's about terrible living conditions in Silvertown and the East End. The landlords are breaking the law by putting up rents and they refuse to do repairs. So...' She paused for effect. 'We are organising a rent strike!'

He didn't look as impressed as she'd hoped. Instead, without a word, he pulled the folder towards himself and started to flip through the pages so quickly they didn't believe he took in a thing. They were wrong.

'Hmm... surveys, testimonials, reports, you girls have been busy.'

'We're ladies,' Cordelia said, struggling not to sound as angry as she felt.

He looked up. 'You one of them feminist girls I've read about? Want more rights?'

She smiled sweetly. 'Yes, I am one of those feminist women. But I'm sure a story that will sell copies for you is far more interesting than my beliefs.'

Mavis was about to nudge her, sure that her approach would antagonise the editor and lose them any chance of publicity. Instead, she butted in. 'We've worked on this for ages, sir. The people of Silvertown and the East End are suffering, rotten homes cause illness and disease. No one seems to care and that includes the council. I'm sure your readers will be interested in the fact that landlords are breaking the law too. Getting some publicity will sell copies for you and 'elp our cause.'

The editor was silent for a moment, considering their story. 'Trouble with this lot...' – he gestured to their folder – 'is there is no human interest. It's all facts and figures. They don't butter no bread.' He sat back and folded his arms, pausing to take a long drag from his cigar. 'So what I propose is to send one of my reporters round to your house.' He pointed at Mavis with the hand that held the cigar. 'I suppose your house needs some repairs.'

'It does. It needs...'

'Don't tell me.' He continued holding up his hand. 'Tell the reporter. I don't know who it'll be. Depends on who's got time.

Whoever it is, you can show them around your house and take them for a look-see at others in the area. Get them talking to the locals, get some good quotes, that sort of thing. Who knows, it might even help you out.'

The two friends exchanged a triumphant look, hardly daring to believe their luck.

'Thank you, Mr Harmer. Thank you very much.' Mavis's voice was choked with emotion.

As they walked back through the newsroom they noticed a newspaper clipping pinned to a bulletin board. The headline caught Cordelia's eye. 'Tensions rise as landlords threaten evictions.' She decided not to bring Mavis's attention to it.

They passed back through the reception area and the receptionist asked how they had got on. 'Any luck with the boss?'

Mavis pulled a face, half pleased, half worried. 'He's sending a reporter round to my place for a bit of human interest for the story.'

Someone approached the desk so the receptionist only had time for one more sentence. 'Good luck, ladies. I heard a rumour that the last person who took on the landlords got thrown out, bed and all.'

As they stepped outside the newspaper office, a gust of wind nearly tore the precious folder from Mavis's hands. She clutched it tightly to her chest, wondering if this gust was a sign telling her to give up hope of winning.

'This must work,' Mavis said, suddenly feeling low. 'If it doesn't we're scuppered. I can't think of anything else we can do.'

But Cordelia's exuberance soon put such a gloomy thought out of her mind. 'Come on, Mavis, let's celebrate with a cuppa and a cake. We've made a big breakthrough today.'

But would it be enough?

28

Jane had been too busy to visit Edith for two or three days. In any case, she was probably wasting her time unless Edith decided to stop sulking or whatever it was and talk to her. Jane had been horrified when she spoke to one of their neighbours.

'Oh, her,' Mrs Ingram said. 'The drunk? No, I ain't seen 'er since she fell into my front door a few days ago. Drunk as a skunk.' Her top lip curled and she shook her head. 'I heard she got arrested for being drunk and disorderly down by the docks last week.'

It was the first Jane had heard of it.

'Typical drunk,' Mrs Ingram went on. 'Never think of anyone else but themselves. I 'ope she never comes back!' With that she went back into her house, slamming the door as if it was all Jane's fault.

Jane didn't know much about alcoholism but knew medical opinion was that it was something people couldn't help. A disease of some sort. If that was true she should try to have more patience with Edith, but that was hard when she seemed to go out of her way to upset everyone.

Clutching her gas mask, Jane sighed and got on to the bus to go to Bromley. It wasn't that far as the crow flies but it seemed interminable, with frequent stops to let on weary workers. The sun was low in the sky, making her squint as she gazed out at the familiar scenery of small houses, tenements and fallen buildings. She glimpsed Eltham Palace and Woolwich Arsenal from the window. How she longed to see trees and greenery – something fresh that promised life instead of reminding everyone of death. East Enders did what they could, planting flowers grown from seed wherever there was a bit of space, but it didn't amount to much.

There had been bombing the night before, and after she got off the bus she had to wait to cross the road twice as ambulances rushed towards the hospital. Standing outside Victoria Ward with the other family members she was too distracted by worry of what Edith would be like to join in the conversations. Would she still be pretending to sleep? And would her head injury have left her with any permanent damage?

But when Jane walked into the ward and up and down the rows of beds three times, there was no sign of Edith. Baffled, she went to the sister's desk, relieved to see Sister Norman was on duty again.

'I'm looking for my mother-in-law, Mrs Wilkins,' she said. 'Has she been moved?' For a second the dreadful thought that she might have died went through her mind, sending an icy shiver down her spine.

The sister looked up and indicated for Jane to sit. 'Let me explain. As you know she had a problem with...' She looked around to make sure no one was listening. 'With drinking. Strange as it seems the accident might have been a blessing. When people who are heavy drinkers stop, they get withdrawal symptoms, but because of her head injury she was unconscious so not aware of them.'

Jane tried to absorb what she was saying. 'Do you mean she's okay now? She won't drink any more?'

'I'm afraid it's not that simple. People often go back to alcohol again. But there is excellent news. The Catholic priest who visits the ward very regularly has found her a place in a convent.'

'What!' Jane's jaw dropped open with surprise and disbelief. 'She's going to become a nun?' Edith had never been to church in her life as far as Jane knew and the family were Church of England anyway.

Sister Norman laughed. 'I'm afraid not. But the convent has a small area where they take people who want to stop drinking. The facilities are very limited. It is mostly about people being away from temptation and in a peaceful environment.'

Edith in a place like that was utterly impossible for Jane to imagine. She was a lifelong East Ender, in and out of pubs every day. 'But...' she started.

The sister held up her hand. 'She will only be there for a few weeks. That is all the nuns offer. And they don't allow visitors at all.'

'But what do they do with them in that short a time?' Jane asked.

The sister sighed. 'I asked one of the nuns once. She said they offered a secluded environment where the women are away from the temptations and stress they usual encounter.' She paused trying to remember the conversation. 'Oh, I do remember they are expected to work; gardening, cooking at very specific times. And religious services several times a day as you'd expect. The nun said they try to help the women have more inner strength.' She pulled a piece of paper towards herself and began writing.

'Here is the address, but please don't go there. They are very strict. I've written the phone number down but I suggest you wait at least a week before calling them. They'll know more by then.'

As she headed home Jane tried to imagine Edith in a convent, even as a patient. Was it possible that she would last the two weeks, or would she leave as soon as the need for a drink overcame her?

Even if she lasted the two weeks what would she do when she returned to the East End? All her friends were drinkers, pubs were a huge part of her life. If they were no longer in her life, what on earth would she do? Who would she even be?

29

Mavis looked around her modest living room with its worn but spotless furniture. She dusted the mantelpiece again, taking especial care of the photos of Joyce in her best dress, Ken in his army uniform and her and Joe at a funfair. What a day she and Joe had! She remembered the thrill of so many attractions, the crowd, the laughter and the music. She'd clung to his arm, feeling a sense of freedom from the worries of war, the danger, the shortages, the struggle of everyday life. He made her feel proud and safe. She remembered the stuffed rabbit he'd won at the shooting gallery, the one that Joyce now took to bed every night. Then kissing the photo briefly she put it back on the shelf ready for her visitor.

Usually someone unfazed by anything life had to offer, she had butterflies in her stomach about her expected visitor.

As the editor of *The London Gazette* had promised, a reporter was coming to interview her about the strike. He wanted to see her home and had asked her to show him some of the neglected properties.

'Be careful,' several people had said. 'He might set out to

make you look like an interfering fool. You know what newspapers are like!'

But the strike campaign needed all the publicity it could get if they were to win against the greedy landlords. She couldn't believe any reporter would fail to be moved when he saw the poor conditions many people had to live in.

Dead on time there were two sharp knocks on the door, and taking a deep breath, Mavis went to answer it.

'Mrs Kent?' the tall, thin man asked with a smile. He wore mismatched but smart trousers and jacket, a trilby hat, and smelled of Macassar oil. He carried a scuffed brown leather briefcase. He held out his hand. 'John Edwards. Good to meet you. Is it okay if I come in?'

She stepped aside. 'Of course, come on in and I'll put the kettle on.'

He walked in and looked around as if he was inspecting everything from the multicoloured rag rug to the tiny kitchen area to the lacy antimacassars on the back of the settee.

Her hands shook a little as she filled the kettle, unsettled by his posh voice. 'You'll want to know all about our fight for the people of Silvertown,' she said as she busied herself. 'Have you been here before?'

'I haven't.' Something about his tone made him sound as if he was glad he'd stayed away.

'Well, Mr Edwards,' she said, continuing with her tea-making. 'I 'ope you're prepared to see the truth about what's going on 'ere. It's not right that people 'ave to live in such awful conditions and something needs to be done.'

The reporter opened his briefcase and took out a notepad and pencil. 'That's why I'm here, Mrs Kent. To get the facts and let our readers know what's going on.'

Mavis placed a small tray on her little table and began

pouring the tea. 'Good, because what's happening 'ere is a disgrace. There are some good landlords, of course there are, but a lot are simply dreadful. They don't do repairs and let their properties fall down around tenants' 'eads.'

He accepted the cup and saucer she handed him, then began scribbling in shorthand on his notebook. 'Can you give me some examples?'

'Well, my roof leaks sometimes. There's a couple live upstairs. It's not unusual in the East End for more than one family to live in one house, even a small one like this. The bombing has made it really tough to find somewhere to live.'

'So your landlord doesn't fix the roof?'

Her eyes narrowed with anger. ''E does not. I 'ave to pay to get someone to do it or the people upstairs get their stuff ruined. Then the damn water can come down to my place. We pay 'alf each.' She paused and looked at him. 'Don't get this wrong. They're not paying me rent, they're paying the landlord just like I am.'

Joyce came in with a friend, breathless from skipping. 'Can I play out a bit longer, Mummy?' she asked.

'Yes, but stay in this street so I can find you for teatime,' Mavis replied, and looked at Mr Edwards. 'You got kids?'

He nodded. 'Three. Little blighters they are too. But what made you begin the rent strike?'

Mavis sat down opposite him, ready to tell her story and fight for the people of Silvertown. It took a while.

'And them landlords who've put up the rents are breaking the law!'

He looked up sharply, his pencil paused.

'That'd make a good headline for your paper, wouldn't it?' Mavis said. '"Landlords breaking the law!" At the beginning of the war a law was passed that landlords couldn't put up rents without good reason. When you walk around the area with me, you'll see there's no good reason.'

When they'd finished their tea and he'd run out of questions, they left the house and headed to the nearby streets. He looked shocked at the extent of the bomb damage.

'Where do you live then?' Mavis asked.

'Havering. We've had very little bombing there. Nothing like this.' As he spoke he was looking at a massive crater in the road.

'A double-decker bus fell in that hole. Full of people it was,' Mavis said, remembering the dreadful day.

He looked at her, wide-eyed with disbelief. 'Full of people? A double-decker bus? How come it wasn't in the news?'

She looked at him as if she couldn't believe how naïve he was. 'You're a reporter. You must know the government doesn't report all the bad news. They don't want to demoralise us what's at the sharp end.'

They passed groups of men working to repair two adjacent houses. A couple were busy nailing planks of wood to support the front of the house while others covered broken windows with pieces of thin wood.

'We've got the Yanks doing repairs. Keeping them busy until the action starts. That's who these blokes are. You can tell cos they look a lot healthier than people around 'ere.'

He stopped and got out his notebook before going up to the repair gang. They looked up at him, glad to stop and wipe their faces. It was a hot day and they were working in full sun.

'Hi,' John called over to them. 'I'm a reporter. Can I ask you a few questions about your work here?'

They all stopped what they were doing and two lit up cigarettes and leaned against the nearest wall. 'Sure thing, bud,' one said. 'What do you want to know?'

Mavis stepped back and listened to the conversation. It

wouldn't help her campaign but anything that brought awareness to the hardship Silvertown faced had to be good.

But they hadn't been talking for more than a few minutes when it went: the air-raid siren. Its wail cut through their conversation like a butcher's knife, its eerie wax and wane sending a chill down Mavis's spine as it always did. In an instant the bustling street was transformed into one of panicked chaos, as people stopped whatever they were doing, gathered their belongings and hurried towards their nearest shelter.

Glancing at John, Mavis saw he was frozen for a moment, his eyes wide with a mixture of fear and confusion. Had he never been in an air raid, she wondered. She grabbed his arm, snapping him out of his stupor. 'Quick, come with me,' she shouted over the siren's piecing screech. 'The Underground. That's the nearest.'

John nodded, his reporter's instincts kicking in as he looked around him. People of all ages and walks of life were scurrying past them, their faces etched with fear. Mothers clutched their children's hands or pushed prams almost crashing into people. Elderly men and women leaned on canes, often being helped by ARP wardens.

Mavis and John joined the throng, dodging around those who were heading in different directions to their own preferred shelters. The sound of the siren was almost deafening, and Mavis felt her heart pounding in her chest. Would Joyce be okay? She would know the nearest shelter, she'd been there many times. She would surely be with her friends and their mothers.

As they approached the entrance to the Underground, they saw a queue had already formed, snaking down the stairs and out of sight in the dim lighting. Fear in the air was palpable as people craned their necks to scan the skies, dreading the sight of enemy planes.

John took the lead, pulling Mavis into the queue, their bodies tense with anticipation. Around them people murmured prayers and words of comfort to each other, or hurried up little ones who hoped to get a glimpse of the aircraft.

Although the wait to get downstairs was brief, it seemed to take forever, each second like an eternity.

When they finally reached the platform, the pair moved around to find a space against the wall where they could sit down and use it as a backrest. The sound of the siren was muffled, but the distant rumble of planes was getting louder by the minute.

'Made it,' Mavis said with a sigh, worrying again about Joyce. John may have been afraid when he first heard the siren but his reporter's instinct had reappeared. He watched and scribbled notes in his baffling shorthand as people moved around, settled down, finding themselves a suitable place. As usually happened, some had blankets to sit on, some had flasks of tea or playing cards.

'Is it always like this?' he asked Mavis.

'It's not as full as it'll get. The smell gets worse, the mosquitoes have a field day but it can be fun. Surely you must be used to underground shelters?'

He bit his lip. 'I suppose I've been lucky. We've got a basement shelter in the newspaper's office and our own Anderson shelter at home.' He paused and licked the end of his pencil. 'Do you think any of these people will be involved in the strike?'

She nodded. 'For sure. I recognise a couple of people and even people who don't come out 'olding banners might still be refusing to pay.' They were interrupted by some children almost tripping over them as they played some sort of war game. 'You know, if I was you, I'd wait 'til the noise dies down then stand up and ask if anyone will talk to you about their complaints.'

Mavis watched him weaving his way in and out of the tired East Enders struggling to get comfortable. She admired the way he spoke, drawing stories out of people. Some were shy, while others wanted to complain into next year. All the while he wrote and wrote in his notebook, filling page after page. He heard stories of damaged roofs, rotting floorboards, broken windows, faulty plumbing and failing electricity – in some cases no electricity at all.

In an hour he had more examples of terrible conditions and wicked landlords than he could ever have dreamed of. Some stories almost made him cry.

Finally the all-clear sounded and he went back to Mavis. 'It'll take a couple of days, but I'll write a really good story about your campaign. I promise.'

30

Mavis didn't have to wait to read the newspapers in the library. The headlines outside the newsagents she passed on her way to work stopped her in her tracks.

Silvertown Stands Strong: Rent Strike Spotlight

By

John Edwards

The headline screamed in bold black letters. Mavis's eyes widened with excitement. He'd actually done it. The reporter had been as good as his word!

'You're famous, girl!' the man in the newsagents said as he handed her the paper. 'This one's on the house. Good work you're doing.'

Two other people queueing behind Mavis congratulated her as well. She felt overwhelmed with everything that was happening as a result of a brief conversation in the library.

Taking her paper outside, the rhythmic clatter of a passing

tram echoed down the narrow street. Her hands shook as she opened the newspaper and read:

The oppressive smell of the Thames and various factories along the riverside hung in the air, a world away from the polished desks of the newspaper office where I usually work. I found myself in the heart of London's East End, in Silvertown, a borough I was barely aware of. Before this assignment, Silvertown had been nothing more than a name on a map, a place I vaguely associated with docks and intense bombing during the Blitz.

I'd come to meet Mrs Mavis Kent, the woman at the heart of the Silvertown Rent Strike. A slight woman, she nonetheless had a firm handshake and a determined look on her face. She ushered me into her home, proof of both wartime austerity and pride. Her spotless home showed she wasn't a wealthy woman, yet it was both welcoming and attractive.

Frankly I'd approached this assignment with a degree of cynicism. Rent strikes? I thought. How would that work? Surely the tenants would all simply be evicted. But as Mrs Kent spoke, her voice trembling with a potent mixture of anger and despair, I felt the beginning of unease. It wasn't just the bombing that left this area so deprived, she explained, it was 'greedy landlords' who illegally put up rents but failed to do even essential repairs.

'Landlords are breaking the law,' she declared, her eyes flashing with fury. 'The government brought in a law at the beginning of the war banning rent increases unless with good cause. You just look around this area,' she said. 'There's no good cause...'

By the time Mavis had finished reading she was almost dancing with delight. This article surely had to help their cause.

Back in the familiar early morning quiet of the library, the newspaper she'd been given felt warm in Mavis's hands. The article highlighted many of the things she'd said and pointed out during her time with the reporter.

'Have you seen the article?' Cordelia said as soon as Mavis arrived at the library. 'You did a good job with him, he mentions all sorts of aspects that could have been overlooked. Well done, Mavis!'

Mavis had only just taken her coat off and the library wasn't open yet, but she was pleased with the boss's praise. Joe had managed to phone her the previous evening and was impressed with what she'd already achieved too. 'You've got what it takes, girl. They should set you up to sort that bloody Hitler out!'

'What really won 'im round,' she told Cordelia, 'was going down the Underground. People there soon told 'im what was what! I thought 'e was going to cry at one point when Mrs Collins from Brunner Road told 'im 'ow her little one died of bronchitis. The doc said it was because of the damp and mould in 'er 'ouse. Shameful.'

'That last sentence is going to put the wind up some of the landlords,' Jane joined in, folding the newspaper to highlight the text in question:

Tomorrow we will disclose the name of some of the greedy landlords who should be ashamed of the way they are treating honest, hard-working East Enders.

'Name and shame the buggers!' Mavis cried. 'No more than they deserve. Some of them'll surely get repairs done just to avoid the publicity.' She paused, remembering that Cordelia's father was one of the landlords. 'Sorry, boss. This must be tough for you.'

By the end of the day twenty people had popped into the library and said they would join the strike.

By the next day three major landlords had backed down and promised they would do repairs. They also agreed to reduce rents to pre-war figures.

31

The sale of a first edition of *Sense and Sensibility* had gained more publicity than Cordelia dared hope for. She had told a local newsman who used the library and he printed a small item about the sale in his newspaper. It was picked up by two national papers and interest in the book was beyond her wildest imaginings. War news was always prominent along with the latest news of Princess Elizabeth visiting hospitals near Windsor Castle where she and her sister Margaret were living for the duration. But even so there was a small article about the book sale.

The auctioneer had let Cordelia know that there was plenty of interest in the book, including from GIs, some of whom enjoyed auctions, hoping to pick up unusual gifts to send home.

It was with some trepidation that Cordelia and Tom approached the building where the auction was being held. A local prominent book dealer was taking charge of the proceedings. 'Your book will bring a good price despite the war,' he told her. 'There are always people with money looking for gems like this.'

The sale was to be held in a large hall that had once been

quite grand although it now looked slightly shabby beneath its faded gilt detailing. Much like London. Tall arched windows let in a pale light but did little to illuminate the long rows of chairs and occasional small tables where bidders would sit.

The air in the auction room was thick with the musty smell of old books, aged leather and the faint, sharp tang of mothballs. There was a hint of perfume from some of the well-dressed attendees mingling with the dusty aroma. The complex tapestry of smells hinted at the history of the items on display.

Their book was far from the only object being sold and Cordelia and Tom enjoyed looking at the other items. Antiques always whispered of lives past – a painting showing lands untouched by war, jewels reminiscent of peacetime galas, love letters from lovers long deceased. Cordelia ran her fingers along the well-polished front of a desk, wondering what letters had been written there. It was a beautiful piece of furniture that spoke of wealth and reminded her of the one in her father's study.

There were plenty of whimsy items too and she and Tom were soon chuckling at furry chessmen in silly hats and a one-eyed teddy bear clutching a tiny book of fairy tales.

'I was so tempted to keep the book myself,' Tom said as they tried to read the minute letters in the fairy-tale book. 'I don't think I've ever wanted anything so much. But I've got over it and I'm really glad the money it raises today will help the library.'

It was impossible to look at some of the items and not imagine the lives of the people who had once owned them. What happened to the child who owned the teddy? Had the teddy been cherished? Had the child lived a good long life? And the jewellery. Why was it in the auction when it was so beautiful? Perhaps it had been a gift from an adoring husband but why hadn't it been left to a daughter? Perhaps the family had fallen on hard times. Looking round it seemed as if any of the items could give an author ideas for a story.

Behind the wooden podium, the auctioneer tidied his papers and looked around, banging his gavel a couple of times warning they had ten more minutes to browse.

As the time for the beginning of the auction neared she looked around at others browsing. There were traders in worn tweeds, ladies in furs, some GIs in uniform. But then she stopped. Standing only a few feet away was Eugene.

'Cordelia! How wonderful to see you and Tom too!' he said, kissing her cheek and shaking Tom's hand.

'How is your family history research going?' Tom asked.

Before Eugene could answer the auctioneer banged his gavel. 'Time to take your seats, ladies and gentlemen,' he called.

'Shall we meet for a cup of tea when the auction is finished?' Eugene asked.

Cordelia's smile was the answer he needed and she was aware of that pull again. That attraction she shouldn't be feeling when Robert was having a terrible time stationed in North Africa. As she walked she pictured Robert there, working in impossible conditions, often in tents. The heat, the sand, insects and unfamiliar diseases made his life a struggle every day.

But thoughts of Robert were pushed out of Cordelia's mind as she searched for a seat, her heart fluttering with anticipation. The precious book that could solve many of the library's financial difficulties was about halfway down the list of items to be auctioned. Finding three seats together they watched, fascinated by the bidding strategies of different people. Some raised a hand, others waved a paper, yet others simply nodded or even raised an eyebrow.

To Cordelia's surprise Eugene bid on an apparently insignificant box she'd noticed. It held some old letters along with a variety of bits and pieces. The sort of things many people would have in their 'junk' drawer in their kitchen. Odd coins, buttons, safety pins, receipts and more interestingly a small stack of old letters tied together with a faded red ribbon. Bidding was slow and Eugene picked it up for what he described as 'peanuts'. Cordelia looked at him questioningly. 'Tell you later,' he whispered.

Then finally, their number was called. Cordelia's pulse quickened as the assistant brought the book to show to the audience. The modest book had been laid on a velvet cushion and despite its age it seemed to glow under the room's chandelier.

The auctioneer waited until his assistant showed the book, holding it high and turning it this way and that in his gloved hands so it could be seen from each part of the room.

'Ladies and gentlemen, now we come to one of the most important items in our sale today. Perhaps the most important. A true treasure that will set many book lover's hearts aflutter and have collectors yearning to own it. This is a first edition of Jane Austen's beloved novel *Pride and Prejudice*, published in eighteen thirteen when the author was a mere thirty-seven years old.

'This very volume would have been one of a handful owned by readers in Regency England, perhaps passing down through the generations of a grand country estate library.

'So, who will be the next owner of this treasure? Do I have an opening bid of twenty-five guineas for this wonderful item? I should tell you I already have some advance bids.'

Beside Cordelia, Tom glanced at her, smiling encouragement, fingers crossed. She dared to look at Eugene again but he was engrossed in watching the bidders.

The bids piled up quickly, and soon Cordelia found she couldn't take in the figures that were being bid, then outbid again and again. As each new bid was called, Cordelia's fingers gripped her handbag so tight she left nail marks in the leather. The numbers climbed dizzily.

Watching the auctioneer and listening to the numbers was like watching a high-wire act in a circus – so dangerous it seemed impossible to believe. Watching to see if the performer would cross or fall to his death.

How far could this bidding go? Finally it slowed down to two bidders on opposite sides of the room.

Somewhere a clock ticked, and with each second the stakes grew higher. The auctioneer looked from one to the other then back again, each time waiting a little longer for a response.

A man nearby checked his watch for the umpteenth time, then wrote something in a small notebook.

But just when the auction seemed ready to move on a third person put up his arm. A late bidder! The tension in the room, already palpable, thickened as people looked from one man to the other.

The three men battled it out, each taking longer than before to increase their bid. Finally, the bidding was down to one man.

The auctioneer looked around the room. His voice rang out, sharp and clear.

'Going once!'

Cordelia's heart raced, her fingers digging into her palms. The moment of truth was here. She looked around frantically. Was anyone going to make a last-minute bid?

'Going twice!' It seemed as if everyone in the room was holding their breath.

She exchanged an anxious glance with Tom. The price was much higher than they'd dared to hope. Would it be enough to make all the improvements they wanted in the library?

The room fell silent. Breaths held. Seconds stretched.

'Any last bids, ladies and gentlemen? This is your very last chance.'

Cordelia's stomach churned. Her pulse pounded in her ears.

'Gone! Sold to the gentleman in the front row!'

The gavel banged. Applause erupted.

Cordelia felt light-headed. She turned to Tom, eyes wide. 'Did that really happen?'

Tom nudged her arm. 'Crikey, Cordelia, that's amazing. All the library's worries are over!'

She turned to him, like a woman rescued from drowning. 'Was that figure what I thought it was?' Could it be true that this book was so much more than just paper and ink – it was salvation for their humble library?

Tom nodded. 'Yes, you're not dreaming. Time to celebrate!'

'And I think more than tea is in order, don't you?' Eugene added.

32

It took some time for the auction to be over so that Cordelia could meet with the auctioneer to deal with the necessary paperwork.

'You won't get the money immediately,' the auctioneer said. 'But I know that dealer of old. He works for responsible buyers so you don't need to worry about someone failing to pay up. I'll let you know when the money has arrived.'

Thrilled at their success and wanting to unwind, Cordelia suggested the three of them walk to Shaftesbury Avenue. It wasn't far and unlike the East End there were plenty of places to eat. Shaftesbury Avenue, a broad thoroughfare, was lined with grand Victorian buildings housing a selection of activities not seen in the East End. It was a hub of activity, with theatres, cinemas, shops, restaurants, cafés and bright notices advertising the latest shows and films. It was a breath of fresh air reminding them of life before the war started.

They strolled along chatting, Cordelia explaining to Eugene that Tom had to take all the credit for finding the precious book.

Eugene shook Tom's hand so firmly he thought the bones would crush. 'That's swell,' Eugene said. 'You did a great job.' He looked ahead. 'If we're going this way, allow me to take you both to the Rainbow Corner for an American burger!'

Cordelia's eyes widened. 'I've been there. Do you remember we bumped into each other...'

'How could I forget? But do you think Tom here would like to see it?'

'Tom would like the food, that's for sure,' she replied.

'So this Rainbow Corner is for GIs. Is that right?' Tom asked.

'That's right, but anyone can go. It's a terrific place, a little piece of home in the middle of a war, in the middle of London.'

Tom stumbled, leaning heavily on his stick to keep upright. 'Damn leg,' he said absent-mindedly. 'So can any GIs go in there? No colour bar?'

'None. Everywhere else in the army there is. Black units are led by white officers. We even have different mess halls and recreation areas.' He paused and sighed. 'Takes a lot of getting used to being here where there's no segregation – not legal anyways. Still, the Rainbow Corner is mixed and we don't get much trouble. I almost feel like apologising in advance,' Eugene continued. 'Compared to the East End, this place is heaven. You'll look around and not believe there's a war on.'

Eugene led the way into the foyer where they were greeted by a different girl from before. 'Welcome, everyone,' she said with a smile. 'Have you been here before?'

'I have,' Eugene said, smiling at her. 'These are my English friends. I'm planning to show them around and treat them to some good old US food!'

The girl grinned and giggled, looking mostly at Tom. 'You're in for a treat then, honey.'

Cordelia noticed that she might not be American but she was picking up some of their lingo.

Eugene led the way. 'We've got plenty of rooms here, Tom. It's over three floors. But if you're like me, you're ready to eat and celebrate.' Eugene stopped suddenly. 'Oh, I should have said. They don't sell booze here, so if you were hoping for some bubbly to celebrate we should go somewhere else.'

Tom looked around, his senses almost overwhelmed by such variety. Not just the variety of people, skin colour and accents but by the riches of entertainment he could see from where he was. Through a door to the left was a room with a whole wall of pinball tables.

'Rescued from seaside piers now they're not in use!' Eugene said with a smile.

Tom shook his head in disbelief. 'I don't know about you, Cordelia, but I'm willing to do without the bubbly to eat here, not to mention look around.'

They went up a flight of stairs to the dining hall. For a minute their happy mood was squashed when two white GIs looked at them. One, sneering at Cordelia, muttered, 'Slut!' It wasn't loud but she was convinced he meant for her to hear.

'Ignore him, Miss Cordelia,' Eugene said. 'Some folks are just plain ignorant.'

The smell of the food was enough to stop Cordelia and Tom in their tracks. Their senses, dulled by years of rationing, were excited by the enormous variety of smells coming from the café – burgers, chips, hot dogs, apple pie, meat loaf and others they couldn't identify.

'Boy, my mouth's watering. I'll have one of everything!' Tom said, taking an eager step forward. Like the rest of the building, the café area was busy and they struggled to find a table, but were lucky when one became free.

'Do we have to queue?' Tom asked, rubbing his injured leg.

Eugene shook his head. 'No, a pretty waitress will come and take our order. Look on the board over there for what's on offer today.'

While they waited their conversation went back to the auction.

'What will you do with the money?' Eugene asked, settling himself in his chair. 'Got any ideas?'

Cordelia laughed. 'I've got a list as long as your arm. Lots of new books if we can get them. Some part-time help...' She stopped and looked at Tom. 'Actually, I haven't liked to say until I was sure the book would sell but, Tom, how would you feel about being a paid member of the team instead of a volunteer?'

His eyes lit up. 'That would be wonderful.' He paused and his ears went red. 'I haven't liked to say anything but I'm going to ask my girlfriend if she'll marry me. My grandmother's inheritance won't last forever so some salary would be just the ticket.'

She smiled and touched his arm. 'Let's talk about it tomorrow when we're back in, but now...'

They were interrupted by the waitress who came to take their orders. She was pretty with blond hair in Veronica Lake curls and scarlet lipstick. She looked like a film star. Although she wore a white overall, she made it glamorous by belting it tight round her slender waist and rolling up the sleeves. Cordelia suppressed a smile when the waitress called Tom 'Darlin'' and he didn't know where to look.

They ordered burgers and fries, as the Americans called chips, and a Coke each.

'Be right back, sweeties,' the waitress said, blowing them a kiss.

Cordelia was sitting next to Eugene and realised that without any conscious intention she had moved her legs to be nearer to him. It was as if there was an invisible force pulling her towards him. She instinctively moved her legs away, hoping the movement would appear natural, a mere adjustment for comfort's sake. Yet even as she did so, a part of her longed to hold on to that closeness, to enjoy its magnetic pull, to savour the undeniable attraction she felt.

It was with mixed emotions that Tom speaking brought her back to the moment. 'We've been talking about a special section of the library with artefacts honouring local people who have lost their lives during wars...' Tom said. 'There are quite a few of them.'

Cordelia took a deep breath. 'Actually, there's something else I've been thinking about for a long time. A van to take books to workers in the factories who can't get to the library during office hours. And perhaps to housebound people too.'

Eugene frowned. 'I hear you have petrol rationing in this country. Won't that get in the way of your plans for a mobile library?'

She nodded. 'We'll probably only be able to go out once or twice a week, but it'll be worth it. It's not far anyway. Mavis, who knows everything that goes on in Silvertown, tells me a lot of the girls in the factory would love some romance books.'

As they enjoyed their meal, Eugene told them he had bid on the box in the hope the letters would give him some ideas for his family research. 'The name is the same, but I don't think it's an unusual one, so it's a long shot.'

All too soon the meal was over and Eugene was excusing himself.

'I'm sorry to leave you two, but you can stay as long as you like.'

'We'll be here long enough to have some of the desserts on

offer. I fancy an apple pie and cream,' Cordelia said. She looked at Tom. 'Is that okay with you?'

He grinned. 'It certainly is. An ice cream sundae for me!'

As Eugene began walking away he lightly touched her shoulder, sending a thrill through her body. When he had gone it was as if the sun had dimmed a little even though there was none shining through the windows.

33

Tom and Cordelia walked side by side, their minds preoccupied with the task at hand. They were on a mission to find a suitable van for their mobile library. But Tom was about to reveal something that might cast a shadow of uncertainty over their success.

'The trouble is, you know I used to work at Canning Book Shop,' Tom said. 'I heard he's started taking books to the factories in the East End. To sell though, not to borrow like we would.'

Cordelia stopped in her tracks, her brow furrowed with concern. 'So he might see us as competition?'

'He might. There's never much profit selling books so he's protective of his territory. He's bound to see our van as a threat.'

It was Saturday afternoon and the library had closed for the weekend. After tidying up, ready for opening on Monday, the two were on their way to a car dealer to look for a van. They were standing at a bus stop waiting for a bus to take them to Stratford where they'd been told the biggest dealership was.

The bus stop was not far from the library and several people paused to say hello, two talking about the latest books they'd read. One was a member of the library sewing group, a keen attendee who never missed a session. She opened her bag and showed them a worn-out dress she'd just got at a jumble sale. 'I'm going to take this to our next sewing session. I've got ideas on what to do with it, but other people might have better ones.'

Their conversation was ended by the bus arriving. It lurched forward, navigating through war-torn streets. Although the Blitz had ended, the whole East End was like a broken mosaic, its once poor but vibrant pieces shattered and scattered by the relentless bombing of the Blitz. Although repair teams worked hard to patch up houses where they could be fixed, great gaps showed where family homes and busy shops had once stood. The scars of war were etched in every corner. However, it wasn't just the war responsible for the poor state of local housing, it was also those negligent landlords that Mavis was trying to do something about.

But life continued. People in the bus chattered about the latest war news, about food shortages, about their family birthdays. Outside they saw children playing on the bomb sites, using them as castles or battle sites. Their laughter was a reminder that life still went on.

The bus suddenly jolted turning right, throwing them against each other.

'Blimey, another building's gone and fallen down,' a woman behind them said, looking out of the window. 'Lucky the driver saw that one in time!'

The conductor called their stop, and they got off along with half a dozen other people. They were opposite a very modest car showroom that could barely be called that. A tired hut stood at the back of the site, the door open, its only window cracked and held together with the blast tape that covered windows everywhere. They had been told it had always sold second-hand cars and had once been the best in the area. However, now a few worn and weary vehicles stood forlornly, but their paint was shiny and well looked after. The only sign of its earlier heyday was a faded sign, hung above the entrance. Its once bold letters now a ghost of their former selves – 'Stratford Motors – London's Finest Automobiles.' The grand title made them smile.

The pair felt defeated before they even stepped into the lot. 'Don't think we're going to have much luck here,' Tom groaned. 'Still, we're here now, perhaps they've got what we need at the back.'

They hadn't gone more than a few steps when the hut door opened further and the owner, a man in his late fifties, came out to greet them.

'Good afternoon, and what a wonderful day it is! Something to be grateful for.' He held out his hand. 'My name's Reg Atkins, how can I help you?'

He had an air of dignity despite the run-down state of his business. His posture was straight and his smile genuine, if somewhat tired. He wore matching grey woollen trousers and waistcoat, no doubt two parts of a three-piece suit. Underneath was a spotless white shirt, open at the neck. The cuffs and collar of the shirt were slightly frayed.

As he shook their hands, he gave a sense of trust and reliability. Cordelia quickly felt relieved that she had taken the advice of Mr Hubbard, a builder they used in the library. He knew everyone and recommended this business.

'I'm looking for a van big enough to use as a mobile library. We are from Silvertown Library.'

Mr Atkins blinked fast. 'Blimey, that's a new one. Good idea though. My missus never has her nose out of a book.' He paused. 'Now, let me think. I know we don't have any vans big enough at the moment but I've been approached by a man, I won't tell you his name, but a man who has decided to retire and close his business. He is thinking of selling a van that might be just what you need. Come with me.'

He took them into his hut and leafed through some ageing car leaflets. Finally, he found what he was looking for. 'It's like this – a Ford. You see them everywhere. I'm guessing this one I have in mind will need a bit of a touch-up though.'

Cordelia and Tom looked at each other. 'Can you call us when you know more, Mr Atkins?' Cordelia asked with hope in her voice. She had indeed seen those vans around.

They walked away with a glint of hope in their hearts. Perhaps this scheme would work.

'Are you coming to the rent protest tomorrow, Tom?' Cordelia asked as they crossed a busy road.

'I can't, I'm afraid. I'm meeting my girlfriend's parents for the first time!' His voice shook a little as he spoke. 'I'm a bit nervous about it, to be honest. Her dad sounds a bit of a tyrant.'

Cordelia placed a hand on his arm. 'Tom, I've seen you deal with all manner of difficult people in the library. Not only that, you sound as if you coped well with your old boss at the bookshop. You can have faith in yourself.'

Despite the evidence of bombing, they decided to walk back to the library. It was a long way, but it gave them time to talk and enjoy the sunshine. 'It's not right, is it, how people in the East End have such a hard life,' Tom said. 'I'm thinking about joining the protest. I don't have a problem landlord, but I want to support the local people.'

'She'll be thrilled,' Cordelia said, stepping round a crater in the road. 'Mavis is so brave doing all this.'

Tom nodded, his own anger at the injustice simmering just beneath the surface. 'Our mobile library will show people that we care, even if the rotten landlords don't. It'll be an important service.'

As they neared the library, they spotted a small crowd gathered outside. Curious, they quickened their pace, wondering what had got people's attention.

To their surprise, they found Mr Hubbard, their builder, standing on a crate, addressing the crowd. 'We can't let these landlords get away with it any more!' he shouted, his voice full of passion. 'You don't need to be a builder like me to know what repairs are needed in our houses. It's time we stood up for ourselves!'

The crowd cheered, their voices rising in agreement. Then they gradually dispersed. The message was getting across to more and more people.

Mr Hubbard spotted them and walked towards them. 'I expect you've guessed Mavis has dragged me into helping her with the rent strike. Not that I mind, them landlords should be ashamed of themselves.'

'I've heard you do bits and pieces of repairs on the cheap,' Tom said, looking at him admiringly.

'Gotta help the old folks, ain't ya?' Mr Hubbard responded. 'Especially them what's got no family to help. A lot of old girls around here lost their husbands and sons in the last war, never mind this one.'

'And now we have a new struggle,' Cordelia said. 'And I'm thrilled you'll be involved.'

34

Mavis walked towards Mr Stanstead's office, the weight of the community's hopes riding on her shoulders. A quiver of fear ran through her as she stepped inside, comforted only by the knowledge she was in the right. Mrs Gregory, a tenant and library user, was with her for support.

"'E's going to try to make us look stupid,' Mavis had said when they were planning the meeting.

Knowing the man's character, she couldn't help but compare him in her imagination to a cunning and predatory animal, a wolf. He embodied the traits of that animal: sly, opportunistic and willing to prey upon the vulnerable for personal gain. Even though she knew he employed rent collectors, she imagined him lurking in the shadows, ready to pounce on unsuspecting tenants, using his power to extract every ounce of profit no matter how much hardship he caused.

'We need to treat him with caution because he bites.'

Mrs Gregory nodded. 'You're braver than me, Mavis. I'll back you up but I might be too scared to say anything.'

His office was stuffy, no windows open despite it being a

warm summer's day. The air was thick with cigar smoke and the smell of whisky. But while large, the room wasn't as opulent as Mavis had expected. Her adversary's desk was big and imposing with a tray bursting with papers, several pens and pencils, but the rest of the room was unimpressive. A smaller desk with a chair sat on another wall and a grey metal filing cabinet was beside it. Both had overflowing ashtrays sending up acrid scents into the room.

Stanstead didn't look up when they entered, his attention on some documents he was looking at with what they took to be his secretary. She was young with bouncy blond curls and scarlet lipstick, glossy and pouting.

'Are you happy with it, Mr Stanstead?' she asked, her voice low and husky. Like him, she ignored Mavis and Mrs Gregory.

He patted the girl's bottom and she grinned and play-swiped his shoulder.

'Naughty man!' she said with a laugh. She picked up the papers, tapped them to a tidy pile and walked out past the visitors as if they didn't exist.

Outside, a cloud moved over the sun and a sparrow hopped along the window ledge looking for bugs. If it found any it would be the only kindness from this man.

Mr Stanstead sat unmoving behind his desk. His flabby stomach hung halfway to his knees. 'Yes?' he said, still not bothering to look up. The heavy gold ring on his little finger caught the sunlight, glittering menacingly.

The sneer on his face, an apparently permanent feature, reminded Mavis of a saying she'd heard – 'You're born with the face God gives you but by the time you're forty you have the face you deserve.' The lines etched across his face were evidence of his lifetime of disdain for others. Deep furrows creased the skin around his mouth, forming vertical lines that were etched there forever. The puppet wrinkles extended from the corner of his lips and descended to his jawline. Deep crow's feet lined his mouth, no doubt as a result of smoking as well as sneering.

'Yes?' he said again, shuffling papers as he spoke, still barely looking up.

Mavis took a deep breath to get in control of her anger. Anger at his arrogant treatment of his tenants and fury at the way that within seconds he was silently trying to tell her she was of no importance.

'Let's not beat about the bush, Mr Stanstead,' she said, her voice steadier than she'd expected. 'You know why I'm 'ere—'

'Yeah,' Mrs Gregory said, interrupting her. 'You're a wicked, wicked landlord. You put up rents but never do any repairs. One day you will regret this. God will...'

Mr Stanstead stopped her with a dismissive flick of his wrist. 'God? What, that God who looks after you all so well?'

Mavis realised she had to intervene before things got heated. Much as she wanted to hit this arrogant man in front of her with his heavy glass ashtray, they had to stay calm.

'You're making a mistake, Mrs Kent, with this protest of yours,' Stanstead went on. 'It's annoying me and all the other landlords, and we don't like to be bothered. Some of them might back down, but the rest will stand firm like me. This won't end well for any of you.'

His henchman, who had come in and moved to stand behind him when the two women entered, nodded his head and cracked his knuckles.

Mavis gulped, her mouth dry. 'Mr Stanstead, we're not 'ere to make enemies or cause bother. We're 'ere because we want fair treatment for the tenants of Silvertown. We've spoken to the council and they say they 'ave written to you about the repairs needed but you've done nothing.'

His top lip raised in a sneer again. 'That lot? The council? Waste of public funds.'

Mavis stood her ground, her heart beating fast, but she refused to be intimidated by this man's veiled threats. She met his cold gaze with unwavering determination. 'You may find us a nuisance, Mr Stanstead, and I'm glad that is the case. We intend to continue our battle until you take good positive action. The tenants of Silvertown deserve better.'

Mr Stanstead leaned back in his chair, rocking on its rear legs. 'You think you can challenge me? You're nothing but an insignificant do-gooder, trying to stir up trouble where there is none.' He shuffled his papers again. 'I've checked and you are not even one of my tenants. If you were, you'd have already been thrown out on to the street!'

Mavis took a step closer, her eyes ablaze with conviction. 'I am 'appy to own the title of do-gooder. I aim to do good and the good we need is fair rent and prompt repairs.'

Mrs Gregory chimed in, her voice trembling with anger. 'You may think you can 'ide behind your money and power, but we will win in the end.'

He raised an eyebrow. 'You think?' he said, and his henchman tittered like a schoolboy. Mr Stanstead stood up. 'Off you go then, ladies. I've got better things to do than speak to you two!'

'We're not finished yet,' Mavis said. 'We've documented the conditions of your properties in Silvertown, the leaks, the faulty electrical wiring, the mould-infested walls.' Her voice grew stronger with her conviction. 'These are not mere complaints. They are legitimate concerns affecting the health of your tenants, people who entrust you with their well-being. It is your responsibility as a landlord to address these issues promptly and fairly.'

Mavis looked around the room, taking in the cluttered desk, the overflowing ashtrays and overall neglect that mirrored his indifference towards his tenants. She had to try to make him understand somehow.

'Imagine for a moment, Mr Stanstead, if you and your loved ones were living in such conditions. Buckets catching the drips from leaking roofs, wiping down mouldy walls every morning, sitting wrapped in a blanket any time of day or night because of the cold winds thrusting themselves through the rotten windowpanes.'

She paused to see if her words were having any impact, but his face hadn't changed one iota.

'Wouldn't you want someone to stand up for your rights, to 'elp you, to fight for justice and fair treatment?'

Her words hung in the air and she hoped that by appealing to his sense of what his own family life might be like, she could break through his dismissive facade and ignite a spark of understanding.

But it was as if they hadn't spoken.

'You finished now?' Stanstead asked. 'Out you go, the pair of you. I've got a lot of things to do.'

Outside his building the two women looked at each other, eyes wide.

'What a bastard!' Mrs Gregory said. ''E 'asn't got a decent bone in his body. I hope he rots in hell.'

Crossing the busy road, they dodged boys pulling homemade carts and a bicycle.

'We can't let him intimidate us,' Mavis said, her voice resolute. 'We need to gather more information, more evidence. If we 'ave enough, the council will have to take action.'

Mrs Gregory shook her head, her mouth downturned. 'They 'aven't been interested so far, 'ave they?' She gave a bitter laugh. 'I bet some of them are making money out of it somehow.'

Mavis looked up at the sky where rain threatened. She got her umbrella out of her bag, ready. 'That lot couldn't find their way out of a paper bag. But we'll just 'ave to show them the way, won't we?' She sighed. 'Some of the landlords have already backed down. He'll do the same one day.'

35

Jane and Tom were finishing preparation for the children's section of the library for another scavenger hunt session. Limited by paper rationing, they nonetheless put in extra effort to make the area look lively and attractive. Tom, a good artist, had even found some books that were too damaged to use, and drawn pictures of characters from books over the text. A string of them hung across the area like bunting.

'You missed a spot,' Jane said, pointing to a small empty patch on the wall.

Tom grinned. 'No, that's my artistic interpretation. It represents how empty life is without books.'

Jane laughed. 'Well, we'd better fill it up quick then!' She admired his work which gave a playful and inviting atmosphere. 'We'll have to tell the little ones not to do that with the books they borrow, but we could give them half a dozen pages each from the books that are past it. They could draw on them.'

Each week had been different. Some children were regulars, some had dropped out altogether, like Willie whose father had dragged him out, some appeared occasionally and there were also some newcomers. Tom had been in charge of selecting the theme for this scavenger hunt and he'd chosen the seaside. It gave a wide range of options – the sea, piers, fish, boats.

Ten children appeared on this occasion. Little Hetty Gregory, of course. She was an avid reader and reading well above her age. Her mother, who had married at seventeen in a 'shotgun wedding', had told Jane she wished she'd been able to stay at school and perhaps even go further. But her mother had pushed her to work in one of the clothing sweatshops the day after her fourteenth birthday. Then she'd got in the family way, so that was that.

Her words reminded Jane of her own struggle to continue her education. No one in her family had ever gone beyond the legal school leaving age. Some had even dodged off before then to earn some money to help the family out.

'It's never too late,' Jane urged Hetty's mother. 'I don't suppose you get much time for reading, but if you have a subject you're interested in, we'll try to get you the relevant books.'

Mrs Gregory had paused. 'But what good would it do, even if I had the energy?'

Jane's heart wept for the limited opportunities Mrs Gregory and so many like her were offered. Poverty and lack of knowledge restricted their choices.

'Trouble is, I'm interested in lots of things. I wouldn't know what to choose,' Mrs Gregory said.

Tom had overheard the conversation. 'Can I offer a suggestion? Why not think about it until you come in next. Jot down anything that interests you, perhaps on the wireless, or the newspapers or just chatting to a friend. It's a good start.' He excused himself to help a struggling child.

Mrs Gregory nodded but looked unsure. 'You know,' she said to Jane, hesitation in her voice, 'I've never told a soul this but I've always wanted to be a teacher.' She got out a hankie and wiped her cheek as she spoke.

Jane was so delighted she clapped her hands together. 'Mrs Gregory, you're a young woman with plenty of years to work towards being a teacher. Come back to the desk when this session has finished and I'll look up courses you can do to get the right qualifications.'

Mrs Gregory's eyes opened wide. 'Wow, is that possible? I never knew. That would be so kind.' She paused and pulled Jane to one side, then lowered her voice. 'Can I talk to you about something else? It's... it's... well, it's awkward...'

'You can tell me anything,' Jane said. 'Whatever you say will remain confidential.'

Mrs Gregory looked away and her cheeks went pink. 'Well, if I ever want to do anything with me life what I don't need is more nippers.' She looked across at Hetty who was telling a girl her age all about the book she'd just read. 'I love my two to death, but I don't want no more...'

'I understand,' Jane said. It was a common problem in the East End and too many mouths to feed made it harder for families to survive. 'Kids don't leave much time for anything what with the housework, queueing for food and everything else.' She held up her hand. 'Hang on a minute. I've got just what you need.'

She went behind the circulation desk and opened the third drawer. There was a small pile of leaflets about birth control produced by the Family Planning Association. She wrapped one in a piece of old paper and handed it to Mrs Gregory.

'This will help. I don't know why they're not available everywhere. Every woman should know about it.'

Turning her back to the room, Mrs Gregory took a quick peep at the leaflet and gasped when she saw the title. She clasped it tight and looked around as if to ensure no one else could see what it was. Then she hid it again and touched Jane's arm. 'Thank you, thank you. You could have just changed the rest of my life.'

'You're welcome,' Jane said. 'And if you've got time this morning you can listen to one or two other children reading. It would really help us.'

Looking at her baby in the pram, Mrs Gregory nodded. He was still sleeping. 'I'll stay while 'e's asleep, but you won't want 'im 'ere when 'e wakes up. 'E'll scream the place down!'

The clock struck the hour, telling Jane and Tom it was time to get the children reading on their own for a while.

'Okay, boys and girls, find a cosy spot. You get ten minutes to read the book you've chosen, then we'll tell you when time is up. Your job then is to tell the boy or girl sitting next to you what you've learned about the book.'

Little Fred Brown put up his hand. He'd only joined the session because his mother had made him. Now, though, he enjoyed reading. Always looking for ways to help the youngsters, Tom had found a friend who had helped him improve his literacy, giving him a lesson once a week for free. He'd proved a quick learner and loved books about pirates.

'Do I 'ave to sit next to a girl, miss? They're soppy!' Fred's nose was wrinkled with disdain at the very thought.

Joyce, Mavis's daughter, was part of the group. She was learning to be a spitfire just like her mother. Her mouth opened wide with outrage at Fred's question. 'We're not soppy!' she declared loudly. 'And you're a smelly old sock what's been left in the poo-poo!'

Fred frowned, puffing up his chest to regain some superiority. 'I am not!' He made a rude gesture at her. 'I just don't want to catch being soppy from *girls*.'

Joyce had her hands on her hips now. 'If it was that easy perhaps you'd have caught being clever from us girls, old smelly socks!'

The children hooted with laughter at Joyce's robust response. Even Tom had to hide a smile behind a cough.

Five minutes later Joyce had her hand up again. 'What does this word mean?' she asked Tom, pointing to a page in her book.

'Gosh,' Tom exclaimed. 'You've got a book there that's very advanced for your age. You must be a good reader. The word is mischievous. It means naughty.'

Joyce thought about that briefly. 'Like rotten Fred when he put a worm down my back!' She stuck her tongue out at the boy in question. He just pulled a face in response and went back to his book.

Mavis was walking past with the returns trolly and overheard the conversation. She struggled to hold back a hoot of laughter but instead went over to Joyce looking serious. 'Now, Joyce, what have I told you to do when someone is mean to you?'

Joyce started, having not realised her mother was nearby. 'Um... stand up for myself. I did! I did!'

'But we stand up for ourselves politely, don't we?' She looked around. 'That applies to all you lot! So what could you have said to Fred instead?'

'Shut your big fat gob!' one of the other girls said with a giggle. She made a familiar gesture with her thumb to her nose, wiggling her fingers in the air.

Another said, 'Shut your gob, the parrots are learning bad words!'

Mavis ignored that and looked to Joyce for a reply.

Joyce looked at her friends is if they would come up with something more helpful than shut your big fat gob.

'I suppose...' she started, looking as if the words would choke her. 'I suppose I could have said that what he said was unkind and girls aren't soppy.'

Mavis clapped her hands. 'Perfect.' She looked around at the other girls. 'Now you all can reply to rude people as cleverly as Joyce did.'

Laughter gradually subsiding, the room hummed with the sounds of pages turning, of children quietly sounding the words they were following with their fingers. Jane took a moment to enjoy the sight. Her old boss, the one before Cordelia, would never have allowed this to happen. A serious man who hated change, he begrudgingly allowed Jane to set up some shelves just for children's books, but nothing else. He'd have been horrified to hear the laugher and fun there now. He wouldn't have cared that they had brought in many new readers.

'But what about the other library users?' he'd said when Jane suggested weekly story time. 'It would hardly be peaceful for them, and library users like their peace and quiet, as well you know. No, I won't hear of it.'

They'd got round that by warning people when the sessions were and only had one complaint from old Mr Jenkins who complained about everything. It was his hobby.

Mrs Gregory had vanished for a while during the session but came back at the end to collect Hetty. As Hetty was getting her things Mrs Gregory went over to Jane. 'I've been looking at this leaflet. How come I didn't know all this stuff? I can't thank you enough. You will never know what you've done for me.'

36

Although she would never have admitted it, Cordelia walked a different way to the library every day now. She knew Eugene and his colleagues were doing repair work in the area and hoped to bump into him 'by accident'. She knew where bombs had caused the most damage so by walking in that area she would increase the chances of an encounter with Eugene and his repair crew.

Just a quick chat with him, she thought. *That wouldn't be betraying Robert... would it? It would just be a chat – something to brighten the day, like the sun peering round the clouds.*

She thought about Robert's latest letter, tucked safely in her handbag. As usual, he had tried to disguise the hardships of life in the badly equipped hospital where he worked, but it was easy for her to imagine. No, she thought as she continued on her way, this behaviour wasn't her, she wasn't the type to chase after men, especially...

She sighed and put aside the memory for a minute.

She had no idea if she would find Eugene on her walk, but nonetheless a fluttery feeling danced in her stomach, making her feel light and jittery as she continued on her way. If she did bump into him, what would she say?

Eugene had helped out in the library a few times with the children's scavenger hunt, and the other librarians were full of praise for him. The trouble was, Cordelia never got a chance to talk to him alone. If she'd been free, and not had a lovely boyfriend in North Africa risking his life for the war effort, she might have asked Eugene if he'd like to meet for a cup of tea sometime.

But it wouldn't do. She was in a committed relationship... She must put him out of her mind instead of behaving like a silly teenager with a crush on a handsome man. Handsome? Was that it? But she knew it was more. It was the way he carried himself, the strength in his shoulders, the kindness in his eyes and his infectious laugh. They all momentarily chased away the shadows of war.

The thoughts didn't stop her ears being alert for American accents as she walked, struggling to hear their voices over the everyday sounds of East Enders hurrying to work. The clipped, hurried footsteps of workers on their way to factories and the docks, their pace proof of the urgency of wartime production. The rumble of lorries carrying supplies, their engaging struggle to haul their heavy loads through the damaged streets. The cheerful banter of costermongers, their voices sore from hawking their wares and the shouts of paperboys announcing the latest news.

She turned into a road she walked along less often and ahead of her were men repairing the roof of one of the small terraced houses. She could hear their voices, but not enough to recognise their accents from where she was.

Outside that and the house next door, two women stood talking while they watched the work. Seeing repairs wasn't unusual – repair teams worked hard after every bombing, organised by the local council. But there had been no bombing for several days. Cordelia assumed this was a continuation of that work. She could hear the men calling to each other as they worked and the accents were disappointingly local.

But then something occurred to her. What road was this? Had she taken a wrong turn in her distraction? She stopped where the women were talking and asked them.

'It's Factory Road,' the older of the two women said, her hair tight within a cotton turban that almost matched her apron. 'Looking for someone are you, ducks?'

Their conversation was interrupted by one of the men on the roof wolf-whistling at Cordelia while the other shouted, 'Come out with me tonight, love. I'll show you a good time!'

'Shut your 'orrible gob!' one of the women shouted at him with a grin. 'You've already got a missus and four kiddies!' With a laugh the men turned back to their work. 'Now, where were we?' she continued. 'Oh yes, you looking for someone in particular, love?'

As she spoke, a little lad of about four poked his head out of her front door. 'I'm 'ungry, Mum,' he whined. 'Can I 'ave some bread and dripping?'

The woman raised her eyes to the heavens. 'In a minute, Connor, I'm just talking to this nice lady.'

'I'm not looking for anyone,' Cordelia said, noticing the boy looked undernourished, his skin grey and his hair thin. The child's legs bowed unnaturally, a telltale sign of rickets, while his frail frame and protruding ribs make her want to weep. The government provided cod liver oil and orange juice for youngsters but sometimes it seemed it wasn't enough.

The woman was still speaking. 'I read the article about the rent strike...'

'Yeah, we're doing that,' the other woman interrupted. Younger, she was heavily pregnant and stood supporting her belly. 'Well, we were, but wonders'll never cease, this morning this pair...' – she indicated the men on the roof – 'turned up out of the blue they did. Going to do all the repairs they said.' She looked at her friend. "Ow many times 'ave we written to our rotten landlord, Maggie? Lost count I 'ave. I never thought 'e'd do a thing. But me old man says 'e won't want that newspaper to splash 'is name on the front page. Ashamed 'e should be.'

With every word a sense of dread enveloped Cordelia. Surely it couldn't be... could it...

Her mouth was so dry she could hardly speak. She swallowed hard, then spoke so quietly they struggled to hear her words.

'Who is your landlord?'

Maggie answered. 'Who is 'e? Well, we've never seen the bugger, 'ave we? Oh no, the likes of 'im wouldn't lower 'imself to come round 'ere, would 'e? No, the rent man comes and collects for 'im.'

A tile slid off the roof and crashed at their feet. Small pieces flew like shrapnel around them.

'Oy, you stupid bastard!' Maggie shouted to the workmen. 'You could've killed me then!'

'Sorry, missus,' he shouted and carried on as if nothing important had happened.

Maggie looked at her friend. 'Them two'll be the death of me. Now, I'm trying to remember the name of our landlord. It's on our rent cards so we must see it every week.'

'I know!' her friend said. 'It's something Curruthers or Carmichael. Something like that. The rent man said 'e's got a title, lord, or sir or something.'

Cordelia's legs almost gave way. These were her father's properties. She should have realised, and she would have done if she'd known the name of the road.

'You look like you're going to pass out or something,' Maggie said. 'Come 'ere and sit on the step. I'll get you a drop of water.'

Cordelia shook herself out of her state of shock. 'I have to get to work, but thank you for your offer,' she said, then walked away quickly in case they somehow discovered their landlord was her father.

As her footsteps tapped along the pavement, she began to think more clearly. So, finally, her father had begun the repairs she had been begging him to do since she learned he was a property owner in Silvertown. She should be pleased, but guessed Maggie was right, he was only doing it to keep his name out of the papers. If only he had done it because his attitudes to people less fortunate than himself had changed.

Then she remembered the cottages he owned in the village near their huge home. She was willing to bet any money that he wasn't doing repairs on them. The villagers, some of whom worked for the family in one way or another, weren't likely to go to the press. She and her mother had pleaded with him to get the cottages updated. Some didn't even have electricity. So far he had refused emphatically.

She was so engrossed in thoughts about what she'd just learned that at first she didn't catch the sound of American accents ahead of her. Then as she got a little nearer she could hear the conversation of the men who were repairing a partially fallen wall.

'I told you that club round the corner from Shaftesbury Avenue was jumpin'. Never seen so many folks swingin' 'til dawn. Boy, did I have a sore head next day.'

'It sure makes me miss home,' another man said. 'But

Harlem ain't got nothin' on London when it comes to wartime spirit. Live today cos you might be a gonna tomorrow, I guess.'

Then she heard his voice. Eugene's. A thrill shot through her and she wondered if she should dodge into a side street. She felt discombobulated after the news about her father's properties and wished it wasn't that particular morning when she bumped into him. But it was too late. As if he was drawn to her invisibly, he looked up and saw her. His eyes widened and his smile showed how pleased he was to see her.

'Cordelia!' he called out, pleasure in his voice. 'What a treat. Come and talk to us.'

Of all days for this to happen. She was already late for work, but she couldn't ignore him. Not that she wanted to when she felt pulled towards him like a helpless magnet.

But her lack of time made her strong for the first time in this man's presence. 'I'd love to stop and talk but I'm already late for work. I hope I'll see you another day.'

His sad eyes showed his disappointment. 'I hope so too, Cordelia and next time leave yourself more time!'

She vowed that every time from then on she would leave ten minutes earlier. She could. Couldn't she?

37

'Thank goodness we had enough money from the sale of that book to buy a trolley,' Jane said, carefully placing another dozen books on it. She and Cordelia were loading the new mobile library. The old Ford van looked cheery with its bright blue paint and white wording 'Silvertown Mobile Library' emblazoned on the sides.

'You're right,' Cordelia replied, dusting the cover of a book. 'How many hours did we spend trying to decide the right mix of books? I dread to think. Mostly your hard work though.'

When the van was loaded Jane looked at it with pride. 'I think there's a good chance we've got something for everyone,' she said with a smile.

The whole enterprise took time to organise. The trips to the factories, twice a week, could only be when all four librarians were on duty. Then two could stay in the library while the other two headed off in the van.

Finally they were ready. The van had been adapted by their friend Mr Hubbard so the side could lift up to show the books. It was with a sense of excitement that Cordelia and Jane set off on their very first mobile library run. They'd chosen a time when several of the Thames-side factories had their midday break. For a week beforehand they had posted notices and the local newspaper had kindly put an article about the event with a photo of the van.

As Cordelia navigated it through the bustling streets, the vehicle's aged suspension creaked and groaned with each pothole and uneven surface. The smell of petrol and exhaust fumes mingled with the acrid tang of smoke from the factories. The smells from the Tate & Lyle sugar refinery were particularly strong – the sweet caramel-like smell of boiling sugar, the smell of coal burning. After a while the inhabitants of Silvertown rarely noticed the smells except when the wind blew directly from the Thames into their homes and shops. But the worst smells came from the soap factory where animal carcasses were used. The stench of them mixed with the smell of chemicals was sometimes enough to make anyone nearby gag.

The narrow streets they passed were alive with activity as usual. Pedestrians hurried along pavements, their faces often tired and grey from loss of sleep due to bombings. Cars, many as old as the van, jostled for space alongside horse and carts that were increasingly used because of petrol rationing. They passed a newsagents with a board outside announcing, 'More rationing coming!' Both women groaned. Was there much else that could be rationed?

'I bet it's clothes again,' Jane said. 'Thank goodness for jumble sales or we'd all be going round in rags.' As she spoke she remembered the gulf between herself and Cordelia. She didn't know, but guessed that she still had some clothes in her family home and probably a friendly dressmaker too. Then she shook the thought aside. Jealousy got you nowhere. She remembered a quote she'd read in some book or other 'Jealousy is fear of comparison, it gets you nowhere.' She mentally shrugged. Cordelia was a good boss, a kind boss who never flaunted her wealth or her title. She was grateful to know her.

Cordelia gripped the worn steering wheel, her knuckles white as she navigated around craters from bombing raids and barefoot children playing in the street. As they turned a corner to the spot they'd identified as best to attract factory workers, the van's brakes squealed in protest and Cordelia winced at the sound. She hoped she hadn't made a mistake choosing it, but the reality was there had been very little choice.

They got out of the van to stretch their legs and looked back at it. Its cheerful colours stood out amongst the drab factory backdrop. From where they stood they could see the factory gates for Tate & Lyle. They'd decided that factory might be their best bet for interesting prospective library users. They knew that the factory employed a lot of girls and women. Women tended to read books more than men, they found.

When the factory hooter punctured the air, they nervously opened the side of the van, glad it was a beautiful sunny day with no rain, something they hadn't considered. The selection of books looked colourful and inviting. They waited anxiously as the workers walked towards them on their way to wherever they spent their breaks.

'Mobile library, girls! Books to borrow free!' Cordelia shouted again and again at the top of her voice. Some were too busy chatting to their friends to notice, others glanced but continued on their way. But about a dozen walked over, their eyes attracted by the artfully curated display. She turned to Jane, having had a last-minute thought. 'If any of them mention they have children let's tell them about the summer holiday activities!'

'What sort of books do you have?' a young woman with her hair tied back in a neat bun asked.

Cordelia let Jane take the lead, as she was on the library floor more and had done most of the work selecting the books.

'We've got a little bit of everything,' Jane replied, gesturing to the shelves. 'Romance, mystery, adventure... even some books on science and history if that's your cup of tea.'

'I like a bit of mystery,' the woman said. 'Never get the chance to go to the library and I can't afford to buy books meself. What've you got?'

Jane selected three books to show her – two Agatha Christie and one by Dorothy L. Sayers. 'Have a look at the write-up on the back and see if you fancy any of these. You can borrow up to two for two weeks. We'll just need your details.'

More women and one or two men began to see what was happening. Some wandered off but more asked about what they had. Soon the two librarians could hardly keep up with the demand. They'd typed brief forms for the borrowers' details and had several pencils available. Before long four people were leaning on the bonnet of the old van providing their names and addresses.

An older man approached the van, his steps getting shorter the nearer he got. Noticing his hesitation Cordelia walked towards him. 'Can we interest you in a book?'

His cheeks went pink. 'I ain't read a book since I left school. The teachers always said I was a dunce. Made me stand in the corner wiv me back to the class. They all laughed at me.'

Her heart went out to the poor man, so badly treated by a teacher who should have been encouraging him. She reached out and touched his arm. 'How do you do with reading other things?'

He frowned. 'Well, I read *The Mirror*, don't I? Mostly the sports pages, of course, and I manage all the instructions in the factory, like.'

Cordelia smiled at him. 'Then you've proved that unkind teacher wrong. You can read.' She indicated the van where there were already gaps showing in the bookshelves. 'What sort of stories do you think you'd like?'

'I dunno. It's bin so long. Got any about sport? Or murder? That sort of thing.'

She looked along the rows, knowing there wouldn't be much choice. Then she spotted it – a murder story set in a football club.

She turned and offered it to him. 'I think you'd like this one. You can borrow it for two weeks. If you haven't finished it then, you can just let us know and we'll sign it out to you for another fortnight.'

Holding it as if it might bite him, the man turned it over and looked through the pages. 'Dunno, some of them words are a bit long...'

'I find that sometimes,' Cordelia lied. 'I just skip over them. It works somehow. Go on, give it a try.' He nodded and she passed him a form, glad they had no long words on it. 'Just give it back when you've done it.'

They were kept so busy it was a surprise when the factory hooter sounded again and the workers looked up with a start then hurried away. Most would have money docked if they were late.

As they walked, the workers chatted excitedly, showing each other the books they'd chosen. The older man walked along more slowly, reading, then he turned back and gave Cordelia a thumbs up. Delighted, she guessed he had read the first page and felt encouraged.

The two librarians watched them all go and smiled at each other, struggling to hold back a tear.

'We did well,' Jane said. 'Let's give ourselves a pat on the back, but first, we need to tidy this van!'

They began looking through the forms and putting the books back in order.

'Did you see their faces when those two girls in the turban scarves realised they could borrow the books for free? They were so excited. And what a pity they didn't know that before.'

Jane nodded, putting away two history books that hadn't attracted any attention. 'That's something for us to think about. Another word to spread.' She paused, holding one of the books to her chest. 'You know, before you took this job our life was a lot easier!'

Horrified, Cordelia looked at her. 'Oh... I...'

Jane gave her an unaccustomed hug. 'Silly. It was easier because nothing ever happened. It was the same thing week after week. Since you started it seems there's always something interesting and exciting happening.'

Cordelia turned the key in the van but it spluttered then died. She looked at Jane. 'Know anything about cars?'

Jane laughed. 'I don't even know how to drive, never mind how to fix them.'

38

'Damn!' Cordelia muttered, getting out of the van and kicking it. 'That Mr Atkins at the car showroom swore this van was reliable. What're we going to do now?'

Jane got out and stood beside her, shaking her head. 'And on our first run too. What rotten luck.' She looked around. 'There's got to be engineers working in a big factory like this. I bet some of them tinker with vehicles.'

'I have no idea how to fix cars but we can at least have a look,' Cordelia said. She bent down to open the bonnet. The catch was stiff. She broke two fingernails trying to open it and her hands were covered in dust and dirt. Finally she got it open and, muttering curses, propped it open. The two women looked inside and could have been looking at a Chinese puzzle.

'Got any ideas?' Jane asked.

Cordelia laughed. 'Not a clue. It's all filthy but I don't suppose just cleaning it will do the trick.' She wiped her hand on her hankie.

'Well, don't ask me to try it, boss. I've got my best blouse on.'

Groaning, Cordelia muttered, 'Here we are, supposed to be

independent-minded librarians but we haven't got a clue when it comes to cars.'

It was Jane's turn to laugh. 'Well, I don't suppose many mechanics understand the Dewey Decimal System. We can't be experts on everything. We need to find someone to help us. Maybe someone in the factory knows about cars. I bet they do.'

They had no time to do more because the sound of a trolley being pushed alongside them drowned out their words.

'Broken down, have you... ladies?' the young man pushing it said. He wore a brown cotton work coat and his dark hair was slicked back with pomade. Unusually, his eyes were slightly different colours, one brown and one hazel.

They looked at him as if he'd been sent from heaven. 'Do you know anything about cars?'

He nodded, his head on one side. 'A bit. The bloke who... lived next door used to show me what he was doing... when he fixed his old car.'

It was impossible to miss his unusual hesitant way of speaking even though he seemed at ease with them.

'You're the library ladies, I guess,' he said. 'Want me to have... a look-see?'

They could have kissed him. 'Yes, please. Do you come into the library?'

'Not yet,' he said, peering inside the bonnet. 'But I keep meaning to. Have you... got any books about... family history sort of thing... I don't know if that's... what it's called.'

As he spoke he took out the spark plugs and began cleaning them on a rag he had taken out of his pocket. 'I think this is... the problem. Should be easy to... fix.'

'I'm sure we can find some books to help you,' Jane said. 'We don't have any in the van at the moment though.'

He was only half listening, busy with cleaning the spark

plugs. 'These are Champion plugs,' he muttered to himself. 'As old as... the van, I reckon. Whoever sold them... to you should have... given it a service.'

Cordelia hated feeling like a helpless female needing a man to help her with a simple task. She resolved to get some car maintenance books out of the library and study them.

'Have you worked here long?' Jane asked him. 'Oh, I'm so sorry, I didn't ask your name. I'm Jane and this is Cordelia, she's my boss.'

'Ben,' he replied, still looking at the task in hand. 'I'm... Ben... Only started last week. Still finding me way around, if you know what I mean.'

Finally he straightened up, wiping his hands on the rag which didn't help much. 'I think that's... all hunky-dory now. Give it a try.'

It started first time. Cordelia hurried out of the car again and kissed Ben on the cheek. He went bright red, even to his ears.

'It was... nothing,' he protested.

'Nothing to you but a godsend to us,' Cordelia said. 'Can we pay you for your time?'

He brushed her offer away. 'Nah, just help me... find them books when I... come in and we're quits.'

Then with a wave, he walked over to his trolley and began pushing it towards a side door in the factory.

'I hope he does come in the library,' Jane said. 'What a kind man.'

39

For the second time, Cordelia walked along the street where Eugene and his friends were hard at work. The sight of them, clad in their army work clothes, but wielding tools rather than weapons, brought a strange sense of reassurance to the battered neighbourhood. Some people still moaned about the Yanks. 'Overpaid, oversexed and over here' was a common saying about them. The sentiment echoed through pubs and markets, blending humour and resentment. But no one complained about the repairs they were doing.

Despite some landlords' names being published in the newspaper, not all had backed down, and some repairs still needed to be done. Additionally, some damaged properties belonged to the church, the council or other organisations. These entities often had limited budgets, especially after three years of war.

As Cordelia walked towards the group, a hush fell over them. Tools lowered, heads turned. Cordelia's breath hitched in her throat when she saw him – Eugene, a ray of sunshine amidst the dust and rubble. One man let out a wolf whistle, instantly slapped down by an elbow from Eugene.

The few steps towards them were agony. Cordelia felt so exposed as if every man there would be able to read her thoughts. *They know,* a voice whispered in her head. *They can see why I'm here.*

Thankfully, Eugene seemed oblivious to her turmoil. He dropped his tools with a clatter and strode toward her, his smile broad and unguarded. He leaned in, rubbing the briefest kiss against her cheek.

'This is a pleasant surprise,' he said. 'Are you on your way to work?'

'You can come to work with me any day,' the man who'd wolf-whistled said, his meaning clear. His leer made her skin crawl.

'Boys! Boys!' Eugene said. 'This is Cordelia who runs the library here in Silvertown, so none of your silliness.'

The library. Right. The library. Cordelia clung to the word like a lifeline. 'Well, yes,' she managed, her voice catching in her throat. Struggling to speak normally she said, 'I'm on my way to work and I'm running late so I'm afraid I can't stop.'

They all jumped as a small section of wall behind them collapsed to the ground, throwing up a cloud of dust.

'We heard about a dance at the Tate & Lyle factory on Saturday,' Eugene said. 'We thought we'd give it a try. Will you be going?'

'Will loads of gals desperate for handsome Yankees be there?' one of the others asked. She decided to ignore that question, although the answer was that there probably would be. It was hard for poor local lads to compete with these glamorous GIs.

She was glad she had already committed herself to go to the dance. It saved her the agony of having to choose whether to go or not. Whether to resist seeing Eugene or not.

'Well,' Cordelia said, trying to sound breezy despite the way her pulse was hammering. 'Of course, I'm happy to dance to help the library.' A strand of hair blew across her face and she pushed it behind her ear. 'And I don't know if you've been told but they're asking anyone who can to donate a book for the library. So bring one if you can, especially children's books.'

'I haven't been in a bookshop for years,' one of the men said. 'But count me in. Do I get a dance in return?'

Eugene nudged him jokily. 'You'll be in line after me then.' He looked at Cordelia as he spoke, his eyes holding hers for a second too long. *I hope it's a slow number,* she thought, hoping none of them were mind readers. 'Maybe at the dance we can teach each other a few steps. I'm a fast learner.'

Fearful she might be blushing, she looked down and glanced at her watch. 'I... I'm... going to be late. Sorry, boys, but I must get going. See you at the dance.'

As she walked away she heard one of them say, 'I wouldn't mind a night with that broad!'

Eugene's sharp response was immediate. 'Wash your mouth out with soap. She's not a broad, she's a lady and too good for the likes of you!'

The crude comment sent a shiver down Cordelia's spine and she unconsciously held her bag closer to her body for protection. How could that man think she was a 'broad'? It made her sound like something cheap, disposable.

All the way to the library Cordelia went over and over the conversation, remembering Eugene's magical brown eyes she could lose herself in. She couldn't remember a thing she'd said beyond reminding them about books. Had she made a fool of herself? Were her feelings for this lovely man glaringly obvious?

As always happened when she thought of him, her thoughts soon turned to Robert, out there in the desert facing untold hardships. She felt ashamed of her lustful thoughts for another man. Eugene's eyes, the way his accent livened up even the dullest words... shame washed over her. Was this what Robert felt, surrounded by nurses while she...

Had she imagined it or had his letters become less frequent, less romantic?

She walked the rest of the way engrossed in her thoughts. She skirted a pile of rubble, once a familiar shopfront, now mirroring the wreckage Eugene was making of her composure. It was so long since she had seen Robert she struggled to remember if she felt the same animal attraction for him as she did now with this American. Had she struggled to stop herself falling into his arms, to stroke his skin, to run her fingers through his hair when she'd first met him in the library? It was impossible to recover those emotions after all this time.

She got out her key to open the library door, but her hands shook and she dropped it. She scrabbled around on the floor until she found it, only to miss the keyhole twice before she succeeded in opening the old creaky door.

She'd barely taken a few steps into the library when Mavis rushed up to her. 'Have you heard?' she asked, her eyes sparkling with triumph. 'Three landlords have backed down. One of them a major one. And...' Her excited voice suddenly faltered. 'And...' She avoided Cordelia's eyes.

'And one of the landlords is my father!' Cordelia said, relieving her of her awkwardness. 'I know. I walked down the road where he owns some houses just now and work has already started!' She wished she felt the same enthusiasm as Mavis, but the knowledge that he'd only ordered the repairs to avoid public shame dampened her pleasure in the news. It always hurt her how he'd never valued her thoughts or ideas, how he'd never shared his plans. Would they ever be able to feel as close as she would like?

Mavis chatted as Cordelia took off her coat and put her handbag away. 'Did your dad tell you he was going to do it?'

'No, we're not in touch very often... to be honest I don't think he'd want me to believe he'd listened to my pleas to do the repairs.' She took a deep breath and stood more upright. 'But let's look on the bright side. The repairs are being done and where three landlords have backed down, others will too.' She put an arm round Mavis's shoulder. 'And it's all down to you, you marvellous woman! Have you told Joe? He must be so proud of you.'

Jane had come in while they were speaking. 'Yes, you deserve a medal, or at least the key to Silvertown.'

Mavis laughed. 'Not that there's many doors to open after all this bombing.'

Bert hammering on the big library door interrupted their conversation, and for now they went to their stations ready to serve their community once again.

Would Cordelia be able to concentrate on her work when images of those deep brown eyes and smooth brown skin kept forging themselves into her brain?

40

A cool breeze waved the curtains as Jane looked out of the window. Edith had written to say she would visit that afternoon, recently discharged from her convent rehabilitation centre.

It was only a few weeks earlier that she had been found drunk and unconscious by the side of the road.

When Jane saw her walking towards the house she took a deep breath to steady her nerves. 'She's here,' she said to Mrs S.

'Want me to leave you to it?' the kindly old lady said. 'I'll go on up to my bed and have a rest.'

Edith's knock on the door made Jane jump even though she'd been expecting it. The first thing she thought when she saw her mother-in-law was that she looked better than she had for ages. Her skin was brighter and her hair had more body. She was more upright than she had been before too. When drinking, she'd either avoided Jane's eyes or had glared at her.

'Come on in,' she said, moving aside. As she stepped into the living room she heard Mrs S's bedroom door close.

She followed Edith into the living room, her mind full of

questions, not least among them was: was Edith going to be as unpleasant as she'd been in the past?

Edith sat on one of the armchairs but didn't take her coat off. 'I'm not stopping,' she said, her voice softer than it had ever been in the past. She wiped a tear that slowly slid down her cheek. 'I've come to collect the rest of my things and to apologise.' She looked up at Jane, hoping her apology would be accepted. 'Is Helen here? I'd love to see her.'

'I'm afraid she's gone to her friends' house for tea.' Astonished at Edith's apology, Jane sat opposite her and leaned forward. 'I'm so glad you're looking so much better. You look like a new woman. Would you like a cup of tea?'

'Just a glass of water, please,' Edith replied. Jane could hardly believe how polite she was being.

Jane went to the kitchen and got out a glass. 'How is your head now? You had a nasty injury.' As she spoke she poured water into one of their few glasses.

'They told me I was out of it for more than two days,' Edith said, accepting the drink. 'I still get pains in my head a lot but the docs say that will pass.'

Jane wasn't sure whether to ask the next question but was too curious to leave it alone. 'How was the convent?' She grinned. 'I couldn't imagine you in a nun's outfit!'

'Well, I wasn't, was I?' Edith's old harsh voice was back, briefly making Jane feel unsettled again. Then Edith took a sip of the water. 'It was hard, being there. The nuns weren't especially kind. Not cruel, but they had their way of doing things and you had to do as they said or leave. For the first few days I nearly gave them a right mouthful...'

Jane could easily imagine that.

'But then,' Edith went on, 'I kind of got used to it and it was easy never having to think what to do next. Got a lot of thinking time too when everyone else seemed to be praying.' She stood up and went over to the window, looking out without speaking. 'I had time to think what a rubbish mum I was to George. I'm going to write to him and say how sorry I am. And I wasn't too nice to you either.' She turned back towards Jane. 'Trouble is I don't remember a lot of what I did. Booze does that to you.'

She got out her hankie, blew her nose and wiped her cheeks.

Jane heard Mrs S moving about upstairs but said nothing. She hoped she wouldn't come down. Better to let Edith go on with what she was saying.

'So are you feeling more confident about your future now?'

Edith sat down again, her hands never still, fiddling with her necklace. 'There's this new organisation. AA it's called. Alcoholics Anonymous. Do you know about it?'

'No, tell me.'

'You have to follow twelve steps towards recovery and go to meetings at least once a week where there are other... drinkers... alcoholics like me.' She stood up again then sat down as if she couldn't keep still. 'There, I've admitted it. It's taken me a long time to say that. One of the things we have to do is put right the wrongs we've done to others because of our drinking.' She undid her jacket, her face pink. 'That's why I'm here. I thought you were stuck up because you worked in the library. I didn't even try to get to know you. The nuns helped me to see that was because I don't feel good about myself. I should have been nicer to you.'

Jane couldn't believe the change in her mother-in-law in just a few weeks. It was as if a magician had waved a magic wand and, hey presto, here was a brand-new person. Surely it wouldn't last, couldn't last. 'I think it's really brave of you to come here to say sorry,' she said, reaching out her hands to Edith. Slowly, uncertainly, Edith took them in hers.

'I put you and your kind landlady through a lot. I can't even remember half of it, but enough to know I wasn't nice.' She let go of Jane's hands and went back to fiddling with her necklace. 'I thought I should tell you what I'm going to do now.'

Jane momentarily went cold. Surely she wouldn't ask to move back in, but no, she had said she was collecting her stuff.

'I've got a sister in Suffolk. Never got on with her much. Too much of a goody-goody, but I wrote to her a few days ago and she says I can go to stay with her and look for somewhere to live there.' A bit of the old Edith appeared. 'I'll have to sew my damn mouth together when she gets too holier-than-thou though!'

Jane nodded. 'It seems sensible to make a new start away from your old temptations. Away from the bombing as well. Will there be AA meetings there?'

'The nuns said there's one near enough to get to by bus.' She sighed and stood up. 'Well, that's one of my steps partly done. I must have tons of other things to put right if I can remember them.'

She went upstairs and packed her few things then quickly came back down.

'So I'm off. I'll write to George but you can tell him I came as well. Perhaps we'll get on better in future.'

41

Cordelia stood outside the Tate & Lyle factory, bracing herself for the evening ahead. The building loomed large, its blackened brick facade softened by the gentle hues of early twilight. Old Father Thames, just the other side of the factory, reflected the shielded lights from the ships docked along the quay, loading and unloading their cargo. The dockside buzzed with a clamour of shouts, thick with East End dialects and sailors' jargon.

The factory workers had transformed the bustling canteen area. The blackout curtains were already pulled across, giving the room a more intimate feel. Tables were pushed to the sides. On each was a candle in a glass jar and a small posy of flowers, many of them wildflowers found alongside the river. A picture of the king was in the centre of one wall and the other walls were adorned with home-made bunting of many colours and patterns.

One long table was set with a white tablecloth ready for staff to bring refreshments halfway through the dance. Many were provided by the workers themselves. On a smaller side table was a gramophone with a pile of vinyl records. Next to it was a pile of about twenty books.

Cordelia had decided to arrive when the dance was in full swing. It was a pity neither Jane nor Mavis had been able to come, but she would know a few people there – those that had come to the book van and of course Eugene and his friends. It was the thought of seeing him that made her nervous. If it hadn't been for the book collection she would have made excuses to avoid attending.

She stood looking around the room at the eclectic mix of people there. Factory workers, some office staff, women whose husbands were away fighting, and of course some British soldiers and American GIs.

She was glad that, when she walked into the room, Jenny, the person who had invited her, spotted her immediately and called her over. 'Come and meet my friends,' she said. 'You can't stand there like a Billy No-Mates, can you?' She took Cordelia's coat and added it to the pile on a nearby table. 'Did you see? We've already got some books and lots more promised before the end of the evening.'

'And some smashing Yanks too,' her friend said with a wink. 'Maybe I can bag meself a rich one!'

When most British people only gained their knowledge about Americans from films, it was no wonder they thought they must all be rich. Just from listening to the GIs when she was in the Rainbow Corner, Cordelia knew that that wasn't the case. She brought her attention back to Jenny's friend. 'Well, I know some of those Yanks. Want me to introduce you?'

The girl's eyes widened and she clutched her throat. 'Would you? That'd be smashing. Lead the way!'

The three of them wove their way around the dancers towards Eugene and his friends, who hadn't spotted them yet.

When he saw her, Eugene's smile widened as it always did. 'You came,' he said as if he'd doubted she would.

'How could I miss seeing you?' she said with a cheeky grin. 'But I want to introduce all of you to these two wonderful girls. Jenny here has arranged all the book donations and her friend...' She realised she hadn't asked the other girl's name.

'Ellie...' she was told.

'And Ellie would love to meet some Americans for the first time in her life.'

'Well, ain't that fine and dandy,' the tall man called Will said. 'You've surely come to the right place.' He took Ellie's hand and kissed it while looking into her eyes. 'Would you do me the honour of the first dance, Ellie?'

She giggled and followed him onto the dance floor where the local band was playing 'String of Pearls'. They were immediately lost in the crowd of dancers all doing the jitterbug with varying degrees of success.

Jenny had started talking to the other men, leaving Cordelia next to Eugene. 'Would my favourite librarian like to dance?' he asked, his gaze sweeping over her, sending a blush creeping up her neck.

She laughed. 'When a slower number comes on I'd love to, but for now I'd just like a lemonade. It's so hot in here.'

As they walked to the refreshments table, he tucked her arm through his. The warmth of his body even through his uniform made her heart beat faster. *Get yourself in control,* she told herself. They passed the table with the books and it gave her a minute to talk about something neutral as they explored the titles. None of the books were new, but they'd still be welcome by library borrowers. As they looked at them, his arm pressed against hers, again distracting her.

He pulled her away. 'Come on, let's get that drink.' At the drinks table, they had to stand close to hear each other.

One of Eugene's friends danced nearby and called over, 'Don't let her get away, Eugene!'

'Don't worry, Hank,' Eugene called back. 'I won't! This one's special!'

Cordelia felt a tingling warmth spread through her as he turned to her and smiled again.

'I'm so glad we both made it this evening.' His unspoken words sent a shiver down her spine.

'I had to come,' she joked back. 'All those books have been collected for the library.' She raised an eyebrow and play-punched him in the chest. 'Nothing to do with you, mister!'

'That's my girl,' he said, chuckling. 'Always thinking of your library.'

It was a dangerous game they were playing, Cordelia realised, this dance of subtle flirtation. Especially tonight, with Robert so far away and her body thick with longing. Out of the corner of her eye she saw one or two of the factory girls she knew were watching her and whispering.

But she turned her attention back to him. 'It's true, I think of the library a lot, but there's always space in my mind for the most charming GI in London.'

The band transitioned into a slow, swaying number and he held out his hand, his gaze holding hers. 'May I have the pleasure of this dance, Lady Cordelia?'

She knew she should say no, should step back from the precipice of temptation. But the desire to be held in his arms, to feel the warmth of his gaze upon her, overwhelmed her fragile resolve. *It's only a dance, nothing more,* she told herself.

'Just one dance,' she murmured, her voice barely audible above the music.

As they moved together, his hand firm against her back, she was acutely aware of his body against hers. The scent of his cologne, a mixture of soap and something woody, filled her senses. His hand felt warm through the thin fabric of her dress, sending a thrill through her. She tried to drag her attention away from the sensations, to listen to the music, to look out for people she knew, but it was impossible to ignore the way his presence affected her, making her heart pound against his chest like a captive bird.

She caught sight of one of the British soldiers and a sharp pang of guilt stabbed her, reminding her of Robert yet again.

Eugene drew back a little as if reading her thoughts. His expression was serious. 'Are you okay, Cordelia?' he asked, his voice low and concerned. 'You're a million miles away.'

'Just a bit tired,' she said with a smile, hoping it reached her eyes. He didn't press further, but his arm tightened on her back again, sending a jolt of pleasure through her. For the rest of the dance, she tried to maintain her distance, both physically and emotionally. But it was a tough battle. His nearness, his scent, the warmth of his gaze chipped away at her defences, leaving her feeling exposed and breathless.

It was a relief when the number finished and she pulled herself from his embrace.

'I'll leave you for a minute. I need to go to the ladies',' she said and turned away before she was tempted to stay.

She looked back from the door. He was at the drinks table pouring himself more orange squash. She hoped he would ask someone else to dance. She might not be able to resist if he asked her again.

42

The moon, a silver sliver peeking through the clouds, cast an ethereal glow on the bomb-damaged streets as Cordelia and Eugene walked from the dance hall. The moonlight softened the harsh edges of rubble and ruin around them. Their shielded torches cast only cones of muted light, illuminating small patches of pavement, leaving the rest in shadow.

There were a few people about, yet Silvertown gently thrummed with life. Muffled piano music came from a nearby pub, competing with laughter of the men inside. A baby cried behind a darkened window and they heard a mother trying to calm it. A tram rattled past, its shielded headlights glowing eyes, momentarily illuminating a couple stealing a kiss in a shop doorway.

Neither Cordelia nor Eugene spoke much as they walked, but she was acutely aware of his presence. When his arm brushed against hers, it made her breath catch. Her senses were on high alert, aware of him beside her, of every detail. The rhythmic sounds of their shoes on the pavement, the way even their breaths were in harmony.

As they neared her building, a sense of dread made her stomach tighten. The closer they got, the more urgent her dilemma became. Should she invite him in? It was late, but did that matter? Rosalind would have thought nothing of it. But she knew such an invitation would be unlikely to stop at a drink. Yet the thought of ending the wonderful evening, of saying goodbye so soon, felt unbearable.

They stopped at the bottom of the steps leading up to her home. The air crackled with unspoken tension. She fumbled in her purse for her keys, her fingers trembling slightly. Eugene stood waiting patiently, saying nothing.

'Well,' she said, aware her voice wavered. 'This is my place.'

He took her hand. 'It was a lovely evening, Cordelia.' His voice was low and sincere. 'Thank you for letting me walk you home.' He made no move to leave. He just stood there, and even in the darkness she could feel his gaze upon her. A question lingered in the air.

Cordelia's mind raced. A wave of conflicting thoughts and emotions swirled within her.

Go on, invite him in. Nothing has to happen.

Don't kid yourself. He'll be impossible to resist.

But it's just a drink, a cup of coffee.

Think of Robert. You can't do this to him.

Robert isn't here. Eugene is.

The inner turmoil raged on, leaving her brain scrambled, her body full of longing. She stole a glance at Eugene. He hadn't pressured her. Hadn't asked if he could go in with her. He'd just waited patiently.

She knew in that moment that if she invited him in, it wouldn't just be for tea. It would be much more. It would be a betrayal of her love for Robert, for the future they anticipated together.

But it was so tempting to throw caution to the wind, just for one night. To pretend the war wasn't happening, that the world wasn't on fire, that this man might not soon lose his life in battle. Oh, to lose herself in the warmth of his gaze, of his touch.

Finally, after what felt like an eternity, she took a step back, putting a safe distance between them. 'Eugene, I've had a wonderful evening, especially dancing with you. But it's getting late. I should go in.'

He reached forward and tucked a stray strand of hair behind her ear. The touch, feather-light though it was, sent a bolt of emotions through her, almost undoing her resolve.

'Sleep well, Cordelia,' he said, and gently kissed her cheek.

'You too, Eugene,' she whispered. But she had to say something before he went, had to make things clear between them. 'Eugene,' she said, touching his arm with her hand. 'I think there is something between us, something special, but it can't go on. I'm so sorry but I can't see you again. I have a boyfriend who is a soldier in North Africa. I can't be unfaithful to him. I'm so sorry.'

There was a long pause, neither of them speaking. The air laden with unspoken emotions.

Then she heard him sigh. 'I understand, Cordelia,' he said, his voice full of regret. 'I think we could have a wonderful future together, but I'm sure you're making the right decision. The noble decision.' Another long pause, then he leaned forward and briefly kissed her cheek. 'Have a wonderful life,' he whispered.

He turned to leave, his footsteps echoing as he walked away. She watched him go, a dark shadow in the darkness of the night. For a second the clouds parted and she caught a glimpse of him as he turned the corner out of sight.

Back in her flat she kicked off her shoes and poured herself a stiff drink, the first of the night. Her senses still tingled with the nearness of the handsome GI. But as she sat down and her breathing calmed she was glad she had resisted temptation. How could she have faced Robert if she had been unfaithful?

Sipping her drink, Cordelia gazed around her small flat, the surroundings comforting. The faded wallpaper, the small table by the window, all reminded her of the life she had chosen. The quiet, the routine, the waiting.

Turning off her light, she walked over to the window and peered out into the night. The street below was deserted apart from a drunk singing incoherently as he staggered along. The blackout rendered everything in shades of shadow and darkness. She could almost hear the echo of Eugene's footsteps, a haunting reminder of what could have been, what almost happened.

She took another sip, the alcohol burning a path down her throat. She knew she had made the right choice, but that didn't make it easier. It was so long since she had been held tight, been loved in that way. She leaned against the window frame, allowing tears to roll down her cheeks, feeling a mixture of relief and regret.

She reached over to the pile of Robert's letters on the table, tied together as they always were with a red ribbon. She ran her fingers across the top one. She tried to remember the sound of his voice, the feel of his arms around her, the smell of his skin. But the memories had faded, replaced by the visceral presence of Eugene.

She shook her head. Her choice was made. It was the right one.

She finished her drink and put the glass down with a determined clink.

As she prepared for bed, she allowed herself one last thought of Eugene. The way his eyes sought hers, the gentle touch of his kiss on her cheek. Then she shook it away. No more.

Slipping under the cover, Cordelia stared up at the ceiling, the darkness pressing in on her. She had made her decision and was relieved that she had. But as she drifted off to sleep a fleeting memory of Eugene appeared, a bittersweet reminder of what might have been.

43

The days since the dance with Eugene had been busy. Nonetheless Cordelia's mind frequently went back to that evening when she might so easily have changed the course of her life forever. So she was pleased that they'd decided to have a night on the town. They didn't need an excuse, although the new books from the Tate & Lyle staff was a good one. A bit of fun was overdue.

First they went to the West End for a meal. The idea of going to the Rainbow Corner fleetingly drifted through Cordelia's mind. She hastily pushed it away. Too much temptation.

'Let's to go The Epicure,' she suggested. 'My friend Rosalind's been there. She says it's got a lot of food from different countries.'

Jane's face fell. 'It sounds expensive,' she said.

'Rosalind says it's reasonable. Anyway, I think it's time to give you both a bonus for being brilliant library workers.'

'What about Tom?' Mavis asked. 'He's always a good worker. I'm so glad 'e's being paid now. So many of our readers love 'im.'

They paused for a moment while a member of the public

came in, but he was a regular and went straight to the stacks to search for his next read.

'Tell you what,' Cordelia said. 'Whatever we spend tonight, I'll give Tom the equivalent of the total divided by four.'

Mavis smiled at them. 'And I've got some news...'

They both looked at her expectantly.

'Nope. Not telling you now. I'll tell you tonight. But it's cause for celebration!'

* * *

The three friends stopped outside The Epicure restaurant, taking in the elegant facade that had so far avoided bomb damage.

'It looks a bit posh,' Jane said uncertainly. 'Will me and Mavis feel comfortable in there?'

Cordelia laughed. 'Our cook, who was the wisest woman I ever met, used to say, "They've all got holes in their bums the same as us, dear!"' The other two spluttered with laughter.

'Too right,' Mavis said. 'I'd like to meet your cook. And some of them, like that landlord Stanstead, are the biggest arseholes! Come on, girls, let's have ourselves a right slap-up meal if we can get a table.'

'I've booked one,' Cordelia said in response. 'It can be hard in the West End, especially now all the Americans are here.'

Jane nodded. 'They've got tons of money to splash around. Do you know their soldiers, just the ordinary privates, get about four times more than our soldiers?' She shook her head. 'No wonder they get all the girls.'

Cordelia tried not to think about 'her' GI as Jane spoke. Not that he was hers, nor would he ever be.

Inside the restaurant, they were greeted by a smartly dressed waitress who took their names and showed them to their table. The spacious room was tastefully decorated, walls lined with rich dark wood panelling that extended up to a high vaulted ceiling. The floor was covered in plush red carpeting that muffled footsteps and gave a sense of warmth and intimacy to the space. The lighting was soft with small, fringe-trimmed lamps around the walls and smaller ones on each table.

A waiter held out the chairs for the three women and took their coats to a cloakroom.

'This is the life,' Mavis said. 'Think they'd let me move in 'ere?'

As they settled themselves the waiter offered each of them a menu. Unknown to the other two, Cordelia had asked for a 'woman's menu' that didn't show the prices. She knew the other two would choose the cheapest food if they saw them.

'Cor,' Mavis said, looking at the menu. 'Some of this is stuff we get in Lyons Corner 'ouse, but I bet it tastes a lot better.'

There were three appetisers, three main courses and sides and three desserts. Their mouths watered and they stopped talking while they studied the menus.

'Why aren't there any prices on here?' Jane asked.

Cordelia grinned. 'Well, in these posh places it is assumed that the fairer sex shouldn't have to think about anything as coarse as money. Only the men get the menus showing prices.'

Jane's jaw dropped open. 'How the other half lives,' she muttered.

Cordelia ordered their drinks while they took their time choosing their meal.

'My mouth's watering just looking at this,' Mavis said. 'I think I'll 'ave smoked mackerel pâté and roast chicken with root vegetables. I'll think about afters after.'

A waitress appeared with their drinks and took their orders.

Cordelia had ordered wine and she picked up her glass. 'Here's to us, girls. The intrepid East End librarians!'

They all took a sip of their drinks, then Jane turned to Mavis. 'Come on, Mavis. You said you had some news to share. What is it?'

A family at the next table began singing 'Happy Birthday' and everyone in the restaurant joined in even though they didn't know the birthday girl. When they'd finished Cordelia and Jane looked at Mavis again. 'So, what's your news?' Cordelia asked.

Even with the dim lighting they saw Mavis go uncharacteristically pink. She smoothed down the skirt of her sage-green dress. 'Well, it's... it's... you'll never guess what... it's just that...'

The other two looked at her wondering if she'd ever get round to telling them her news.

Mavis took a deep breath. 'Joe proposed!'

Cordelia and Jane whooped so loud everyone in the restaurant turned to look at them.

'That's wonderful news!' Cordelia said. 'When's the wedding going to be?'

They were interrupted by the waitress bringing their appetisers. Mavis looked at hers. 'Blimey, that's a bit fancy, isn't it? Look at all them trimmings.' She laughed. 'I'll 'ave to do that next time Joe's 'ome. 'E'll wonder what's wrong with me.' She spread the snowy-white napkin on her lap and picked up her knife and folk. 'Always start on the outside with cutlery. I read that in a book.'

'So,' Jane said, 'come on then. When's the big day?'

'Mmm,' Mavis muttered. 'That is the best pâté I have ever 'ad in my life. When? Next April unless this rotten war sends him abroad. But it'll be a small do, that's for sure. I 'aven't told Joyce yet but I think she'll be pleased to have a daddy. She gets on well with Joe.'

'I'd love to make her a bridesmaid's dress,' Jane said. 'Let's start looking for material when we can.' She paused as the waitress topped up their glasses. 'How small a do?'

Mavis grinned. 'Not so small that I can't invite you two and Tom, that's for sure. But don't expect anything posh like this place.'

The rest of their conversation was about wedding plans, and other achievements.

'The book van's been a right success.' Mavis said. 'I looked at the figures the other days. It's brought in loads more readers. Did that bloke who got the van started that first day when it broke down sign up?'

'Ben? Not yet, but I keep looking out for him. Plenty of time.'

'We've achieved a lot this year,' Jane said, wiping her mouth with her napkin. 'But the biggest thing is your rent strike, Mavis.'

'Almost all the landlords 'ave given in now,' Mavis said, looking pleased with herself. 'It was touch-and-go with some of them. It helped that Mr Wheeler's solicitor friend wrote them a stern letter. And the advice he gave me was invaluable. We've still got to win Stanstead round, but I've 'eard a whisper that 'e's weakening.'

'You are an absolute marvel,' Jane said. 'I meant it when I said they should put up a statue to you in Silvertown. Or at least give you a medal. I can't imagine how many households are better off because of you.'

'And live in better accommodation,' Cordelia joined in. 'And live healthier lives.'

'There's a way to go,' Mavis said. 'Not all the repairs 'ave been done, but I reckon with the threat of newspapers over their heads, they'll do them.'

Let's hope they don't get bombed flat, Cordelia thought.

Two minutes after they left the restaurant, the air-raid siren wailed.

44

The siren wailed its terrifying song, sending everyone scurrying to the nearest shelters. Mavis and Jane looked towards Cordelia, expecting her to know shelters in the West End as she went there more often. She didn't know many, but she knew of one very close.

'Come on, girls,' she shouted over the din. 'We're off to John Lewis.' They both looked at her as if she'd lost her mind. John Lewis was one of the biggest department stores in London, not one East Enders went to.

An ARP warden was at the door to the basement urging people to hurry in. They went downstairs, past several rooms to the most luxurious shelter any of them had ever seen.

'This is better than my 'ouse,' Mavis said, looking around at the décor. The area was separated into three, with each section painted a different pastel colour. There were a few camp beds complete with bedding and a variety of odd chairs and small tables. Some had obviously been repaired and they assumed they had once been for sale.

The three friends pulled three chairs together and looked at each other wide-eyed. 'Well, this is a lot better than the Underground with the smell and mosquitoes,' Jane said. 'Or the Anderson shelter we've ended up in a few times. We had to wade through a few inches of water and it was damp and cold even on a hot day.'

Having settled, they looked around. The people in the shelter were a much more mixed bunch than would ever have been in the departments above. Magazines of varying ages were here and there, along with glasses and jugs of water.

'If it wasn't for worrying about Joyce we could stay 'ere all night,' Mavis said. 'Come to think of it, this place is good enough to get married in.'

'You didn't tell us how Joe proposed,' Cordelia said. 'Was it romantic?'

Mavis laughed. 'I wish! I'd 'ave liked a swanky restaurant, candles on the table, a piano playing in the background...'

'What did you get instead?' Jane asked, knowing the proposal must have been far from romantic.

'We was walking past St Marks when a couple came out. They'd just got married. She looked really pretty. I could see 'er dress was made of parachute silk, and she 'ad a massive bunch of red and white roses for a bouquet. I made Joe stop and look for a minute; I like a good wedding, me.'

'And...?'

Mavis smiled at the memory. ''E stood there for a minute looking at the couple then turned and said, "Why don't we get 'itched? We've known each other long enough."'

The other two burst out laughing, their giggles echoing off the shelter walls.

'Leave it to Joe to make a proposal sound like renewing a library book!' Jane chortled, wiping tears of laughter from her eyes.

'I can just imagine it! Right there in the middle of the street. No fanfare, no getting down on one knee, no ring...'

Mavis was laughing too. 'That's Joe. Practical to the last. But you know what, I was still happy as pie. We'll be a no-fuss family, just us and Joyce, except when Ken comes to visit, of course.'

The shelter shook slightly with bombs dropping, but they seemed some distance away.

'I 'ope we're not copping it again in poor old Silvertown,' Mavis said. 'And I'm glad my neighbour will 'old on to Joyce, take her down the shelter with her.'

They were in luck, it was a much shorter raid than sometimes happened. An hour later the all-clear sounded and they were freed from their very comfortable prison.

'Come along with me, my fellow librarians,' Cordelia said with a grin. 'We must verily leave this low-roofed place and wend our jolly way back to our humble abodes.'

The other two almost pushed her over.

Outside they instinctively looked east. The East End was frequently in flames after an air raid, the fires lighting up the sky so much they could be seen across the whole city.

'It doesn't look too bad,' Jane said. 'Fingers crossed there haven't been many deaths.'

Although she sounded calm Cordelia knew both her friends would be worried about their daughters.

They made their way to the Underground, the familiar musty smell greeting them as they stepped onto the platform. As the train rattled along the tracks, they passed station after station, some transformed into makeshift shelters. Families huddled together on blankets, some people slept while others read or played cards. The face of every single person showed worry and exhaustion.

Half an hour later they were standing outside their library.

Or what was left of it.

The three women stood in the evening light, staring at the remains of their beloved workplace. The building that had survived the Blitz and so many other bombings. The facade was pockmarked with shrapnel holes and one entire wing had been reduced to rubble. Shards of glass crunched underfoot as they slowly approached it. Pages from books fluttered through the air like leaves in autumn, torn and tattered. Other books lay on the floor burned or soaked from the firefighters' attempts to stop the whole building going up in flames. It was a heartbreaking sight. One the three friends would never forget.

'All our books...' Mavis said, her voice breaking. 'All our work...'

'Don't go in there, ladies,' an ARP warden said, his voice cutting through their numbed brains. 'It ain't safe. It could fall on you. Seen it 'appen more than once.' He shone his torch on their faces and recognition dawned on him. 'Oh, you ladies are the librarians, ain't you? Seen you in there loads of times. Well, the good news is we put out the incendiary fires pretty damn quick, excuse my swearing.' He stopped and looked up at the cloudless sky. 'Bomber's moon like this was 'andy for them Nazi flyers, but it means your books should stay dry overnight. That's got to be a blessing if nothing else is.'

Hardly able to breathe, Cordelia shook her head. 'But will the books be stolen overnight? Will we be able to come back tomorrow and rescue them?'

'Yeah,' Mavis said. 'You know what those tea leaves are like around 'ere. They'll nick anything, even our books.' She began to sob and pushed a hankie to her mouth to stop herself.

'Don't you worry,' the warden said. 'We'll keep an eye on the place. You all come back in the morning when they can look proper, like, and let you know if it's safe to go in and get your books and stuff.'

Someone came and spoke to him and, calling 'Keep safe' to the three of them, he walked away.

Cordelia pulled her friends towards her and they linked arms together. 'This is an awful way to end a lovely evening with your news as well, Mavis. But we're not done, not by a long way. There's still a fair bit of money from selling that book. Our people need us, the community rely on us.'

Jane took a deep breath. 'I hate seeing our lovely library like that, like it's wounded. But you're right. We're not done for. If we can't carry on here, we'll find another building. People will help us just like we've helped them.'

Mavis stopped sobbing. 'You're right, girls. It'll take more than that awful 'itler to stop the girls of Silvertown Library!'

The three women stood together looking at their beloved building.

'I feel silly saying this,' Jane said, steadying herself despite the ache in her heart. 'But it feels like a bereavement looking at that, like someone we love has died.'

'Not died,' Cordelia said. 'Just injured. I feel the same way.' She hooked arms with her friends again. 'You know how when someone you loved dies, they say remember the happy times? We can do that with our library. We've had so many happy times. Helped so many people. And I've never had two such good friends as you. I may not say it often enough, but I value you both every single day.'

'We value you too,' Mavis said with a grin. 'I think we've rubbed some of the posh edges off you now.' She laughed. 'And you're right, we'll help people again whether it's here or some-where else. We're tough women and we'll carry on.'

A cloud moved from the moon and the light cast long

shadows around them, but the three librarians stood tall, their hearts resolute.

'The library isn't just about bricks and mortar,' Cordelia said, her voice firm with conviction. 'It's about knowledge, education, and helping the community. If the damage is too bad to carry on our work here, we'll find somewhere else.'

They would rebuild, stronger than ever before.

ACKNOWLEDGEMENTS

I would like to acknowledge the very kind help and support from my husband Rick, who is also good at thinking of plot ideas. Also, my close friend and writing buddy Fran Johnson; Maggie Smith, a superb editor; and of course Emily Yau, my lovely editor at Boldwood.

ABOUT THE AUTHOR

Patricia McBride is the author of several fiction and non-fiction books as well as numerous articles. She loves undertaking the research for her books, helped by stories told to her by her Cockney mother and grandparents who lived in the East End. Patricia lives in Cambridge with her husband.

Sign up to Patricia McBride's mailing list for news, competitions and updates on future books.

Visit Patricia's website: www.patriciamcbrideauthor.com

Follow Patricia on social media here:

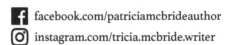
facebook.com/patriciamcbrideauthor
instagram.com/tricia.mcbride.writer

ALSO BY PATRICIA MCBRIDE

The Lily Baker Series

The Button Girls

The Picture House Girls

The Telephone Girls

The Air Raid Girls

The Blackout Girls

The Bletchley Park Girls

Christmas Wishes for the Bletchley Park Girls

The Library Girls of the East End Series

The Library Girls of the East End

Hard Times for the East End Library Girls

A Christmas Gift for the East End Library Girls

A Better Tomorrow for the East End Library Girls

Sixpence Stories

Introducing Sixpence Stories!

Discover page-turning historical novels from your favourite authors, meet new friends and be transported back in time.

Join our book club Facebook group

https://bit.ly/SixpenceGroup

Sign up to our newsletter

https://bit.ly/SixpenceNews

Boldwood

Boldwood Books is an award-winning fiction publishing company seeking out the best stories from around the world.

Find out more at www.boldwoodbooks.com

Join our reader community for brilliant books, competitions and offers!

Follow us
@BoldwoodBooks
@TheBoldBookClub

Sign up to our weekly deals newsletter

https://bit.ly/BoldwoodBNewsletter

Milton Keynes UK
Ingram Content Group UK Ltd.
UKHW040156211124
2904UKWH00001B/1